Chelsea Wives and their Mistresses

Chelsea Wives & their Mistresses

SARAH BRAMLEY

Q

QUARTET

First published in 2012 by
Quartet Books Limited
A member of the Namara Group
27 Goodge Street, London W1T 2LD

A catalogue record for this book
is available from the British Library

ISBN   978 0 7043 7264 1

Typeset by Antony Gray
Printed and bound in Great Britain by
T J International Ltd, Padstow, Cornwall

1

Dedication

For a dear friend, who I will always remember
with frustration and love.

Acknowledgements

Thank you to everyone who encouraged me with their enthusiasm and positivity, notably my family, Amanda, Azzy, Eliza, Gary, Marc, Nicky, Paula, Steve and Zahra.

Prologue

Cara Brooks waited anxiously in her silent drawing room at Wellington Square, Chelsea. She glanced at her watch, encrusted with round brilliant cut diamonds; it was 11.10pm. She slipped it off her slim wrist and lightly threw it to the other side of the sofa, fed up of watching the mocking minutes go by. Moving uncomfortably on the black leather sofa, she loosened her silk bronze robe, which her husband, David, had bought for her thirty-fifth birthday the previous year. David and her son Giles were on a skiing trip in Lech so she had the house to herself for a week, which she often appreciated. She picked up her phone, which rested beside her, and checked again for any possible missed calls or text messages – but still nothing. She sighed loudly, holding back from sending another demanding text. She had an image to uphold and she never liked to chase anyone, regardless of how much she desired them. After massaging her tense right shoulder for a few hopeful minutes, she lifted herself heavily from the sofa to retreat back to her bedroom. She assumed that Alessandra was caught up with friends at the dinner party in Mayfair so she would either be arriving much later or, quite possibly, not at all. That was the problem with Alessandra and indeed herself – they had their own separate lives to manage as well as attending to each other.

She turned off the lights in the drawing room and walked along the wide corridor in bewilderment, although her mood was slightly lifted by the row of original works by a well-known fashion illustrator, which she had recently ordered. The gold-framed illustrations looked just immaculate against the pure white walls, each lit by slim picture lights, which made her feel as if she were in one of her favourite art galleries. Barefoot, she stepped onto the stairs leading to the second floor, wishing she had made other plans for that night. She would've liked to have caught up with some friends who apparently had some rather humorous stories to tell from their trip to Juan-les-Pins. They were all out that night, no doubt having a great time in some club or restaurant, she thought rather jealously to herself. The video entry phone suddenly rang, startling her.

'Alessandra!'

With pent-up excitement, she quickly walked back down the stairs, brushing her hands through her golden brown hair to give it more volume after playing carelessly with it on the sofa. She skimmed along the corridor to the spiral staircase, lightly holding onto the banister to the ground floor. Her landline phone began to ring but she delighted in ignoring it as she walked towards the front door with just one thing in mind. She smoothed down her silk robe in the mirror in the entrance hall to ensure that she still looked pristine after being curled up on the sofa for over an hour, and then gazed eagerly at the video screen mounted on the wall. She smiled affectionately and composed herself again before opening the door to a young woman, displaying an apologetic expression.

'Alessandra.' Cara gave her a stern look to express her frustration, although they both knew she could never get too annoyed with her. 'Come in – you should have called or texted me.' She deepened her sensuous voice in a bid to further signal her seriousness. Standing to the side, she held the door open to the tall slim woman wearing an embroidered jersey dress under a long cream coat, which discreetly displayed her shapely tan legs as she walked in. 'Did you not get my messages?'

'Yes I did. Cara I'm so sorry I'm late but my friend didn't prepare the food till much later than planned and then he drove us to another friend's party in Kensington,' Alessandra replied in a flustered state. 'I got here as soon as I could!'

'Well you could have let me know what was going on.' Cara

crossed her arms, trying to contain herself from just throwing them around Alessandra during the lecture. Although she was annoyed, she was overcome with relief.

'Sorry, I was just so caught up with the evening. I did try calling you a few times but for some annoying reason I didn't have any reception so I only got your messages about fifteen minutes ago, babe.'

Cara maintained her angry stance as she fought a mix of joy and upset, waiting for Alessandra to make more effort in heightening her excitement, which had faded during the wait.

'Cara you know I've been looking forward to seeing you?'

'Well that's been made perfectly clear, don't you think?'

Alessandra groaned and started to pull off her coat. 'Are we going to be standing here all night?' Five seconds of stubborn silence followed. 'Well maybe I should just go home so you can calm down then?'

With a surrendering sigh, Cara loosened her dipped eyebrows and uncrossed her slender arms playfully. She held out her arms to draw Alessandra into her. She instantly felt her emotions rise with Alessandra's soft and floral scented hair flowing around her cheek. Being with Alessandra was always a breath of fresh air from her family life, which sometimes made her feel trapped. She tenderly kissed Alessandra's lips. 'Don't be silly; you know I can't resist you my darling – I want you here but next time do try harder to let me know if you're going to be so late, OK?' She clasped her hand gently around Alessandra's defined jawline. 'So did you have a fun night then?'

'I did actually, great wine and conversation,' Alessandra replied, relieved that Cara was quick to forgive her. She pulled slightly away from Cara and took her bag off her shoulder. 'I'll tell you more in a second . . . I bought you something from my break in Rome so maybe this will make up for tonight, I mean, it was going to be a gift of love but now it's a gift of apology! Not so romantic now.'

'Oh darling now you've made me feel guilty, you shouldn't have bought me anything,' Cara exclaimed, containing an excited smile. She was used to exchanging gifts with Alessandra, however. 'You're very sweet.'

Alessandra reached into her bag for a white gift box, which she held out to Cara. Both of her parents were Italian so she was in Italy often, but she grew up in St John's Wood where she resided with her husband, whom Cara had never met nor desired to.

'Alessandra, thank you.' Cara lit up as she opened the box to reveal a three-row, circle pendant necklace. 'Gosh it's *so beautiful*, how lovely of you, thank you darling.' She leaned in to kiss Alessandra on the lips again. 'It really is sweet of you – so did you have a good time with your relatives?'

'Of course but I've already told you I did; do you not listen to me?' Alessandra quipped.

'Well you sounded so happy on the phone; I just wanted to see your matching smile.'

Alessandra happily wrapped her arms around Cara's waist. 'I'm so glad you like the necklace, I've been looking forward to giving it to you.'

'I absolutely love it. I'll put it on tomorrow – got a charity gala to attend so I'll wear a dress to go with it.' Cara grinned down at the necklace then carefully placed the box on the contemporary console table. 'You can help me choose a dress actually while you're here – you might as well make yourself useful,' she said jokingly, deepening her voice again.

'I hope you don't intend on giving me too much of a hard time tonight,' Alessandra winced. Although she delighted in the prospect of going through Cara's dresses; she loved her dress collection, which was of such great variety. Cara loved her high fashion brands but also enjoyed wearing cultured pieces from her travels, notably her sculptured Moroccan dress.

'I'm still deciding whether to or not actually,' Cara said,

slightly raising an eyebrow. 'Would you like a drink or anything by the way?' Cara moved away from Alessandra and edged towards the stairs, leading down to the lower ground floor.

'No I think I've had enough to drink for one night already.'

'Not a glass of water or anything? I'm going to get one for myself – it'll be good for you.'

'Yes OK then,' Alessandra shrugged. Cara was only five years older than her but she had the tendency to mother her nonetheless.

While she stood in the entrance hall, Cara walked down into the kitchen and brought out two small bottles of still water from the fridge. With the fridge door still open, she paused to calm and cool herself, before shutting the door and walking back up the stairs.

'Come on beautiful,' she beckoned warmly to Alessandra. Alessandra took off her embroidered silk sandals and followed Cara in anticipation, up to the third floor.

Cara could feel herself becoming more aroused with each step she took towards the bedroom. She'd been yearning to see Alessandra over the past two months but she'd had to travel continuously around Europe to manage her property portfolio. As it wasn't always easy to arrange to see Alessandra, she embraced every opportunity. She looked over her shoulder to smile alluringly at Alessandra and took hold of her hand as they carried on walking up the stairs.

Alessandra looked around her as she followed Cara up into one of the five bedrooms in the elegant five-floor grade II listed property, located in the heart of Chelsea. Cara was a woman of exceptional taste and her London home reflected that, with its light minimalist interior partnered with modern works of art and the latest technology. Cara was born in Chelsea and, although she had travelled a lot, she always returned to where her heart was. Alessandra followed Cara into her spacious bedroom and quietly shut the door behind them. Cara placed the two bottles of water on each bedside table, the silence in the room accentuating the sound of every movement. She hoped she would finish a bottle that night – although she enjoyed slow and sensuous love-making with Alessandra, she was in the mood for a more fiery night.

Alessandra placed her bag on the table by the door. She unclipped her wavy brown hair and glanced at Cara standing by her usual side of the bed. She watched with contained sexual hunger as Cara slipped off her silk robe, which drifted delicately onto the parquet floor, revealing her ever glowing, slender physique.

Cara could feel Alessandra's heated energy colliding with hers as she lifted herself under the soft white duvet, which she had neatly prepared for the night. She dimmed the lights to encourage Alessandra to get into the bed with her, unable to cope with the silence and charged atmosphere any longer. She looked over at Alessandra as she took off her jewellery by the door, feeling her whole body weaken with the desire for her delicate hands to be stroking her breasts. Alessandra's exposed arms and legs were looking more exotic in the dimmed lights. She needed them wrapped around her tightly. It had been too long. She tapped the pillow beside her excitedly.

'Come on now Alessandra! What are you waiting for darling?!'

Chapter One

Two Years Later

'Darling, are you coming?' David called out to Cara on the landing of the second floor.

Cara sighed heavily. She swept her tousled golden brown hair to the side and clipped on her white gold pendant necklace. She then carefully picked up her matching pendant earrings and carefully put them on each ear. She was going to yet another party with David – the sixth in two weeks. They were nearly always the same; the same people, the same conversations and, worst of all, the same assumptions that she was happy. Nevertheless, she stood up proudly in her full-length, ivory dress and looked at herself approvingly in the dressing table mirror. Regardless of how she felt inside, she had an image to uphold and she did rather enjoy being seen and photographed at society events. She picked up her satin clutch bag and her heels before heading out of the bedroom and down the stairs to the entrance hall where David was now waiting, and as patiently as he could.

'We must leave now Cara,' David urged, standing smartly dressed in a black dinner suit, his grey coat folded neatly over his arm. 'We don't want to arrive just in time for the dinner!'

'I know,' Cara replied with slight exasperation. 'I told you I was running late.' She bent down to put on her heels by the bottom step then stood up to slip into her long evening coat, which David held out for her. 'Thank you.' She turned to face him. 'Do you think my dress is OK for this evening?' she asked fleetingly. She quickly rummaged through her clutch bag again to ensure she had everything she needed.

'Yes you look divine,' David said hastily, reaching for the

front door. 'We always arrive late at this party so we must hurry.' He held the door open for Cara while admiring her elegance as she walked out into the cold February evening. She was so beautiful he sometimes didn't really notice what she was wearing.

They were on their way to an annual dinner party hosted by James Halpern, the founder and Managing Director of a prestigious property company, who liked to bring his closest friends within the property industry together. The party always presented a great opportunity to network and to be photographed for the reputable *Living the Desire* property magazine. David had co-founded a Mayfair-based hedge fund and had been involved with property, but it was Cara who had made it into a full-time successful career. She particularly enjoyed designing the properties in London to the taste of exceptionally wealthy and time-constrained foreigners, who simply wanted a base in London without having to do any further work to the property. David locked their front door at 8.00pm and walked briskly to his car. He held open the door to the passenger seat of his black Maserati for Cara.

'I hope Giles behaves himself tonight,' Cara said with concern as she stepped into the car. She wrapped her coat tightly around her to stop herself from shivering.

David quickly got in at the other side and started the engine. 'I told him he mustn't stay out late but he knows he has to be alert for his tennis match tomorrow.'

'Good. I do trust his friend's father to drive him home on time as well.'

David smirked slightly. 'Yes, although we may stay out rather late tonight.' He pulled away from Wellington Square towards Eaton Terrace, feeling a sense of achievement.

'If he asks us to stay over we must say no David. I have a lot to do tomorrow; I have to help organise an exhibition for this weekend, then I have that launch party for the bar on Walton Street . . . '

'Darling it would be fun to stay over. We can sleep at his like last time?'

'David, I'm not staying over again and I don't recall sleeping at all last time!'

David pulled a face as he concentrated on the road. They had been married for seventeen years but, despite their warm and familiar love for each other, they both knew they were on the verge of separation.

'Well you know he'll ask us Cara so I'll leave it to you to turn him down on his big night.'

They'd had a volatile year with growing disagreements leading to greater uncertainty with their future together but, because they had known each other for so long, regardless of what happened they knew they would always remain friends, or at least give it a good try.

'David, don't get into a mood about it, whether we stay over or not won't exactly make a huge difference to his night and I'm sure he'll have others to drink into the early hours with. I do want to return home tonight, OK?'

They had met at a fashion after party at The Ritz, London, when she was just nineteen and he was twenty-eight. She had fallen in love with David who, at five foot, ten inches, had a charming look about him with his deep-set hazel eyes presented by dark thick eyebrows and stubble around his strong jaw. He used to have a nice muscled physique, although he had relaxed a little over the years and his once lean stomach was now a bit rounded. His earlier strong jawline was also now hidden by the weight he'd put on around his face, although this made him look quite adorable. They had married a year after their first date and soon after Cara became pregnant with their only child, Giles, who was now sixteen years old. With her classically arranged features and elegant tall physique, she did a bit of modelling when she was in her late teens but her parents, who were involved within the property industry, encouraged her to get into the field.

She did so in her late twenties and never looked back, for property development utilised all her skills and passions, such as creativity, self-management and the ability to make *a lot* of money.

Cara stood confidently by the table of canapés in the double reception room in Eaton Terrace. A rather familiar crowd of about twenty-eight or so guests stood engaged in conversation, all drinking champagne served by two enthusiastic waiters. She gazed at the decor of the large, bright and busy room; James had an interesting way of combining contemporary design with antiques that amused her. In exercising her passion, her eyes skimmed across some young eager faces she hadn't seen before, as they mixed with her well-established friends. One female acquaintance she spotted by the door had evidently taken more trips to Harley Street since last year's party.

'Cara!' James exclaimed cheerfully.

Cara turned to see him approaching her quickly from the other side of the room; his gallant aura paving the way. 'James!' She matched his vibrant tone and leaned in to greet him; she had known James for eleven years through his friendship with David. 'You're looking very well! How have you been?'

'Very well thank you, and may I add that you look absolutely stunning as usual.' James took a step back to look her up and down.

She contained her emerging smile and sighted his latest girlfriend, whom she had met once before, walking towards them. Her name was Daisy – twenty-six years old and gorgeous with wavy platinum blonde hair, which tonight was held up elegantly in a French twist.

'Hello Cara,' Daisy said politely, standing two inches taller in a gold chiffon dress.

'Good to see you again Daisy.' Cara leaned in to embrace with her.

'Good to see you also.' Daisy flimsily kissed Cara's cheeks

before leaning back and wrapping her arm protectively around James's slim waist to lead him away, but he stood firm.

'So you must have just arrived?' James asked, finishing his glass then handing it to Daisy. He quickly smoothed out his eyebrows, which were as silky as his flicked back brown hair.

'Arrived about fifteen minutes ago.' Cara glanced at her watch. 'Enough time to realise you've redesigned this room since the last time I was here?'

'Yes indeed I have, how very observant of you! Made changes inspired by antique and fine art fairs among other events,' he beamed. 'Do you like it?'

'I love it, particularly your new paintings; the European landmarks match your sculpture collection very well.'

Daisy wrinkled her delicate nose silently.

'You have more guests this year by the way,' Cara continued as she gazed across the busy room. 'Some people I haven't seen before, which has somewhat excited me.'

James nodded proudly, casting his strong narrow-set eyes around the room at his numerous guests. 'I'll introduce you to the ones I'm particularly fond of. I've invited the eldest son of our friend Maurice – he's over there by the window,' James motioned discreetly. 'He's about to become *a lot* more involved in his father's business.' He lowered his voice. 'But that's one to discuss later.'

'Yes of course,' Cara said, diverting her intrigued eyes away from the young man.

'And apparently he's dating a much, much older woman you know . . . over twice his age I heard.'

'Oh?'

'Well I'm desperate to meet her but he hasn't brought her along – annoyingly. I do think some women look better the older they become you know.'

'Do you really think that James?' Daisy intercepted, almost in a daze.

'Yes, why we have an example here – I've seen photos of Cara when she was in her twenties and believe me when I say she's come a *very* long way since then.'

Cara shook her head with a tight-lipped grin. 'You're certainly the perfect host.'

'Cara my love, you know I'm teasing,' James laughed, embracing lightly with her. 'So where's that suspect husband of yours hiding?'

'He's had to take a call so I expect he's found a quiet corner somewhere.'

'Tell me, does David still play tennis at the Harbour Club?' James asked while feeling the slight, child-like tugs from Daisy.

'He does, yes. Why, do you still go?'

James winced. 'I've been meaning to get back into the game but I've been a bit lazy with my sporting activities lately, although I place all the blame with Daisy here.' He motioned at Daisy by quickly tilting his head towards her. Daisy tilted her head away at a faster speed so he didn't knock his head into hers.

Cara grinned slightly at the perfectly timed choreography. 'Didn't think you had it in you to be lazy James?'

'I know.' James turned to Daisy. 'Maybe you could motivate me to play darling?'

Daisy produced a smile. 'Depends on what's in it for me James, you know that?'

Daisy and James laughed in sync, although she still looked anxious to pull him away. Cara knew why – James had a reputation for being a bit of a playboy and clearly she saw her as competition. As well as being married James really wasn't her type, although he could certainly be considered handsome with his firm features and a smooth, clean-shaven face.

'Well tell David I'm on the lookout for him won't you. Listen Cara darling, I'll catch up with you both later at dinner – a lot to catch up on!' He trailed off with a wink as he allowed Daisy to happily lead him off.

Cara picked up a canapé and placed it delicately into her mouth, taking a moment to appreciate the ambience of the room. James had classical music playing throughout the property as usual, and had brightened the room with new yellow patterned curtaining for the two-front aspect floor-ceiling windows. She suddenly lit up as a young captivating woman walked towards her, smiling generously in a stunning draped dress. 'Hi,' Cara grinned.

'Hello,' the woman said gracefully. She quickly chose a couple of canapés to put on her plate. 'Bye,' she beamed softly, before walking back into the crowd.

The brief interaction made Cara suddenly feel very alone as she stood away from the centre of the crowd, waiting for David to return. She locked eyes with a dark, enchanting-looking man as he spoke with a friend of hers under the central chandelier; she exchanged a friendly look with him and glanced away. The crowd this year were unexpectedly tempting. She was about to immerse herself with the guests when David appeared back beside her.

'Sorry about that – important call. So have you seen the main man yet?'

'He came up to me a minute ago before Daisy dragged him off to her private garden.'

David looked bemused. 'How is he? I should find him.'

'Seems very happy . . . said he would look out for you but I expect he'll be back any second.' Cara glanced at her watch and waved at an acquaintance from across the room.

'I should think so.' David sipped his champagne and looked proudly across the room. 'He should have greeted us upon arrival, don't you think Cara?'

Cara nodded lightly and reached for a canapé. He looked at her quizzically; she appeared deep in thought but, as usual, he had no idea what she could possibly be thinking about. 'I've noticed a lot of the other guests looking at you tonight,' he complimented, in an attempt to snap her out of her own mysterious world. 'You know, I was surprised to come back and find you standing alone!'

Cara picked up her glass. 'Let's speak to Sander and Beatrice – I saw them arrive earlier,' she replied distractedly.

David put his empty glass down and followed her across the room to their mutual friends. He hoped that she would be in a more vibrant and flirtatious mood with him that night, despite their current delicate situation.

After a night of meeting with friends and engaging in fresh conversations with the new guests at the party, David found himself reluctantly driving back home at 1.15am. David opened their front door and Cara walked in briskly. She rested her clutch bag on the console table in the entrance hall.

'Giles hasn't returned any of my calls so I hope he's in bed asleep; I'm going to check.' She took off her heels and headed to Giles's bedroom on the second floor.

David put his shoes to the side and pulled off his cashmere scarf and coat. He walked after Cara.

Cara gazed at Giles asleep in his room and quietly shut the door. She turned to walk back to her marital bedroom on the third floor and nodded at David as he walked along the corridor towards her. 'He's asleep,' she said quietly, motioning at him to walk back towards their bedroom.

'Good night wasn't it?' David took off his tie and flung it onto the bed.

'Same as last year really,' Cara replied lazily. She picked up her night dress from the bed and walked into the en suite to get some time on her own. Her head was feeling heavy with thoughts about her marriage to David. She had watched and envied couples at the party who just seemed so in love with each other – the passion in their eyes were as clear as the sparkle of the diamonds on her bracelet. She removed her bracelet carelessly and it dropped to the tiled floor. She groaned and ignored it adamantly. She'd had enough of her inability to change things for the better and knew that she had to make big decisions, which she would finally stick to instead of going around in circles. But she had been with David for so long, which made it difficult emotionally for her to really move on with someone new. After ten minutes of deep thought, there was a sudden knock on the door, which startled her.

'Darling are you OK in there?'

'Yes David, I'll be out in a minute.' She bent down to pick up her bracelet from the floor and placed it on the marble counter-top. The next time she found true passion with someone, she was certainly not going to drop it again.

After a further fifteen minutes, she finished freshening up and walked back out to join David who had used another bathroom while she took her time in the en suite. She climbed into bed with him and pulled the white duvet over her so it reached her chin. David glanced over at her but she had her back to him. She was only in the mood for sleeping that night, although he had become used to this over the months.

'I enjoyed the party – food was fantastic as usual and James was looking very well wasn't he?' David pushed for a conversation.

'Yes, he was. We must invite him over for dinner soon.'

'I was thinking that actually. I do like his girlfriend Daisy as well.'

Cara rolled her eyes. 'We'll invite her too. Let's talk about it tomorrow darling – good night,' she said tiredly.

Cara woke at 7.30am with David snoring lightly beside her. She frowned slightly. She felt guilty for pulling him away earlier than usual from the annual party but she really did need a good night's sleep for a constructive day. She quietly got out of bed and walked to the en suite to freshen up. She was meeting her friend Elle Milne-Smith at 9.00am at Duke of York Square, where the charity art exhibition was going to be held the next day. She climbed back into bed for a few minutes' rest. David had awoken.

'Good morning,' he murmured tiredly.

She turned over and looked at him with affection. Even though she no longer felt passionate towards him as she once did, there were times when he looked exceptionally endearing. She stroked his black ruffled hair and kissed his broad shoulder.

'Did you sleep well?' David yawned.

'Yes I did actually. I was just thinking about the party; it was nice to see everyone wasn't it? Felt more vibrant than last year.'

'James knows how to put on a good show! I had a great time last night.'

Cara felt bad for cutting his fun night short as she examined his tired, yet cheerful face. When she got into bed she had gone straight to sleep when she knew that he wanted to discuss and prolong the night. She stroked his hair again and kissed him gently on his cheek. 'And you'll have a great time this morning,' she said tenderly. She gently pushed him onto this back – she would make last night up to him that morning, regardless of how she felt about their relationship.

Chapter Two

Sirena Marquez laughed courteously with her new colleague, Joseph, as he told her what it was like working at Lion Star PR, the agency she had joined two weeks ago. She had been working in Reigate, Surrey, where she was born and grew up, since she graduated two years ago. Since then, she had been trying to get into PR for fashion publications but, with little experience in

PR itself, she ended up at Lion Star PR, located on Oxford Street, whose clients were within the consumer food and drink sectors. She saw this as a valuable stepping stone nonetheless, and intended on signing up for a weekend or evening course at London College of Fashion, which was conveniently located close to her office.

'So I bet you're glad you accepted a job with us now that you know what we're really like,' Joseph laughed, taking his drink off the bar counter.

'I may actually just move back to Surrey tonight,' Sirena quipped.

'Don't scare her off,' Marcus, her new manager, interrupted. 'We want her to last longer than two months.' He glanced back at Sirena. 'Jenny left because she didn't like being locked in the office overnight every time she made a mistake – I hope you're tougher.'

'In that case, so do I!' Sirena replied, noting his arms, which were as thick as tree trunks. He was an immaculate man who clearly liked to take care of himself, which included going to the gym every morning and evening. Sirena glanced as discreetly as possible at her watch. It was getting late and she really couldn't spend another hour or so at the bar off Oxford Street. She needed a break from her colleagues before seeing them again tomorrow morning and for the rest of the week. She was still feeling overwhelmed with her move to London and starting a new job.

On arriving back to her one bedroom flat in Putney, she didn't waste any time in climbing into her pyjamas and tying back her voluminous hair, which she had down for the whole day. She got into bed and looked at the bare walls, which she still needed to decorate with pictures and photos. She hadn't had much time to decorate the flat as she had started her new job only two days after moving in, but she loved her new independence. Before moving to London she had split up with

Cameron, her boyfriend of two years. They attended the same university and met in a bar in Exeter, but over time it had become evident that the relationship just wouldn't last. Cameron was fun and also very smart but something was missing. He had also decided to go travelling for a year, which she didn't want to do as she had done all of that in her gap year before university, so her career had to now take centre stage.

At 7.45am Cara lay in bed staring at the large plasma television opposite her bed, watching a morning talk show on mute. She had arrived home late from a friend's dinner party in South Kensington, when she should have been packing for her trip to Lombardia with Giles. The flight was at midday so, after ten minutes, she pulled herself up straight in bed to prepare herself to get out of her warm bed.

She nudged her foot against Amber who lay leisurely on the end of her bed. 'Do you want breakfast?' she asked playfully.

In recent months, Amber had become the strong focus of her innate motherly affections and had been the only witness to seeing her cry secretly at night in her bed, since she had made the decision to finally change her life. Lately as the days went by, however, she wondered if she had made the right decision at all, although her close friends were always there to remind her that she *definitely* had. She gazed into Amber's cute dark eyes and smiled affectionately. Amber, her Cavalier King Charles Spaniel, just stared back at her with a slightly bemused expression. She felt a sudden vibration beside her; it was her friend, Elle, calling. She answered straight away.

'Hi darling! Feeling OK this morning?' came a vibrant voice.

'Elle darling, I've got a flight to catch in a few hours . . . tell me why we drank so much?'

'Why did *you* drink too much you mean! Are you all right?'

'Yes I'll be fine,' Cara hesitated, 'just feel a bit disorientated, that's all.'

Elle giggled faintly. 'Darling I've got to pick up a sculpture now from a gallery, but shall we meet quickly before you leave?'

Cara gazed at her Bulgari watch, carelessly laid out on the bedside table. 'OK, I'll be in until about ten so just come over when you're free for a quick goodbye.'

She swiftly ended the call on making the arrangement and dragged herself out of bed and into the en suite. She looked at herself in the mirror and sighed deeply; the nine months since James Halpern's party had taken their toll and she felt more tired and run down than ever. She had chosen to separate from David soon after the party, which they both knew was coming for a long time, but he hadn't taken it as well as she had. She was seeking passion in her life again and could no longer deal with David's growing mood swings, and despite his love for her, her uncertainty with her life had also become an increasing problem for him. He had moved out of their family home for three months during the separation, but they had reached an agreement to remain under the same roof as a family where, despite their disagreements with each other, it was a place where they all felt the safest. After all, they had known each other for eighteen years.

She pulled off her camisole and removed her matching knickers. She then stepped into her shower room and stood just close enough for the water to barely touch her. She watched the warm droplets of water as they began to hit and trickle off her breasts and recalled a memory of being in the shower with Alessandra, in one of the other bathrooms in her home. At times she wished that she hadn't ended things with her, as she had brought energy and excitement into her life, as well as a toned and youthful body. But Alessandra had suddenly made things very complicated for her so it was a decision she *had* to make. She tapped the digital control panel to increase the water temperature and moved closer in; as each intensified hot drop of water hit her soft skin, she recalled what it was like to feel incredibly passionate towards someone. She was truly missing what she once had and threw away a few years ago as her life since had felt tedious, despite her work projects and attending various events and parties in London and around the world.

Feeling more refreshed, she stepped out of the shower room onto a white towel and reached for her matching white bathrobe, hanging idly on the door. She was going to spend the rest of the morning leisurely packing for Italy and double-checking that Giles had packed his passport this time. Although he was going to be seventeen in February, he still needed her organisation skills at times.

'It's turning out to be a rather busy morning,' Elle remarked, stepping into Cara's entrance hall. After a warm embrace and a kiss on each cheek, Cara casually led the way to the reception room. She had just changed into a pair of jeans and a cosy cashmere jumper. 'I know. Can't be with you for long Elle as Giles and I are leaving soon.'

'Yes of course darling,' Elle replied, following closely behind Cara. Elle was forty years old and resembled a youthful sleek panther. 'I actually just wanted to check that you're fit for travel.' She took off her Burberry trench coat in the spacious reception room and laid it over the arm of the cream sofa, revealing her fitted red sweater that showed off her physique well. Elle was blessed with a dark sultry beauty with classic features inherited from her English parents. Her slim physique was similar to Cara's, although she stood an inch shorter than Cara at five foot, seven inches.

'Yes I'm fine thank you,' Cara smiled, pointing lazily to a cup on the bespoke coffee table for Elle. 'Coffee was the saviour, as my father used to say.'

'And a whole lot more, babe.' Elle sat down on the sofa beside Cara, sweeping back her dark brown fringe that had fallen across her face. She reached for her cup of tea. 'So have you finished packing?' she asked in her matching sultry voice.

'I've spent the last hour packing, can't wait to get on that plane now you know?'

'I certainly wouldn't mind flying off right now. Have to sit through a dinner with my ex and his wife tonight. The children are looking forward to it, though. Where's Giles by the way?'

'He's up in his room, packing I do hope. I know he's looking forward to this trip – we both are.'

'Well it would appear that everyone has something to look forward to today except me then.' Elle turned in her seat and locked her seductive hazel eyes on to Cara. 'So, what did you think of Steven last night?' She gave Cara a mischievous look while arching one of her dark alluring eyebrows. Her feminine yet playful elegance constantly swirled around her. 'You know he kept going on about you in the car . . . I was rather amused until he was almost in tears.'

'No Elle, as I recall telling you last night – I'm not interested!'

'Darling you need someone to take your mind off things. You should give him a go; he's such a lovely man, among other things.'

'I'm sure he is lovely,' Cara giggled unsurely, 'but he's so incredibly boring! Don't you think?'

Elle laughed. 'He's not a born entertainer but he is very handsome, though?'

'He's all right but I'm not desperate!'

In responding, Elle noted Cara's split second expression of frustration; she was desperate all right. Although Cara always had a herd of admirers after her, which included industry tycoons and key international political figures, they were merely good for the attention only. For Cara, sleeping with any of them or considering a relationship was a different matter.

'But what I am desperate for is more sleep. I'm probably going to doze off on the plane later.'

'Well you sound a lot more awake than you did this morning.'

'I had a long shower, which has helped – *believe me*. Plus the coffee . . . I might have another actually before we leave.'

Elle nodded. Cara sounded a lot more alert but she didn't particularly look it. 'How have things been with David? I didn't get a chance to ask you last night. Makram told me this morning that he's meeting him for lunch so who knows what they're plotting,' she smirked.

'Oh, he didn't mention that to me but, yes, things are OK between us. He's in the City this morning.' David was a good friend of Elle's second husband so it wasn't a surprise to hear that they were meeting each other.

Elle gazed into her cup thoughtfully. Cara guessed the question that was coming.

'So, no more thoughts about moving out yet? You haven't mentioned it in a while.'

Cara groaned. 'No. I just can't be bothered to think about it, you know? Us all living together is good for Giles anyway.' She turned to gauge a reaction from Elle, who just nodded. Cara looked away. 'Well we're friends and we know where each other stands, so until we both meet someone else . . . '

'If you feel that it's better for you then of course don't move, but I just worry for you Cara.'

Her friends never kept it a secret that they felt it would be best for her to move into a place of her own – and she agreed that it would be best for the long term, but she knew that living on her own would only make her feel even more lonely. She felt it best to remain at Wellington Square until she met someone else who could ignite the fire within her, although this was proving to be a long process.

'You shouldn't worry about me, Elle, there's really no need.

Anyway, I've been invited to St Kitts for the New Year . . . I wasn't going to go but I do need a long break.'

'Oh is that with your friend who lives in . . . gosh I can't remember, in Jordan?'

Cara nodded and took her time to respond. 'Yes. You know, I probably will go.'

Sirena smiled and turned back to her computer. She was looking forward to her first big night out in London since moving from Reigate. Her friend Natalie, whom she had known since school, worked for a small publishing firm in Marylebone and had ensured that they would get into an exclusive club in South Kensington, which was an area of London unfamiliar to her. But Natalie grew to know the London night scene well while working in London, as she became friends with people who worked on the PR side, looking after guest lists for the various private members clubs. With long dark blonde hair and a shapely figure, Natalie turned heads wherever she went and was certainly one of Sirena's more adventurous friends who she could rely on for exciting nights out.

After freezing in the queue for over fifteen minutes, Sirena and Natalie contained their excitement as they walked through the entrance and down the stairs to the main dance floor of the club. The interior was beautiful with crystal chandeliers hanging from the ceilings and a small VIP section with tables making a clearing for a smaller dance floor. After Sirena took a visit to the bathroom she found Natalie talking to a very smart-looking man in an all black suit with silver white hair. As Sirena began talking to Natalie, the man walked away and over to his seemingly reserved seating area in one corner of the dance floor. Her conversation with Natalie was then interrupted by another smart but younger Arab-looking man, whom Natalie then began talking to. As Sirena casually looked around the busy dance floor she caught sight of the man with silver hair looking over at her. He signalled at her with his hands to sit next to him; she didn't really know what else to do as Natalie was now talking to the other man so she curiously walked over, squeezing through the crowd. He immediately handed her a glass of champagne from the bottle in a large silver ice bucket on the table.

'What's your name?' he asked, leaning into her over the loud house music.

'Sirena,' she shouted back, her softer voice more drowned out.

They both drank from their glasses and engaged in a few silent seconds to scan the crowd around them.

'Where are you from?' he asked, giving her his full attention again.

'Here . . . the UK.'

'I thought you were from the Middle East – you look like my niece!'

She took an instant liking to this man, not just because he so freely gave her champagne, but because he had a very warm aura and came across as very confident. They continued to sit with each other for a further forty minutes or so and got into various conversations, which they often struggled with due to the loud music, but they were enjoying each other's presence. Natalie suddenly threw herself down beside Sirena with a thud.

'Where've you been?' Sirena asked wistfully, glad of her presence.

'Have you been here all along? I've been dancing with these really funny guys!' she replied enthusiastically as she danced to the music in her seat.

'This is Natalie.' Sirena introduced her to the man whose name she still didn't know, which resulted in a moment of awkwardness. 'Natalie this is . . . '

'We were talking earlier.' Natalie smiled over at him and caught sight of the champagne on the table. The man handed her a glass with a confident smile.

Sirena sat in silence looking at the people dancing in front of them; all glamorous and well dressed. It would be nice to meet someone special tonight, she thought. The man she had been speaking to was very nice but she wasn't attracted to him. It had been a long time since she'd felt attracted to anyone.

As late December drew closer after a few more nights out, Sirena soon discovered that goodwill to all men had little meaning during the heightened busy Christmas period, as home driven commuters collided with dazzled shoppers along the most famous street in the world at rush hour. Her heart sank while battling her way along Oxford Street to the tube station after work, when she witnessed a young man's Selfridges bag take off like the Snowman and go flying in the air, only to fall and be trampled on by herds of commuters and shoppers as he began scrambling about to retrieve his purchases.

At the same time this sense of urgency also created a great sense of excitement and she held on well to her Christmas spirit – and her bags. A week before Christmas, Sirena happily packed for her return home for the festive holiday season.

Chapter Three

It was the New Year and the beginning of January. Sirena had returned to London after her relaxing holiday at home in Reigate. Having now been in London for a couple of months she was keen on exploring areas of London unfamiliar to her. She had heard of Chelsea and knew of its status as one of the most fashionable boroughs in London so, out of curiosity, she decided to head there. On Saturday morning, she got off at Sloane Square tube station and walked up the King's Road. She walked past Duke of York Square and down Cheltenham Terrace to absorb the atmosphere of the elegant residential areas. To get back onto the King's Road, she walked back up Walpole Street where rows of tall white and brown brick houses, protected by black railings, stood side by side and rows of BMWs, Ferraris and Minis parked proudly. She felt very relaxed walking around the area; the hectic environment of Oxford Street and the plain feel of Putney were certainly not present there. With the Christmas money she'd received, she couldn't resist visiting the Calvin Klein store on the King's Road.

To take a break from exploring and shopping – and to take shelter from the icy cold weather – she decided to rest in a coffee shop for a while before making her journey back to Reigate for the rest of the weekend. She walked further up the King's Road, passing Caffè Nero, but it was too busy so she carried on walking to Starbucks.

Inside Caffè Nero, Cara was sitting on her own flicking through an interior design magazine with her shopping bags beside her. She had returned from St Kitts a few days ago and was still readjusting to the English winter weather. She took a bite of her chocolate brownie and looked up to see who was around her. There were a small group of friends in a corner, laughing and joking with each other and an older couple, sitting quietly beside her as they read their newspapers. She smiled slightly to herself and drank her latte, pondering her own life. She knew that she should be in Switzerland attending to her chateau by the lake, which she was trying to sell, but she had other priorities to attend to in London. Gradually she collected up her magazine and bags, and left the coffee shop. She walked back home to Wellington Square, just off the King's Road, and retreated to her bedroom where she quickly packed clothes into her gym bag before she was to head to KX on Draycott Avenue. She picked up her keys and quickly walked down the stairs to the ground floor.

'Oh, hi Cara!' David had just walked through the front door, startled to suddenly see her as she walked towards him.

'Hey,' Cara said hazily, lifting her gym bag over her shoulder.
'Off to the gym I see?'

'For an hour or so – have to visit a friend after for a quick catch up so driving. So, where did you get off to?' Since their separation they had become more amicable towards each other and it was working well for them.

'Met with Paul for lunch at the Poissonnerie – I left him behind with that overly dramatic character . . . oh his name has escaped me . . .'

'Gregory? You said you were . . .'

'Ah yes! Thank you, yes Gregory,' he interrupted. 'He's just got married to his fourth wife would you believe? He's only forty years old so that's one for every decade!'

Cara rolled her eyes. She had met two of his previous wives at parties who to her were evidently after one thing only: his extraordinary wealth. 'I thought you said you were going to Sussex this weekend?'

'You know I quite simply couldn't be bothered and it's far too cold – thought you, Giles and I could have a nice dinner somewhere tonight instead, seeing as we're all in town now?'

'Err . . . yes that should be fine,' Cara hesitantly replied. She edged closer towards the front door. 'Let me know where you want to go but yes that's fine with me.' She gave him an indolent smile and walked out towards her car. Before starting the engine, she glanced back at David who was watching her leave at the front door. He gave her a small wave. She waved back and pulled away to Draycott Avenue. As she drove she couldn't help but wonder if David had cancelled his trip to Sussex just to spend more time with her. If so, she wished he hadn't. It was mainly her decision that they separated and she could feel that he was beginning to try to win her back again, and so soon after the separation. But that was David.

Sirena travelled home to Reigate after her tour of Chelsea to liven herself up, seeing as her family and friends all remained in Surrey.

'That club in Kensington was amazing – we should go back there soon!'

Sirena turned to hand her a cup of tea with a wince.

'Thank you – it's bloody cold outside.' Natalie wrapped her hands around the hot cup.

'So what did you get up to last night?'

'Well, that's actually why I'm here – I researched some parties and events online and I found an amazing one, which is this Wednesday coming at the May Fair Hotel!'

'Really! What sort of party?'

Natalie always knew where to go for fun.

'Networking for professionals – like you and I,' Natalie said hurriedly to create a sense of urgency.

'Networking?'

'Yes, it looks amazing and I think it'll be really fun. It says here . . . ' She fumbled about for a piece of neatly folded paper in her bag and closely read the content. 'It says that these parties are great for getting to know like-minded professionals who work in the City. Professional guys, Sirena. Just what you and I need!'

'You think?! I would rather check out a new club – these things are usually quite dull.'

Natalie looked despondent.

'But it would be useful do some networking,' Sirena continued thoughtfully.

'Great, I'll meet you there after work – I can't wait!' Natalie was evidently thrilled. Although Natalie was very attractive she was also fussy, which resulted in her single status for long periods of time and her enthusiasm for such random nights out. She was dating her manager, Chris, but only on an ad hoc basis, which she had rather hoped was more serious – but she wasn't going to wait around for him to decide. Natalie left Sirena's house for the stables after she finished her tea but also left

Sirena with the party information. She picked it up and read it.

Networking for Professionals at the May Fair Hotel. This popular monthly event will take place on Wednesday, 7.00–11.00pm. £15 on the door or £10 payable online – book early to avoid disappointment.

It did actually seem quite exciting and the May Fair Hotel looked beautiful, Sirena thought. The prospect of meeting influential business people was also what she needed so it was an event to look forward to. The clubs could wait.

'So how was your gym session?' David asked. He stretched his arms out while puffing his chest to illustrate his question.

'OK, I might get a new yoga trainer you know.' Cara frowned at Giles as he put some of his fried vegetables onto her plate. David had asked her to eat with him and Giles at a Thai restaurant just off the Fulham Road, after her busier than planned day. 'You should eat more vegetables, Giles.'

David put some of his vegetables onto Giles's plate. 'Sounds good, a friend was telling me how good her trainer was yesterday.' He took a quick bite of his chicken in green curry. 'I'll ask her for details tomorrow.'

'Oh I've just remembered, I've got a Thai yoga massage booked for tomorrow,' Cara continued. 'I've already arranged lunch with a friend.'

'Well it's a good thing we chose a Thai restaurant!' Giles remarked. He defiantly moved the vegetables on his plate to the side.

Cara's phone vibrated hard on the table. It was a text from Vladimir, one of her friends in property who also tapped into other areas such as restaurants and bars.

I won't be back in London till late Tues so let's meet Wednesday 7pm, Eaton Square

'Vladimir's rescheduled the meeting on Tuesday to Wednesday,' she frowned. Elle had informed her earlier that she would be holding a special dinner party on Wednesday night.

'When does he not reschedule? I don't know why you weren't expecting it,' David quipped.

'I'm not surprised, just annoyed. I spoke with Elle earlier – she invited me to her dinner party on Wednesday . . . '

'Just go to the party,' Giles shrugged. He made another attempt to flatten down his brown hair, which the sleet had frizzed up. 'Or change the date of the meeting like he has?'

Cara looked at him, momentarily deep in thought. 'And you better get straight back to your studying after skiing,' she said sternly. 'I hope you make sure that you have everything ready by Friday.'

'You should meet Vladimir – you and Elle see each other all the time. Meetings with Vladimir are often very beneficial.'

'I'll speak to Elle later,' she said contemplatively. David was right.

Cara retreated to her bedroom and called her friend Helen Clancy, but there was no answer. She was in the mood for going out after her dinner, and knew various friends were out in clubs and restaurants that Saturday night. She pondered who to call next, but David called her from the bottom of the stairs. 'Yes?'

'Giles and I are going to watch a film – do you want to join us?'

Cara hesitated for a few seconds, standing by the door. Staying in and watching a film was hardly exciting. She proceeded to walk out to the landing. 'Sure, I'll be down in a second.'

Her lazy decision had been made. She knew she had to spend more nights out in town with friends if she was to actually meet someone new – and she needed it to be soon as it had been nearly a year since she'd last had sex. She had no idea if David was sleeping with other women – of course he never brought anyone back to the family home – but she often wondered when he would go on business trips abroad. She knew she only had to raise one eyebrow if she needed sex from him, but she certainly didn't want to confuse the situation between them. Sexual thoughts were teasingly running through her mind; making love to a gorgeous woman and trailing her hands over a soft slender body. She had worked herself up and excitedly shut her bedroom door to spend a few more minutes on her own.

Chapter Four

Cara strolled leisurely out of Chanel on Brompton Road, clutching her bag and new top. She felt revitalised after her facial and arm massage at a spa earlier that Tuesday morning, and planned to spend the rest of the day making updates to her wardrobe.

'Cara!' a clear-spoken voice called from behind her.

She turned around to see a tall cheerful man in a long grey coat, strolling vibrantly towards her.

'Cara – how lovely to see you!'

It was Michael Lauder, her close friend of ten years. Michael hit on her every now and again, and once succeeded when they were on a yacht together in Antibes. 'Michael! What are you doing here?'

'Just walking through – on my way to the big meeting,' he said as he glanced at his watch, with deep brown eyes. 'And you're buying me gifts I see?'

'Yes – a lovely sequined top. So the deal is still going through then?'

'Indeed,' he replied confidently, flashing his trademark smile that exposed his brilliant white teeth. 'And what about your Swiss chateau?'

'*Still* trying to sell it.'

He nodded at her brightly, loosening his patterned scarf around his neck. While he was a yacht tycoon he perceived her as the equivalent in property. 'I'm sure you'll sell it soon, certainly if your history is anything to go by, but you'll have to tell me more over a drink or dinner instead of a fleeting conversation!' He gazed at her warmly in the chilly wind, as she delicately swept her hair away from her face. 'I take it that I'll be seeing you at Elle's tomorrow evening?' He enthusiastically clasped his cold hands together.

'No,' she sighed. 'I have a meeting to attend now, which will probably run late – it's with Vladimir.'

'Oh?' he replied with a raised eyebrow. 'Well that's a great shame; I was looking forward to us having a good catch up. But if you do manage to finish in time, do come over won't you?'

Cara nodded, although she knew this probably wouldn't happen. 'Of course I'll let you know if I can make it, even if it's just for dessert.'

After the brief catch up, Cara carried on walking down Brompton Road back to her car. She knew she was going to be missing out on Wednesday night. Michael could be so entertaining and, recently, she had been thinking about him more often. Although he wasn't normally her type physically with his blonde hair and fair complexion, they had some chemistry and she knew she would probably have fun with him in bed. But there was just *something* missing and she would feel strange with another man after being with David for so long. The thought of getting back in touch with Alessandra was becoming more desirable, but it had been so long since they had parted ways.

Sirena arrived at the May Fair Hotel on Wednesday feeling slightly apprehensive. She had received a text from Natalie declaring that she was going to be late due to a heavy workload, but she didn't want to hang around her office later than she had to after a hectic day. She walked through the main entrance into a grand lobby and asked at reception for directions to the party. She was directed to the May Fair bar and could see through the windows as she drew closer what seemed to be a couple of organisers talking by the main doors. She reminded herself that she was still very early – it was only 6.15pm and it wasn't due to start till 7.00pm.

Making her way down the stairs to the lavish bathroom, she pulled off her winter coat then checked on her hair and make-up. Her hair was swept up in a clip but she took it down; she felt a lot sexier when her long thick hair flowed over her narrow shoulders. Before she left her office she'd changed into a pair of slim jeans and a tight-fitted v-neck jumper. Feeling confident she entered the bar and was greeted by two organisers, clutching clipboards. She took a quick look around; there were only about eight or so people from what she could see, but snow had begun to fall more heavily so she rather wished that she had gone straight home after work. But the bar was warm and very stylish, with large windows exposing the falling snow. It wasn't a bad place to be.

The organisers directed her to the other side of the bar where the event would be taking place; it was sectioned off till 7.00pm, however. As she had arrived early, they suggested she stay in the main part of the bar so she walked towards the bar counter to order a drink. She noticed a woman sitting alone at the other end, on one of the black bar stools that aligned the long bar. She noticed her beautiful golden brown tousled hair, which reached beyond her defined shoulders; it looked nice resting on her light apricot top. Sirena picked up the drinks menu as she sat down. She glanced over at the woman who was looking into her champagne glass, seemingly deep in thought, but she suddenly gazed over at her and they fleetingly met each other's unfamiliar eyes. Sirena felt overwhelmed by the woman's striking face; her eyes were beautifully brown and prominent, yet somehow sad. She looked very elegant and glamorous with her Louis Vuitton bag resting on her lap, her tan arms exposed by her short-sleeved top.

'Hi are you here for the party as well?' Sirena asked the woman with a hint of hope.

'No . . . ' she replied curiously. 'What party is this?' She was suddenly enthusiastic.

'Oh, it's just a networking party,' Sirena replied, disappointed that she wasn't attending but delighted by her enthusiasm all the same. 'Nothing too exciting!'

'Oh right, didn't realise there was a party going on here.' She turned in her stool to look around the quiet bar, sighting a *RESERVED* sign in the lower section of the bar. She had wondered why it was blocked off.

'I'm early . . . been hanging around the hotel since six-*fifteen*.'

'It's been very quiet in here but the snow will delay people.' The woman turned back to face Sirena and picked up her glass of champagne. 'I didn't want to come out today myself because of the blizzard, but I had an important meeting,' she said proudly with a captivating, sensuous smile.

Sirena nodded with a little interest. 'Oh right, what was the meeting about?'

'It was more of an exchange of knowledge really and some exciting developments. I had it here,' she said as she twirled her hand around in a circle motion. 'Now I'm indulgently treating myself for a successful outcome.' She suppressed a smile and took a sip of her champagne. 'And for some reason I'm craving tiramisu all of a sudden.'

Sirena giggled. 'I love tiramisu . . . wouldn't mind that now myself actually.'

'It is yummy. So a networking party . . . isn't that usually another name for a singles event?' The woman looked suddenly intrigued again.

Sirena was instantly flustered. 'I don't know but I'm actually here for a friend who found out about it online.' She didn't know why she felt embarrassed about the party.

'I was going to say, someone as attractive as you should be so inundated with offers you shouldn't have to bother.'

'That's very nice of you to say, but I *am* interested in networking as I . . . '

'Of course,' the woman interrupted with a smirk.

'No really – I am!'

'Yes OK. So why did you get here so early then and where's your friend?'

'Well I've just come straight from work and my friend Natalie has loads of work on so that's why she's going to be late.'

'Oh you're just eager,' she grinned, finishing off her champagne. Sirena was humoured by the woman's cool and cheeky attitude towards her. She looked back and saw the organisers still talking among themselves.

'My name's Cara by the way, what's yours?' she asked to draw back Sirena's seemingly trailing attention. She was captivated by her.

'Sirena.'

Cara smiled, shaking Sirena's hand. 'Sirena's a lovely name; what would you like to drink?'

'Oh that's OK, I'll get mine.'

'No please let me, Sirena,' Cara insisted. She took out her Louis Vuitton wallet.

'No really it's OK.' Sirena reached for her purse in her bag.

'Sirena you're verging on being *very* rude.'

Sirena laughed. 'OK fine.' She took another quick scan of the menu. 'The Fresh Fruit Martini looks nice, thank you – very kind of you.'

'You've caught me in a good mood so make the most of it.' Cara motioned the barman who walked over. She had an extraordinary air of grace about her, Sirena thought as she watched her. 'So Sirena, what do you do if you don't mind me asking?' Cara turned in her seat to fully face Sirena again.

'I'm an account executive.'

'Do you enjoy it?'

Sirena thought for a few seconds. 'It's very varied . . . I enjoy the creative aspects.'

Cara nodded, unsure of Sirena's job. 'It's important to enjoy one's career.'

'Yeah I know, so my parents keep telling me.'

'Well they're right to . . . you should always listen to your parents.'

'I'm actually trying to get into fashion PR, though, but it's so competitive.'

'If you believe in yourself, there is no competition,' Cara said with a glint in her eye. 'Think like Muhammad Ali but dance through life like you're in *Swan Lake*. Or you can of course punch your way through but you don't quite seem the type . . . '

'If I was, I probably wouldn't tell you!'

'So you're a composed dancer like me?'

'Are you a dancer in *Swan Lake*?' Sirena asked with surprise.

'No! I'm in property and have been for many years!'

'Oh!' Sirena laughed. 'Wow; around London?'

'Yes and overseas, depending on the markets,' Cara replied, rolling her eyes.

'Oh wow, what countries?' Sirena didn't know anything about property so her questions were limited.

'Switzerland, France . . . ' Cara replied, twirling her hand in a circular motion again. 'You seem to be very excited about property – you've lit up more by talking about it than when you spoke about your career, which is interesting.'

'Oh did I? I guess it's because property development seems a lot more adventurous than an office job.' Sirena shrugged.

'Yes I can imagine. I've never worked in an office before, you know – I mean in a company. I would just get into trouble all the time, throwing paperclips probably. A bit like being at school actually when I used to love causing mischief – made me realise what I could get away with.'

Sirena giggled as she reached for her cocktail. 'Thanks for this again.'

'That's OK – good choice.' Cara produced a sensuous smile and analysed Sirena more closely as she took her first sip from the glass. She was taken with her. 'So you're single then Sirena?'

'It's not a singles party!'

'Apologies!' Cara grimaced jokingly, although wishing the gorgeous girl answered the question seriously. 'Sorry, I don't even know you and I'm teasing you.'

Sirena glanced away, blushing all of a sudden.

'Where are you from by the way?'

'Half Spanish, half English. You?'

'That's a lovely mix, you have a striking look – you definitely look more continental. I have French and Italian in me.' Cara grinned.

'Oh wow, so can you speak French and Italian?' Cara's Mediterranean genes explained her tan skin.

'I speak more Italian than French. I've always spent more time in Italy with relatives – I have more fun in Italy and more conversation in France, funnily enough,' she smirked playfully. She loved that Sirena shared a continental European connection and she spoke well. 'So do you live close by here?'

'Close to Mayfair?'

Cara nodded, glancing at her watch.

'I live . . . ' Sirena's phone began vibrating; it was Natalie calling so she asked Cara to excuse her as she took the call.

Cara glanced around the bar again; still no new arrivals. Poor girl, she thought to herself as she turned back to watch her. She couldn't take her eyes off her, although she had to leave any second for Elle's dinner party. Thankfully Vladimir had moved the meeting forward earlier that afternoon as well as changing the location, which, again, was more convenient for him as he had an earlier meeting at a friend's office in the area. Of course this last minute change was of no surprise as she had to cut her lunch with a close friend short earlier that day.

Sirena gave Cara a sideways glance while talking to Natalie; she could see that Cara was about to leave as she put a jumper on and then her long cream winter coat. She got off the phone as quickly as she could.

'Sirena, I didn't realise the time – I've got to attend a friend's dinner party now. Sorry I can't wait with you until your friend arrives.' She gave Sirena a look of sympathy while retrieving her bag from the bar.

'Oh, that's OK; she just called to say she's on her way.'

'OK that's good,' Cara hesitated as she looked into Sirena's promising brown eyes. She couldn't just walk away from someone so beautiful and intriguing. 'Sirena I hope you don't mind . . . it's been brief but,' Cara giggled awkwardly. 'Sorry, I was just wondering if . . . gosh, sorry I'm rambling!'

'It's OK!'

Cara composed herself quickly. 'I would really like to carry on our conversation, I mean, I know it was brief but you've intrigued me and I can assure you that doesn't happen often!'

Sirena contained her bemusement. 'Oh right, well I would like to hear from you also,' she smiled happily.

'Oh would you?' Cara asked brightly.

'Yeah,' Sirena shrugged. 'I enjoy meeting new people so why not?'

'Oh great – well I haven't got any cards on me this evening. Can I take your number before I dash off? Sorry for the rush, my friend will seat me in a corner if I turn up late.'

'Lovely friend! Well I don't actually have any cards on me either.' Sirena searched for her number in her phone, feeling overwhelmed yet flattered by the woman's directness. 'Sorry, I'm just finding my number – I never remember it.'

As Sirena flicked through her phone, Cara stood discreetly admiring her. Sirena looked very young but she was reluctant to ask her age; the only information she wanted to walk away with now was her number. Sirena handed Cara her phone and Cara intently typed in her number after saving Sirena's into her phone.

'Thank you.' Cara handed Sirena back her phone. 'Well it was lovely speaking with you – I look forward to us meeting again Sirena.'

'Good speaking to you also,' Sirena smiled. 'Have a good night.'

'And you have fun tonight.' She gave Sirena a cheeky tight-lipped smile before turning to walk away.

Sirena continued to wait at the bar and exchanged small smiles with the barman while she waited for Natalie. She would have participated in small talk with him but was more inclined to go over the moment she had just shared with the mysterious woman who had attracted her within seconds, and then baffled her within the last few minutes. She looked at Cara's number in her phone and felt strangely excited, but she had no idea why they had exchanged numbers – and why Cara would want to see her again.

Chapter Five

At Lamont Road, Chelsea, Elle woke feeling triumphant with her dinner party the previous night. Although Michael didn't turn up with an excuse of food poisoning, Cara had managed to get to hers on time so she had a rather wonderful night catching up with the lives of her close friends. She was particularly interested to hear that Cara had met a random girl at the May Fair Hotel who'd injected hope into her just through mere conversation. Cara seemed to be especially enthusiastic, which she hadn't been over someone for a *long* time.

She threw on her light blue cotton bathrobe and sat up in bed to face the paperwork in front of her. She had just purchased a new property in Kensington, which she was going to redesign for a wealthy foreigner to snap up. She knew what attracted the Russians, the Arabs, the Chinese and so on through her husband, Makram El Haj – a westernised Lebanese property tycoon. It was only on meeting Makram that she gradually became involved in property. She had bought her first property three years ago so she was still quite new to the business. Previously she had been involved in health and fitness and ran a small business in her four-bedroom apartment in Chelsea Bridge Wharf, Battersea.

Makram was making her breakfast in the kitchen before he had to dash out for a meeting. He felt he had to be extra kind to her as he had promised to be at her dinner party but cancelled at the last minute due to work pressures.

'Thank you darling,' she replied as he brought in a tray of fresh fruit and toast.

'Made with love and anxiety. I've got to head out by quarter past.' He glanced at the bedside clock beside Elle.

'You're very late this morning,' she replied, not looking up as she read through contracts; something she disliked doing and usually gave to Makram to take care of. She took a small bite of her toast.

'Meeting was pushed back so no point leaving any earlier.' He adjusted his sleeves as he stood by the bed. 'What are your plans for the day then?'

'Going to measure up at the Kensington property for a few items and then probably relax for a while in a spa pool to soothe my entire body; may have a long massage as well.'

'Can't you just dot a few scented candles around the room?'

Elle took a couple of seconds to glance at Makram with a baffled expression. 'Yes if I wanted to soothe my senses but I'm talking about my body darling!'

'Whatever.' He threw on his suit jacket. 'Don't soothe too hard and I'll see you tonight then baby.' He kissed her on the cheek.

Elle reached for his belt and pulled him in. 'I'm missing you already,' she said teasingly. She began to undo his belt. 'I haven't given you *your* special massage this morning.'

Elle had met Makram when she was thirty-one years old and he became a step-father to her now sixteen-year-old daughter, Lily, and eighteen-year-old son, Jasper. She was previously married to Piers, a retail magnate she divorced when she was twenty-eight years old. Thankfully, he was now living in Hampshire with his new wife. Makram was going to be forty-two in just over a month so he was slightly over a year older than Elle. With a masculine physique and classic chiselled features, he was a handsome and powerful man – just Elle's type. He had an ex-wife in Lebanon and a son. Elle and Makram had never planned to have any children together, which suited Elle; two was more than enough. Sometimes she considered her twenty-five-year-old mistress, Lyra Kennedy, to be a child at times – particularly when she was in one of her sulking sessions.

Cara walked back to her contemporary breakfast bar with an espresso in hand. Still dressed in her cotton pyjamas, she felt warm inside and different to the way she woke the previous morning. She felt like a match had been lit within her all of a sudden. She brightly flicked through her phone to double-check she still had Sirena's number. She grinned benignly; it was there in black and white. She was glad that Michael hadn't turned up to Elle's dinner the previous night as it meant she could talk freely about Sirena – the girl with whom she had only briefly spoken but felt a strong attraction. Only a limited number of her friends knew of her sexuality and she preferred that it stayed that way. She would feel uncomfortable if David ever found out and it certainly had to be hidden from her son. She began to eat her cereal quickly; she had a few things to buy for Giles before he was to leave for St Moritz on Friday.

Sirena's phone vibrated on the big round transparent table. She quickly grabbed it, apologising with a wince as she hid it under the table to read the text.

Hi Sirena, it's Cara from last night . . . I'm assuming u remember me? So did u meet anyone exciting at the party? Xx

After the meeting adjourned, Sirena swiftly sent Cara a reply.

Hi Cara, of course I remember you. No I really didn't meet anyone exciting! I think the snow did put a lot of people off. Did you have a good night? x

Cara responded immediately.

Dinner was great although meeting u was the highlight I have to say. I would like to see u again if u would like to? x

What a lovely reply, Sirena thought – and quite direct. Cara certainly seemed to be an unfolding mystery. She hesitated with what to reply back. She *was* interested to meet again but Cara hadn't yet given her a reason as to *why* they would be meeting. She had only displayed enthusiasm, which was nice all the same. She didn't know how to ask why they were meeting without coming across as suspicious or slightly offensive, but meeting someone new was always exciting – and she did need to make new friends in London, after all.

*

'Take good care of yourself, OK my darling? Remember to always wear your padding and don't ski if you're feeling tired OK?' Friday afternoon had arrived promptly for Cara, as she hugged Giles tightly in the entrance hall.

'Yes Mum, see you in a week.'

Cara turned to embrace David lightly. 'And the same goes for you. Take care of yourself and please call me as soon as you arrive.' She glanced at her watch; it was 2.00pm.

'Yes of course, look after yourself and Amber also.' He bent down to stroke Amber and gazed up at Cara. 'You'll have to come with us next time?'

Cara didn't reply as she handed Giles sixty Swiss Francs she had spare from her last visit to Switzerland. He knew perfectly well why she didn't want to go to St Moritz with them. She loved St Moritz but the last time she was there with David it was a romantic getaway and she didn't want reminders. 'Right, you're all set.' She rolled up the sleeves of her crisp white shirt and placed both her hands into her back pockets. David looked at Cara with slight irritation while zipping up his winter jacket. He took hold of the handle of his suitcase.

'Come on Giles, the taxi's waiting,' David said enthusiastically.

Giles picked up his suitcase and opened the front door, letting in the cold air. Cara shivered instantly and folded her arms tightly, although she hoped her life would be warming up very soon.

'OK, have a great time and please don't forget to call so I know you've arrived safely?'

David rubbed her arm and walked down the steps outside the front door. 'Speak soon Cara – I'll let you know if we bump into Richard and Elizabeth also. See you next Saturday.'

Cara watched from the front door as David and Giles stepped into the taxi. As soon as the taxi was out of sight her thoughts immediately turned to Sirena and their date the next day. David and Giles going on holiday and meeting Sirena couldn't have been better timed. She had the house completely to herself and, if she used her world class charm and beauty successfully, she would also have someone to take to bed. She reached for her phone.

Hi Sirena r u up to anything exciting today? x

Hiya, I'm staying in . . . too cold to go out! You? x

Oh I know, can't stand this arctic weather! Looking forward to tomorrow. Are u OK to meet at the Jumeirah Carlton / Gilt bar at 8? x

Yes that's great, see you tomorrow then at 8pm x

Puzzled, Sirena typed the Jumeirah Carlton into Google on her BlackBerry.

Synonymous with sophistication and luxury, the five-star Jumeirah Carlton Tower Hotel is situated in the heart of Knightsbridge . . .

Wow, she thought. It looked amazing. Cara certainly had good taste.

Chapter Six

Cara rushed out of her house to her spa appointment ahead of meeting Sirena that day. She had her day planned out, which consisted of various quick beauty treatments. Sirena had given her that feeling she had lost over the years, so she delighted in making the extra special effort for the evening ahead. She knew the situation was random and had no idea if Sirena was interested in women, but wanted her in bed that night regardless.

It was looking very positive so far as Sirena had agreed to

meet, but she wasn't exactly used to being turned down by anyone and was always fighting admirers off. But despite her confidence, she was also nervous. She took an instant liking to Sirena and it was usually rare for her to take to someone so much and so quickly. She was desperate for this to amount to something, even if it was just sex. This was also the first time that she had come on to another woman, which reflected how determined she had become to find someone.

She had met Alessandra at a party in Capri and taken a very keen liking to her – and she wasn't shy in showing it. They stayed in touch after the party and met again a few months later in London at another party held by a mutual friend. Alessandra had invited her back to her place in St John's Wood, while making her intentions very clear. Being curious she readily accepted and ended up in bed being pleasured by the gorgeous woman, like she was being rewarded for something. After that night she went back to Alessandra's again and again until Alessandra took *that move,* which forced her to reluctantly put a stop to their fiery relationship.

On approaching her car, she received a text from David.

Hey Cara, Giles and I are about to hit the slopes! Jealous? x

With a smirk, she stepped into her car and shut the door.

Sirena stepped out of Knightsbridge tube station and walked down Sloane Street to the Jumeirah Carlton. She arrived just before 7.45pm after the short walk and the doorman brightly let her in, watching her admirably as she walked the red carpet and marble floor of the lobby. After quickly tidying her hair in the bathroom, she walked into The Gilt cocktail lounge, which was fairly cosy in size yet very impressive, with a mixture of gold, cream and black decor and purple velvet chairs. The dim lighting created a romantic atmosphere.

*

Cara pulled up at Cadogan Place and took a final look at her reflection in the car mirror. She was immensely nervous but luckily had an innate ability to appear composed. She quickly applied an extra layer of lip gloss and took out her chewing gum. With a deep breath she picked up her Versace shoulder bag from the passenger seat and gracefully stepped out of her car.

Sirena anxiously raised her left arm to glance at her watch; it was 8.25pm and Cara still hadn't turned up. But as she was about to call Natalie to air her growing concerns, Cara walked into the lounge and strode towards her, looking as statuesque as she did at the May Fair Hotel. She stood up to greet her and Cara vibrantly leaned in to kiss her on each cheek.

'Hi Sirena,' Cara said, as alluringly as possible.

'Hi – you look amazing.' Cara was wearing a beautiful coral shade, half-belt dress, which contributed to the elegance swirling around her with her beautiful wavy hair adding to her natural glamour.

'Thank you and so do you,' Cara replied rather shyly. She was blown away by Sirena as much as she was when she first set eyes on her. They both sat down at the table. 'Sirena it's a pleasure to see you again – I *very much* enjoyed meeting you on Wednesday you know.'

'It's good to see you again, too,' Sirena replied politely. She made herself comfortable in her seat again. 'I had arrived so early at that hotel!'

'Well sorry I'm so late tonight. I had a hectic day and was stuck in traffic.' Cara apologised as she twirled her hand in the air. 'I was going to text you but my phone had fallen out of my bag and I couldn't find it in the car while driving . . . '

'That's OK,' Sirena intercepted, not wanting Cara to feel bad. 'I got you a glass of wine while I was waiting.'

'Oh thank you.' Cara gazed at the wine. 'I'm actually in the mood for a cocktail, though.' She picked up the gold drinks menu and gazed at it fleetingly. She looked at Sirena over the menu. 'I love your dress by the way.' Sirena was wearing a jersey wrap dress, which looked very flattering on her, but she also loved the way the dress discreetly revealed Sirena's pert breasts. She averted her eyes back to the drinks menu, although she really couldn't help feeling so desirous yet nervous.

'I love your dress also, where's it from?' Sirena replied enthusiastically.

'Chanel, which reminds me, I need to call my friend Vivienne later about some paintings.' She flicked through her phone quickly. 'Do you like it in here by the way?'

'Yeah it's really nice . . . the whole hotel is amazing.'

'I love the decor here.'

'Are you involved in bars as well then?'

'You remember I'm in property – how sweet. Well I tapped into bars and restaurants years ago and mainly deal with residential properties – but I get involved with other projects when they arise.' She tousled her hand in the air, displaying her animal print bangle. 'I love design and being creative you know? Cultural influences and so on.'

'I'm interested in different cultures too – love to travel.' She was inspired by Cara's passion towards her career as she spoke more about how much enjoyment it gave her.

'Are you from London yourself?' Cara asked, changing the subject.

'No I'm from Reigate in Surrey but moved to Putney in November last year.' Sirena took a small sip of one of her two glasses of wine.

'Oh so you haven't been in town for long.' She would have much preferred Sirena to live in her borough. 'I actually have a lovely house in Sussex. Although I'm not there often, when I do go it's usually at the weekends if I need a break from London. I have a lovely pool there, too – gosh just talking about it relaxes me! So what is it that you do again? Something to do with accounts . . . '

A waiter came over and Cara ordered a cocktail while Sirena stuck with her wine.

'Account executive.'

'Yes and I recall you saying you enjoyed it.'

'To a certain degree, but I need the experience so my current job is good for me you know?' She wondered if this verbal nudge would lead to Cara explaining the reason for them meeting – perhaps she had a contact to help her with her career.

'Yes of course.' Cara understood but had no experience of this need, as she had always worked for herself apart from the odd part-time job when she was in her teens and modelling. A few seconds of awkward silence fell on them before Cara jumped in. 'So where do you normally like to go out in London, apart from singles parties?'

Sirena gave her a suppressed smile; Cara's cool and cheeky attitude had emerged again, although she quickly changed the subject so obviously a career contact was not the reason for their meeting. 'I haven't actually been to too many places since I moved here but I tend to just go anywhere really – wherever friends want to go. I went to a good club in South Kensington not so long ago.'

Cara nodded. 'I'm good friends actually with many club owners around the area.' She produced a proud smile as she momentarily fiddled with her bangle. She felt almost in love as she gazed into Sirena's eyes, which were deep and alluring, pulling her in to kiss Sirena's shapely lips. Sirena's dark, thick eyebrows had a slight natural arch, which gave her an assertive, fiery look – rather like a Bond girl, only Sirena wasn't with James Bond; she was with her. 'So how are you finding Putney?'

Sirena paused as she thought about her response. 'It's OK. I haven't actually been out to bars in Putney at all, though!'

'Yes I haven't been to Putney for a while now but I can't imagine there are a great variety of shops? For clothes, I mean.' Cara's cocktail arrived and there was a moment's silence as she took a sip. 'Hmm, cocktails are good here,' she murmured. 'So where do you usually go shopping apart from Putney?' Sirena's answer was going to give her a clue as to her lifestyle.

'Oxford Street normally.'

Cara pulled a face. 'Gracious I never go there, well, apart from to Selfridges. Too many people don't you find? I would get such a headache.'

'I go into Regent Street also,' Sirena replied, trying to improve her initial response. She cleared her throat. 'So where do you normally go shopping?'

'Kensington, Knightsbridge,' Cara shrugged. 'I go to particular places for particular things.' She discreetly admired Sirena's naked lean arms. Her tan skin looked tantalisingly smooth, and could surely only feel luxurious against her own soft skin, like the way her silk night robe felt after a long tiring day. 'Gosh Sirena, you know I really have had a hectic day,' she smiled, leaning back against her chair to compose herself. 'Barely had time to walk my dog!'

Sirena giggled. 'Do you just live with your dog then in Chelsea?'

Cara looked at Sirena earnestly, quickly snapping out of her pleasurable thoughts and placed her cocktail back on the table. 'I have a son who is seventeen next month.' She gazed at Sirena deeply to assess her reaction.

'Really?' Sirena replied with an expression of slight surprise. She didn't imagine Cara to be a mother. She looked far too glamorous; so youthful in appearance and aura, whereas her own mother spent most days with household chores instead of going out to glamorous venues.

'Yes I live with my ex-husband, David, and my son.' Cara displayed an awkward smile. 'I'll get my own place soon.' She paused thoughtfully. 'When David and I were together it just wasn't working but, now that we're not, we do get on better with each other.' She giggled and leaned away from the wall into a more relaxed position. 'Funny really, but we're *very much* separated.'

'Oh. Why did you break up if you don't mind me asking?'

'No it's OK. We were always heading in the direction of separation. We'd been married for seventeen years and I guess we'd just grown apart, but I'm much happier now. So what about you? I'm assuming you're single as you were at that singles party?'

'It wasn't a singles party for the last time!' Sirena groaned, guessing the question was probably the cue to expose the reason of them meeting – to discuss Cara's mystery single friend, no doubt. She picked up her glass of wine and, as she drank, caught the eye of an extremely handsome man at the bar, talking with the two barmen.

Cara looked on as Sirena stared. 'You would've thought this place was, though,' Cara said in a low voice.

'Sorry, I split up with my boyfriend a few months ago so yes I'm single and thus no children.'

Cara giggled slightly. 'I should think so! You do look very young – I'm assuming you're twenty-one or twenty-two maybe?'

'No, I'm actually twenty-four!'

'Oh OK.' Cara hid a mischievous expression; she had never dated anyone so much younger than her before. 'Wish I was twenty-four again,' she sighed playfully.

'How old are you if you don't mind me asking?'

'How old do you think I am?'

'Well I would say late twenties but seeing as your son is turning seventeen, maybe a bit older . . . '

Cara raised her defined eyebrow slightly. 'I'm thirty-eight.' She looked at Sirena to catch her initial response, grimacing inside that she hadn't followed her plan of knocking a couple of years off. 'I did have Giles very young.'

'Well you really do look a lot younger,' Sirena responded with a look of pleasant surprise.

'Thank you, I do get that a lot I have to say,' Cara enthusi-astically replied with high appreciation. 'So as you're single you must be on the lookout for hot, young guys, I suppose?' Cara hid her discomfort in her question. 'Well, I'm assuming . . . '

'Well, I'm not *really* on the lookout – but it would be nice to meet someone . . . '

'Uff, I'm just bored of men,' Cara interrupted with frustration. She leaned back against her chair again. She reached for her cocktail and took a long sip while looking into the long glass, which she could now see the bottom of. 'Do you not get bored of men sometimes?'

'Oh yes, completely!'

'Oh, do you really?' Cara brightened up.

'Absolutely – bored of always dating the wrong ones.' Sirena rolled her eyes.

'Oh, right . . . '

'Sometimes I just wonder if I'll ever meet someone I really connect with, you know?'

'Yes, I do know . . . but you're still very young Sirena so you shouldn't be worrying about that. You just need to go out and meet people . . . like what we're doing – we just met in a bar and here we are?'

'I guess,' Sirena smiled. 'And you're still young – and look so much younger – so you'll find someone else easily.'

'I don't know, men just don't seem to excite me but maybe I'm just going through a phase of being fed up with everything.' Cara looked around the bar, fiddling with her bangle. 'Some-times I find myself looking at other . . . ' Hesitating, she glanced back at Sirena. 'The gorgeous little kittens and puppies in Harrods; they just instantly make me feel better – such cute faces,' she laughed lightly.

'Animals make me feel better too – I have a really cute Spaniel at home called Scarlett.' Feeling puzzled, Sirena finished one of her glasses of wine. So far there had been no mention of a single friend but instead a declaration of frustration from Cara. 'So why are you fed up then? I guess the divorce . . . '

'Oh I don't know, well . . . I really, just don't know. I'm probably just suffering from exhaustion with everything,' Cara shrugged. 'Sirena I've got a table booked for us at nine-thirty at the restaurant here – is that OK with you? I thought we could have dinner together?'

'Yeah that's fine. I'm always hungry anyway!'

'You're very sweet,' Cara replied warmly, relieved that the night was progressing smoothly onto the second stage. 'I'm glad we've been able to meet again. I do enjoy your company – I liked you as soon as I laid eyes on you Sirena, I hope you don't mind me saying.'

'I liked you too – it's funny how you can just feel some sort of . . . '

'Connection?'

'Yeah, I guess,' Sirena replied warmly. She did feel something towards Cara and maybe a *connection* was the right word to describe it.

At 9.15pm they walked across to the Rib Room on the other side of the hotel. While Cara spoke with the hostess, Sirena looked around the spacious restaurant at the elegant diners and the decor; gold-framed pictures decorating the light-coloured walls.

They were promptly shown to their table. They were in silence for a few seconds as they adapted to their new environment. Sirena's hands were resting on the table and Cara was almost tempted to place her hand over hers – she was more attracted to her than when they met at the May Fair Hotel and hoped that she had made it clear so far that they were on a date together. She still had no idea if Sirena even liked women despite her earlier attempt to coax a clue, but she would certainly try her luck anyway. 'What would you like to drink?' She picked up the green-cased wine list. 'I'm going to have a glass of champagne – would you like the same?'

'Yes,' Sirena replied, wincing at the price – which would normally be the cost of her entire dinner at a restaurant.

'Are you sure?'

'Yes, champagne is fine. Thanks.'

Cara lifted her shoulders and beamed at her. Sirena scanned the menu and winced inside again at the prices. Cara immersed herself in the menu.

'I'm going for the roast Gressingham duck, which is just divine.'

Sirena took another minute to read through the menu. 'OK I'll go for that, too,' she said, calculating the cost in her mind.

'What about a starter?'

Sirena continued to scan the menu. 'The oak-smoked . . . '

'The salad of lobster with avocado is very delicious,' Cara interrupted. 'Do you want to try that?'

'Yes that sounds good actually.'

'Great,' Cara smiled. 'I thought you would like that.'

Cara watched Sirena closely as they ate their main together. She liked the way Sirena moved; she exuded a lot of dignity and class. It was important to Cara that whoever she was with had natural sophistication; otherwise, no matter how exquisite looking the person, if they lacked a certain degree of inner quality she would not be interested. She was always an advocate of like-attracts-like. 'So, what drew you to London Sirena?'

'My career really, but I had always planned to move to London after university.'

Cara nodded as she swallowed her food. 'Did you really, well I love London and you'll love living here. I can guarantee it.'

'That's good to hear,' Sirena laughed lightly. 'How do you plan to guarantee it?'

'I'll show you around town and introduce you to my friends . . . I think you'll get on very well with them,' Cara beamed. 'Moving to a new place for one's career is one thing but your social life must be quite another.'

The waiter collected their dessert plates from the table. Cara watched across the table as Sirena reached for her bag. Their night was coming to an end unless she acted quickly.

'Would you like to come back to mine after here?' Cara asked calmly yet determinedly. 'I would love to carry on with our conversation – I can feel quite lonely in the house on my own you see. My ex and son are skiing at the moment. We would normally go together but I've been so busy here in town, plus it's a bit difficult going on holiday with an ex.' She grimaced.

'I expect it would be . . . '

'But if I had gone with them I wouldn't be sitting here with you now would I?' she interrupted, giving Sirena a warm smile with a mischievous glint in her eyes.

Sirena smiled back and thought fast while she picked up her bag from the floor. Going for dinner with a woman she had just met was one thing, but going back to her home was quite another, despite how lovely she was. 'I would say yes but I actually have to be up really early tomorrow to head back to Reigate,' she replied apologetically. She had enjoyed Cara's company and was also drawn to her, but now she just felt bewildered.

Cara hid her disappointment deep inside. 'Oh right, that's fine Sirena.' She paused for a few seconds before retrieving her wallet from her bag. 'So, are you doing anything exciting in Reigate then?'

'Yes, I guess, just a family event . . . ' Sirena looked away to grab a few seconds before looking back at Cara. 'So no actually, not exciting – family events don't really tend to be!'

Cara smirked softly. 'Well I guess we better head off if you have to be up early. I can't believe it's nearly eleven already! I'll drive you home unless you drove here also?'

'No I've got a travelcard so I'll just get on the tube.'

'Don't be silly, I'll take you. I don't want you travelling back so late at night on your own,' Cara said in a motherly tone. 'What would your mother think of me?'

Cara adamantly yet dejectedly cleared the whole bill and they left the hotel. Cara walked Sirena to her car across the road, stopping by a silver BMW where she began to fumble about in her bag.

'Sorry darling, just checking that I have my keys. Always leave them around . . . ah found them.'

They carried on walking past the BMW until they approached a black Bentley parked a few feet away. 'Is *that* her car?' Sirena thought. Cara effortlessly directed her keys at the Bentley and its headlights flashed. Cara held the door open for Sirena and she got in as gracefully as she could. She sat down on the black leather seat and admired the car from inside, particularly noting the Bentley logo on the wheel.

Cara got in at the other side and pulled away towards Putney. 'Well thank you for a lovely evening, Sirena, I had a nice time with you.'

'I had a great time – thank you for dinner, it was very kind of you.'

'Oh that's all right, it's nothing. So you would like to meet again?'

'Yes of course; you're my guarantee that I'll love living in London!'

Cara lit up inside. 'That's right. I'll be in touch tomorrow to arrange for us to meet again, but I need to get you home first so you'll have to direct me!'

Chapter Seven

Cara sighed heavily as she lay awake at 6.00am. She couldn't sleep on arriving back at her house as she tossed and turned with feelings of excitement, frustration and guilt. Although she was no longer with David, she still couldn't help but feel a little unkind in her quest for another partner. The night with Sirena hadn't gone exactly to plan but it was a great night nonetheless and she had agreed to a second date, which surely meant something. With a groan, she lifted the duvet over her shoulders to attempt to get at least a couple of hours' sleep.

At 11.00am Cara was awoken abruptly by her home phone next to her bed. She flung the duvet off and reached out to answer.

'Cara!' David's familiar voice was on the other end.

Cara paused to gather her jumbled, tired thoughts. 'Oh hi David, how's it going? Is Giles having fun?' she asked with slight awkwardness.

'Giles has been spending *a lot* of time on the slopes improving his skills, so yes he's having a great time here as usual. Shame you couldn't come really, the atmosphere is fantastic. We're about to have lunch so I need to hurl Giles off his skis!'

'Well, sounds like it's all going well then! Say hi to Giles for me won't you?'

'You sound tired. Are you all right?' David asked curiously. Cara was usually out of bed early in the mornings – the older she got, the less sleep she seemed to need.

'Yes just couldn't sleep last night, that's all.'

'Ah! So you are missing us?'

Cara rested her head back on the pillow. 'Just Giles actually,' she teased.

David laughed. 'Is that so?'

'Look David, I've got to go . . . have a busy day.'

'OK well I'll call you again tonight or tomorrow?'

'Yes that's fine, or I'll call you. Have fun!'

She ended the call. David's voice was the last she wanted to hear at that moment. The brief conversation with him alongside her thoughts about the previous night had suddenly thrown her. She reached for her phone to contact Elle.

Elle sat patiently in the Harbour Club adult restaurant, waiting for her swimming partner to arrive. She began to massage the back of her neck, which felt a little tense. Her thoughts turned to Lyra. She was looking forward to seeing her again soon, to feel her sensuous hands all over her body. Her phone came to life with a text from Cara.

> Hey babe, great night with Sirena but not sure if she likes me. Will try to arrange a second date later. Still in bed being lazy xx

Elle winced slightly. She knew that Cara had a lot of hope for that night. She sent her a quick reassuring reply and sipped her water contemplatively.

'Elle! What are *you* doing here?'

She gazed over; it was Michael Lauder. 'Why do you say it like that?!'

Michael laughed and sat down at her table, resting his gym bag on the floor. 'So sorry about your dinner, Elle; felt awful but I came down with some sort of food poisoning . . . meat not cooked properly. Feel a lot better today, though.'

'Is that why you're dressed like a vegetable?'

'Sorry?' Michael glanced down at his green T-shirt and shorts. 'Oh! A runner bean to be precise!'

Elle laughed. 'Very wise while you're recovering – with good exercise.'

'So the dinner went well, did it? While I had my head in a bowl.'

'Very well; Cara took your place so your cancellation had little effect anyway,' Elle smirked jokingly. 'But we all did worry about you so you were not forgotten!'

'Cara went?'

'Her meeting had been pushed forward so she called to say she would be on time. In fact she called just after you said you couldn't come.'

'Oh right.' Michael tried to hide his anguish, but Elle picked up on it.

'She was very excitable – kept us all amused.'

'Because of a good meeting with Vladimir I'm assuming,' he replied distractedly. 'Well it must have been a great evening – your dinner party. We should all arrange to get together again soon?' He sat up straight in his seat, in a bid to compose himself again.

'Of course Michael but we get together all the time anyway!'

Michael managed a small smile. He had lost out on an opportunity to serenade Cara among good friends. 'How are things with her and David by the way? She doesn't talk about it much.'

Elle shook her head with a sigh. 'They're getting on with each other but she's adamant they won't get back together again, but who knows what's going on in her head sometimes.' She couldn't mention Cara's new interest to Michael.

'Quite,' Michael nodded in agreement. Cara was a complete mystery sometimes, even though they had known each other for so long. Now that she had separated from David, whom he didn't particularly like, he hoped that she would just get on with her own life – and preferably with him.

Sirena thought about Cara while having a quiet dinner with her family in Reigate. She was absolutely gorgeous and captivating, but also still rather baffling. She clearly just enjoys meeting new people, she thought to herself. It crossed her mind that Cara might be interested in her sexually, given her keen interest and especially after she invited her back to her place, but she couldn't be sure. She had enjoyed her company anyway and her thoughts turned to other things, until a text from Cara arrived minutes later.

Hi Sirena, did u get a good night's sleep? Hope you're having a fun time with your family x

Sirena felt excited as she read the message – but also unexpected guilt. She didn't have a family event to attend but she was at home so not *completely* dishonest. She just needed an excuse at the time.

Yes I had enough sleep. Thank you again for last night, I had a great time xx

Good I'm glad . . . I had a great time too. Just wondered when u would like to meet again? My diary becomes full soooo quickly xx

I can meet you on Thurs or Fri if you're free then? x

Let's meet for dinner at the Dorchester on Fri as I have a friend's party to attend on Thurs. Hope that's all right? x

Chapter Eight

Sirena waited at a table in The Promenade at The Dorchester, looking around in amazement at the elegant and grand interior, as well as the smartly dressed people dining around her.

'Hello darling, good to see you again,' Cara said happily on approaching. Sirena was looking as sexy as ever; this time in slim-fitting white jeans and a peach sleeveless cowl-neck top.

She wondered if Sirena had made the effort particularly for her.

'Good to see you again also,' Sirena smiled. She embraced lightly with Cara, engulfed by her alluring presence that evening. She felt speechless all of a sudden and glanced away to regroup her delighted thoughts before looking back at Cara.

'Have you had a good week?' Cara asked, straightening her printed silk cross-over dress as they sat down at their table. She silently relished Sirena's attention. She was all too used to that look Sirena had displayed and then that look away. At that moment, Sirena was like an open picture book; easy to read and pleasing on the eye. But she also desired depth, which was just as important as a pretty face.

'Yeah it's been OK; just been working really . . . how about you?'

'Oh my week has been hectic . . . meetings, deadlines. Nice to have a relaxing evening tonight, though.' Cara smiled warmly. 'Some friends are out in town tonight, probably going to a club later but I wouldn't have had the energy tonight you know?'

'I feel quite tired also actually, been so busy at work.'

Cara nodded. 'You must have holidays booked for this year to take a break from it all?'

'I'm going to Mallorca with a couple of friends in August; what about you?'

'Oh I usually book trips at the last minute as I never know where I'm going to be or what I'm going to be doing, you know? Summers are always so hectic so I need to be flexible with friends.' Cara fleetingly gazed across the restaurant and spotted an acquaintance, a well-known sportsman. She hoped no one else she knew was around to potentially interrupt her date. She grinned back at Sirena. 'So have you been out much during the week?' Cara asked brightly, although she hoped Sirena hadn't, knowing guys would be all over her. Given Sirena's age, she rather hoped Sirena wasn't too much of a party girl.

'Not too much – just a couple of nights out in bars after work.'

'Gosh! I've been out every night this week; I wanted at least one night in you know?'

Sirena grinned with tight lips, suddenly feeling like an introvert. 'Well I was going to go to this club in Marylebone but probably next week now. So you must be exhausted tonight then?'

'Yes I am rather. My ex and son are back tomorrow so I guess I've been making the most of my total freedom.'

'Oh really? You must be looking forward to seeing your son again, though?'

'Yes of course I am but I have enjoyed the responsibility off my shoulders. I hope David's been looking after him; Giles injured himself the last time they went skiing together,' she winced. 'But boys at Giles's age can be hard to manage. So what are your plans for tomorrow?'

'Nothing really, just relaxing at home probably, especially after the week I've had!'

'So you don't have to be up early for anything? I remember last time you had a family event?'

'Yeah I did, but I don't have any particular plans for tomorrow, which I know sounds a bit boring.'

'No, not at all,' Cara giggled lightly. At least that was cleared up.

At 10.15pm, Sirena was feeling a little tipsy after a few glasses of Laurent Perrier Brut NV. Cara, however, was able to hold her drink after fourteen more years of practice. Cara continued to analyse Sirena as she did on their first date; her thoughts about her were brought back to life as she embraced being back in Sirena's youthful company. 'I love your hair by the way, it looks so healthy.'

'Thank you, I love yours too . . . looks very healthy also.'

'Thank you Sirena, I do love long healthy hair,' Cara replied, reaching her arm out to feel Sirena's soft dark brown hair. She suddenly felt the touch of a hand placed firmly on her shoulder.

'Cara – don't give the girl split ends!'

'Franco! What are you doing here?!' She grimaced inside. Another friend, a flamboyant restaurateur, had made an appearance. She stood up to embrace him warmly, standing at least three inches taller. She introduced the soft-featured man to Sirena.

'Sirena I don't know how much you know about this woman but don't be fooled by appearances – she's no heart-breaker. She's a hair-breaker so slap her hand when it nears your hair again OK?'

Cara rolled her eyes humorously as she sat down. 'I would break yours if you had any.'

'Oh how nasty. Now what are you both doing later tonight?' he asked with a slight accent.

Cara gazed at Sirena while trying not to display her desperation for him to go away. 'Well, we're just having a quiet night aren't we?'

Sirena nodded at Cara then smiled back up at the man.

'Ha! The last time you told me you were having a quiet night, Cara, I heard your night included Annabel's, a police station and Playboy Club . . . '

'Franco it wasn't how . . . '

'Can't remember now which order that was all in,' Franco jumped in, 'but anyway, I'm going to see Hazel now; she's having one of her *quiet* parties so why don't you both come over?'

'I'll see how Sirena and I feel later and call you?' Cara knew her cheeks had become a mild shade of red.

'OK well make sure you do now. By the way, I have a Russian friend who's looking to move to Belgravia ASAP. Can I pass him your details?'

'Yes of course,' Cara replied succinctly, ushering him away with her tone. 'Please do – now go and . . . party!'

'Yes indeed I will. OK bye lovely darlings and pleasure meeting you Sirena.'

'I would love to get into property actually.' Sirena turned to Cara after Franco left them alone again. 'I imagine you get to meet so many interesting people, like him!'

'Yes he is an interesting one! I can show you my place in Belgravia by the way, or I can show you my home in Chelsea? I live just off the King's Road. I can show you examples of my work?' She wanted to get out of the public arena and into private surroundings; they were yet to have dessert but Sirena was certainly better than anything on a menu.

'Really?' Sirena hesitated inside.

'Yes of course darling! Come on, I'm going to show you the best homes in London – the parties will follow.'

'Well how can I refuse then,' Sirena giggled, reaching for her bag. She did feel like a change of environment, but she also wanted to stay in Cara's presence, which she was particularly enjoying that night.

'Exactly,' Cara said with barely suppressed joy. 'I hope I inspire you tonight.'

Cara paid the bill and walked Sirena to her Bentley. She drove them merrily to her home at Wellington Square, where rows of majestic white houses stood proudly around a large enclosed central area of greenery and a small water fountain. Sirena pondered her previous thoughts of Cara living in a large detached house as they walked up the stairs to the front door, but as they entered she was in awe. She contained her amazement at the presentation of the entrance hall; high ceilings, perfect parquet flooring and vibrant paintings adorning the white walls. It was as immaculate as Cara appeared to be.

'The interior was very different when we first moved here; it expressed the property's period charm but, as you can see, I prefer to live with a contemporary style,' Cara commented, enjoying Sirena's reaction to her home.

'I love it already,' Sirena replied. 'And this is just the entrance hall.'

Cara smiled softly and led the way to the first floor. Sirena sat down on a black leather sofa in the large spacious drawing room and flicked through *Vanity Fair*, which was on neat display among other publications on the coffee table. The room was bright with two French windows leading to a balcony. A large screen suddenly came down from the ceiling and Cara changed the channel to MTV. Cara then balanced herself on the sofa to take off her heels. 'It was quite a challenge to redesign the rooms around the original features and so on but I managed to create my vision – minimalism is a state of mind, after all,' she giggled. She sat down next to Sirena on the sofa. 'I was never really keen on overly decorative pieces, which seem to clutter a room I feel.' She lightly stroked the arm of her sofa.

'I like a minimalist environment too actually, although I guess it depends on where I am.'

'Yes of course,' Cara grinned. 'Would you like a drink or anything by the way? Sorry, I should have asked earlier.'

'Oh that's OK; a drink would be good thanks.'

'Wine?'

'Yeah OK,' Sirena hid a slight wince; she actually would have preferred a soft drink.

Cara left the drawing room to leave Sirena to take in the ambience of her proud home, returning five minutes later but accompanied with Amber who rushed excitely over to Sirena.

'Aw!' Sirena exclaimed. She bent down to stroke her.

'Come on Amber, leave Sirena alone!' Cara said playfully.

Sirena carefully placed the copy of *Vanity Fair* back on the coffee table and took hold of the glass from Cara's hand. 'Amber's so cute!'

'She's my baby.' Cara bent down and picked Amber up in her arms. 'Although she can be very naughty,' she said affectionately, looking fondly at Amber. She put her down and sat next to Sirena, giving her arm a friendly stroke. 'So did you enjoy dinner?'

'Yes I did,' Sirena smiled. 'But next time I'll have to pay . . . feel a bit guilty.'

'Don't be silly darling. It's my pleasure to take you to dinner.' Cara took a long sip of her white wine. 'I'll take you to my other properties another time so you can see how I've designed them in comparison to here. Would you like that?'

Sirena nodded and took a sip of her wine. She was already feeling a little tipsy so didn't want to drink more than she could manage.

'How are you finding life in London so far anyway? Am I making it a little more exciting for you or are your bags packed with a one way flight ticket?'

Sirena laughed. 'It's been great so far . . . busy and pretty much how I expected it to be! I do miss being close to my friends, though; they're all still around Surrey.'

'Well it's time to make new friends then. You've made a good one already so you'll be fine. I'll get you into all the best parties, clubs and restaurants. I know *everyone*.'

An hour had passed and Sirena had finished her second glass of wine at Cara's home, which made her feel even more lightheaded. Cara had finished her third and was about to pour Sirena another.

'I can't drink any more, Cara. I really have had too much already!'

Cara laughed affectionately and put the bottle down. 'I have as well actually . . . my head is spinning a little. You can stay at mine tonight if you want to?'

'No I'm OK. I'll just call a taxi.' Sirena looked around for her bag, which was somewhere on the floor by the sofa.

Cara panicked; she *needed* Sirena to stay over. 'Darling please stay – I have plenty of room for you.' She groaned inside – she wanted Sirena in her bed. She didn't know how she was going to seduce her, seeing as she hardly had the experience.

'Well . . . ' Sirena fleetingly questioned Cara's motives in her mind, but she felt safe and it would certainly be more convenient for her to stay over. 'OK. I'll travel back to mine in the morning, but is that definitely all right?'

'Yes of course darling, I like company so you're more than welcome. Now let me show you around quickly.'

Sirena followed Cara upstairs to the third floor. Cara opened the door to her spacious marital bedroom, revealing cream patterned walls with some floor-to-ceiling mirrored panels, two large sash windows and elegant furniture placed around the proud king-sized bed. Sirena caught sight of Cara in a mirror, looking at her admirably by the door.

'Wow this room is great.' Sirena accidently dropped her bag on the floor, making Amber jump slightly. She bent down to pick it up. Cara lightly stroked her arm when she stood tall again.

'It's one of my favourite rooms but I guess one's bedroom usually is?' Cara quipped. She was finding it hard to contain her frustration.

'Well if this was my bedroom it would certainly be my favourite.' Sirena giggled to mask her confusion at Cara touching her affectionately.

'I'm very sorry to say that your room for tonight is on the lower ground floor. My ex sleeps in the spare room on this floor. Come on darling.' She reluctantly walked Sirena back along the corridor, wishing she had made the most of Sirena's reaction to her bedroom. She led Sirena down the stairs while talking about the way she designed her house, but also wondering how on earth she was going to make her move. She revealed another beautifully presented bedroom to Sirena on the lower ground floor. She knew she had to act quickly or else she would be sleeping alone, and what did she have to lose? If Sirena didn't like her they wouldn't see each other again – they didn't move in the same circles so no one would find out. 'Sirena, would you rather sleep in my room?'

'Erm, I'm not too fussed really . . . would you sleep in here then?'

'No I only sleep in my room!'

Sirena hesitated. 'So we would both sleep in your room?'

'Well, my room is a lot more comfortable . . . ' Cara trailed off, feeling her heart beating faster with each second of awkwardness.

'I'm not sure what you . . . ' Sirena paused. 'You mean sleep in the same bed?'

'You don't have to, obviously!' Cara quickly intercepted. 'It's just that I thought . . . well, it would be nice wouldn't it?' She felt the knot tighten in her stomach with anticipation and panic. It wasn't her usually doing the asking and she certainly wouldn't be doing it again. She bent down to play with Amber as she could feel herself turning red.

Sirena took a moment to make sense of her jumbled thoughts. 'Cara, I've never . . . I mean, I'm not . . . '

Cara frowned with embarrassment before standing back up to face the result of her foolish actions. 'Listen it's OK, this room is very nice. There are some clothes in the drawers and toiletries in the en suite – just let me know if you need anything else OK?'

'OK . . . thanks.'

'Right, well good night then – see you in the morning Sirena and thank you again for a lovely evening.' Cara gave her a quick kiss on the cheek and walked away with Amber in tow. The unfamiliar feel of rejection made her legs weak with every step towards her bedroom. She walked quickly in fear of collapsing.

Sirena shut the door when Cara was out of sight and sat down on the edge of the bed, taking in what had just happened.

Cara threw her bedroom door shut and sat down on her bed. Sirena wasn't into women and she didn't want to sleep with her. The night hadn't gone to plan *at all*. She now just wanted to sleep off her frustration and proceeded to get changed into her comforting cotton pyjamas. She got immense satisfaction from making love to Alessandra, and seeing advertisements of beautiful women everywhere was making her yearn even more for her own female lover again. She wearily climbed into bed and turned off the lights. Her head hit the pillow and Amber lay at the foot of the bed in her usual position. She could hear her heart still beating fast and rubbed her chest to calm herself. She certainly hoped Sirena was feeling all right alone in the bedroom but she couldn't face her again that night to check. She curled up in the bed to sleep.

Chapter Nine

With a groan, Cara lifted her head from the pillow and sat up in bed. Nearly two hours had passed without any sleep. For goodness' sake, she sighed, rubbing her forehead. She glanced at Amber who had woken from her sudden movements. She stroked her apologetically, wondering if she would ever see Sirena again after the morning. Yawning, she left her bedroom to get a cold glass of water. When she reached the lower ground floor, she glanced at the spare room. She felt guilty for trying to seduce Sirena; she certainly wouldn't be trying that with another woman ever again. She continued to walk quietly into the kitchen.

'Sirena!' Cara jumped.

'Oh hi!' Startled, Sirena quickly finished filling her glass and stepped away from the sink.

'Gosh you made me jump,' Cara laughed. She composed

herself as she stood in her pyjamas, wishing she was wearing something sexier. 'I didn't expect to see you!' She ran her hand through her hair, suddenly self-conscious. She gasped inside at the sight of Sirena's full body, perfectly on show as the silk rested on her delicately, barely covering her thighs. Sirena was wearing her cream chemise, revealing tantalising parts of her body she hadn't seen.

'I'm just getting some water – a bit thirsty after all the wine.'

'Oh . . . well I can't seem to sleep. Are you comfortable in your room?' She asked this with a little concern, not knowing what else to say.

'Yes, it's really comfortable.' Sirena stood further aside from the sink as Cara walked over to get a glass.

'Good,' Cara grinned, fighting her attraction as she stood closer to Sirena. 'I must say I do feel bad for leaving you alone on this floor while I'm right at the top.'

'It's all right . . . I really like the room. Your whole house is amazing.' Sirena shuffled on the spot. 'And I found this to put on!'

'I know you look so gorgeous in it,' Cara smiled softly. 'And here I am in my moon and stars pyjamas – very flattering.'

Sirena giggled. 'But very comfortable – I've got lots like that.'

'Oh are you warm enough? I should've checked what you had to wear . . . '

'No it's OK, I'm fine and I love this top.'

'You can take it home with you.'

'It's yours! I'll leave it in your room. You must look really great in it . . . '

'No please – it's yours.' Cara said sternly with affection. 'I've got too many chemises.' She could see Sirena's nipples through the silk. She looked back towards the sink, becoming increasingly flustered. She had walked into a teasing session.

With a groan, she rubbed the back of her neck tiredly. 'Gosh I do need a good night's sleep.'

'Are you OK tonight? You seem as if you have a lot on your mind?'

'I do have a lot on my mind with various things,' Cara sighed, 'and with my ex returning tomorrow . . . well, later today now, but you don't want to hear any of that at this hour.'

'Well if you want to talk about it . . . '

'No I just need to . . . sleep, probably.' She placed her glass under the tap. 'Did you just want water by the way or do you want something to eat as well? I can quickly make you something if you're hungry?'

'No water is fine thanks.'

'OK.' Cara smiled. She wanted to splash some water over herself. Her feelings for Sirena were intensifying and she knew Sirena could sense it. They were too strong for Sirena not to. 'Well good night again, see you in the morning.'

'Good night to you too, hope you sleep well.'

Cara felt immense frustration watching Sirena walk away from her. She had to have her. 'Sirena?'

'Yep?'

Cara faltered. 'Did you enjoy dinner with me tonight?'

'Yes of course – why?'

'I like you.' Cara left the tap running to help counteract the awkwardness that followed, with water overflowing from the glass. 'Sorry.' Cara shook her head in an attempt to shrug off her sudden declaration. 'You probably have no idea what I'm going on about. I . . . I've had too much to drink,' she stuttered. 'You know, I probably shouldn't even be having water.'

Sirena remained silent.

'Look, good night Sirena . . . please go and get some sleep before I hold you back any more with my rambling. I'm so sorry for how I've been tonight; I'm really not usually like this . . . I don't know what's come over me.'

'It's OK . . . good night.' Sirena turned to walk away but stopped. She glanced at Cara with compassion. 'No I . . . I do know what you mean.'

Cara paused. 'Sorry?'

'I do know what you're trying to say.'

Cara turned off the tap and faced Sirena again before looking away, feeling too embarrassed to lock eyes with her. 'Gosh, this really is awkward; I shouldn't have said what I did.'

'No it's OK.'

'Is it? I don't understand, Sirena.'

'You know, this is rather awkward. I don't really know what to say . . . I've never really, I mean, I've never been with another woman . . . in that way . . . '

'Sirena, sorry, I'm just . . . ' Cara rubbed her forehead and turned to lean against the kitchen counter. 'You probably want to just go now.' She still avoided looking at Sirena. 'I can call you a taxi if you don't want to stay.'

'No I want to stay, Cara.' Sirena could see how fed up Cara was, which made her look attractively vulnerable. She was drawn to Cara as she was certainly the most gorgeous woman that she had ever set eyes on, and although she had never slept with a woman before she was more than intrigued with Cara.

'Oh . . . well thank you, I mean, thanks for not running off after everything tonight. Gosh I feel so embarrassed right now.'

'Cara it's fine,' Sirena said gently.

Cara paused in the silence. She felt so ungraceful for creating the awkward atmosphere, yet also comfort as she breathed in the air of magnetism between herself and Sirena. Despite Sirena's hesitant stance, she was encouraging her to continue with her intentions. 'Sirena . . . can we go into your room?'

Sirena nodded. 'If you want to?'

'Do you? I mean, do you want us to?'

'Yes.'

Cara tried to maintain a calm and controlled exterior as she followed Sirena into the spare room. She shut the door and took hold of Sirena's hand, gently pulling her in towards her. She didn't want any more stumbling silences or exchanges. 'I'm so attracted to you,' she said longingly. Their lips touched for the first time with a short, tender and curious kiss. 'Are you OK?' Cara asked softly, gently resting her hands on Sirena's refined shoulders. She leaned in to kiss her again before Sirena could answer, this time more intensely. Her sweet smooth lips were too pleasurable to resist any longer. 'Come on darling.' Cara lightly brushed her hand down Sirena's arm to her fingers and she led her to the double bed. She sat down on the edge slowly with Sirena standing up in front of her. 'Sirena are you all right with this? If you're not I'll go back to my room . . . '

'I'm fine Cara,' Sirena said reassuringly. She sat down close beside Cara. 'I really am fine, just feeling a bit . . . erm, I just don't . . . '

'Sirena please relax with me,' Cara said softly, wanting a passionate night instead of one overtaken with anxiety. 'I'm so attracted to you.' She gently clasped her hand around Sirena's jawline. She kissed her sensuously, enjoying every second of their lips touching. Her hands trailed inside Sirena's chemise, feeling her back and shoulders, which were as luxuriously smooth as her own. 'Come into the bed,' she whispered. She eagerly moved further back onto the bed to encourage Sirena to quickly get in with her.

'I've just never done this before.' Sirena winced as she lifted herself onto the bed. She could feel Cara's desire for her so intensely that her nerves were washed away as quickly as they surfaced. 'I've thought about it but I've never . . . '

'It doesn't matter; it's all right,' Cara intercepted, leaning closer into Sirena. She lay beside her and put her arm around her naked waist under her chemise. 'I'm just glad you're here with me,' she whispered. She began to caress Sirena's waist, containing her excitable emotions first experienced years ago, which were now flooding back to her. 'I want you to feel relaxed.'

Sirena sighed with the feel of Cara's hands on her, overwhelmed by the attraction she was feeling towards the older woman beside her.

'I want you so much, can't believe you're here . . . '

'I'm glad I came over,' Sirena gasped with the feel of Cara's unfamiliar feminine lips sweeping across her neck. She groaned more strongly as Cara kissed her hungrily.

'You have a sensitive neck,' Cara giggled softly. 'I'll remember.' She rested on her elbow to lean up. She locked her left hand with Sirena's, admiring her slim fingers entwined with hers. She needed Sirena to caress her all over.

Sirena grinned happily, meeting Cara's satisfied smile. She gently moved her lips around Cara's warm face, feeling aroused as Cara's eyes closed gently like she was in a meaningful dream. She could sense how much Cara was embracing this night with her. She removed her chemise and lifted herself under the warm covers with Cara.

Cara began to stroke Sirena's body more eagerly, allowing her contained excitement to escape, and gasped as Sirena reached into her top to feel her breasts. She sighed contentedly with the feel of another woman's hand under her clothing after so long. She kissed Sirena on her soft cheek before sitting up and taking off her top to reveal the most gorgeous breasts that Sirena had ever seen – full with natural firmness. Cara lay back down, leaning over Sirena to gently caress and kiss her smaller, supple breasts. Her nipples were cutely erect. She shivered with delight as Sirena groaned and writhed on the bed, showing she had sensitive nipples too. She took her time enjoying Sirena's breasts before moving her lips patiently to Sirena's lean stomach, admiring her feminine form along the way. Memory flashes of Alessandra jolted her. She sat up to pull off her pyjama bottoms, revealing her long slender legs. She slid her knickers down, which to her delight encouraged Sirena to do the same. Lying back down, she wrapped her arms and legs soothingly around Sirena, closing her eyes to indulge the smooth sensation of every part of her body. She just lay hugging with Sirena for a while, taking a moment for them both to embrace their emotional connection. She ran her fingers delicately along the dreamy dip of Sirena's back.

'I love having my back stroked,' Sirena gasped, kissing Cara's jawline and neck in return.

'Do you,' Cara whispered lovingly. She lifted Sirena's thigh up to between her legs and moved down on her rhythmically, breathing heavily by Sirena's ear as she stroked her back more intensely. The feel of another woman's naked body over-whelmed her mind with pleasure as the secretive nature of the act thrilled and aroused her. The past few years of hiding and coping with her frustration and sadness left her memory, as she drew herself tighter into Sirena, enjoying the kissing, which was feeling more sensuous. She hadn't felt so sensitive in bed in years and hoped it would never end this time. She slowly moved Sirena down towards her stomach, groaning in delight with the feel of Sirena's hand between her legs. Her toes curled with the ripple of pleasure as Sirena started to move her hand in a circular motion, massaging her. 'Darling you're perfect,' she said breathlessly into Sirena's ear. 'You're mine now.'

Chapter Ten

Tired and elated, Cara drove back to Chelsea the next morning after taking Sirena home. She attempted to call Elle but couldn't get through so she called her friend, Helen Clancy, but she wasn't answering either. She was bursting to inform her close friends about the night she had just shared with Sirena.

Helen watched as her phone rang on the bedside table. She knew Cara was probably calling to share details of her night with the girl she met and, although she was interested, she didn't think it was appropriate as the man she was seeing lay beside her in bed. She sent Cara a quick text to compensate.

Hi darling, can't talk right now – M is over. Call later . . . hope u had fun last night . . . xxxxx

Cara groaned as she read the text; she thought Helen and Max had stopped seeing each other for good. She sent Helen a quick reply before getting out of her car.

Since when were u back in touch with Max?? I slept with u know who last night . . . spk later, babe xxx

Helen quickly read her reply. While she found Cara's attraction to women intriguing, she had no desire herself to actually sleep with one. Max suddenly put his arm around her, holding her in tightly against his chest.

Elle read an excited text from Cara with a perfectly arched eyebrow. She was more than pleased that Cara had *finally* been laid, and was intrigued by the girl she'd taken a liking to. She couldn't help but wonder how it would turn out, despite the fact they had only just slept with each other for the first time. She also knew what Cara was like and the fact that she was still living with David would surely lead to complications if she really liked this girl. She recalled a time three years earlier when she and Makram with her two children were having a quiet evening with Cara and her family at Wellington Square. Alessandra had turned up unannounced but thankfully it was Cara who had gone to the door. It was very awkward for Cara as she had to quietly usher her away, seeing as everyone was seated in the reception room closest to the front door. A few weeks later, however, Cara had abruptly ended the affair with Alessandra.

'Come here beautiful.' Makram tiredly drew Elle into him, kissing her neck sensuously.

'Oh so you're awake now?' Elle gasped lightly. 'Maybe I should have woken you up sooner.' She closed her eyes with a satisfied grin as he began to caress her back.

'Perhaps you should have.' He gently held her left breast in his hand, feeling her nipple become erect. 'Do you need to be anywhere this morning?'

Elle writhed on the bed, enjoying the sensation of his tender lips trailing from her neck to her shoulders. She had planned to see Lyra that morning – not that she would be able to go into her apartment. She still lived with her mother, Lizette. 'Well, I was actually waiting for this sexy, strong guy to turn up.' She turned to face Makram and excitably reached under the covers. She knew her plans for the day would change.

Cara embraced David and Giles as Amber excitedly ran around their feet. 'Did you both have a lovely time?' Cara asked vibrantly. She helped move Giles's travel bag nearer towards the stairs. 'Amber's been waiting for you all day.'

'We always have a splendid time so you missed out,' David teased. He pulled off his winter jacket and draped it on top of his suitcase. He ran his hands through his hair. 'We bought you a small present actually – do you have it Giles?'

'Yes it's somewhere in my bag.'

Cara turned to him, intrigued.

'We'll give it to you when you next come with us,' David said.

'Terms and conditions in place? Are you at least able to tell me what it is?'

David was about to object but Giles jumped in too quickly. 'Ski sunglasses.'

'I already have two!'

'Are you saying two is better than three?' David quipped.

'I might be,' Cara raised a brow at David. 'OK well just give it to me when I next go skiing with you then, which will be never.' Cara shook her head in amusement. 'So did you bump into anyone?'

'Elizabeth and Richard were there as we thought they might be – Giles and I had lunch with them a couple of days ago. They both send you their love. I'll tell you properly later about how they are and so on and also show you our photos. I just need to get out of these clothes first.'

'Yes of course.' She rubbed David's back warmly.

Giles headed towards the stairs, leaving his parents together.

David picked up his jacket and took hold of the handle of his suitcase to walk to the stairs. 'So how have you been?' Cara certainly seemed well enough and she was wearing one of her oversized polo neck jumpers he rather liked. It made her look exceptionally warm.

'Good,' she smiled. 'Been very busy. Are you hungry by the way? I was going to suggest that we all go out for dinner but you both seem exhausted.'

'We are! Let's stay in and keep the night easy. I'll probably get an early night if you care to join me?'

Cara frowned at him. 'David stop it.'

'Being in St Moritz brought back memories of the way we were – I really do miss us Cara.'

Cara bent down and picked up one of his bags. 'Let's take these upstairs,' she said in an irritated tone. 'Then we can all talk about your trip . . . and only your trip OK!'

Later that evening as Sirena was getting ready to meet friends in town, she received a text from Cara.

Hi beautiful, thinking about u a lot . . . can't wait to see u again. Hope you're all right? xxx

Sirena's stomach churned with excitement and she quickly typed a reply. Sleeping with Cara was certainly unplanned but it was an experience she wanted to repeat. Cara had ignited a hidden desire within her.

> I've been thinking about you all day. Look forward to seeing you again also . . . have a nice evening xxx

Cara read the reply excitedly while mixing ingredients together for a dessert for herself, David and Giles. She was feeling an equal measure of happiness and relief since her night with Sirena. She was taking in the fact that she, a thirty-eight-year-old had just spent the night with a twenty-four-year-old girl. The fact that Sirena was fourteen years younger than her made her feel rejuvenated as she suddenly felt she was in her twenties again. She humoured herself as she pondered that this was probably how a man felt when he was with a much younger woman.

They had already planned their third date for the coming Tuesday at The Connaught, although Sirena preferred to meet at the end of the week when she didn't have work the next day. Cara couldn't wait that long, however; she also wouldn't have her home free to herself now that David and Giles were back. She would either have to go back to Sirena's or stay at The Connaught. She didn't particularly want to go to her private country home or use one of her properties that she was developing. David suddenly walked into the kitchen, which made Cara jump as he headed straight for her.

'Hurry up, woman!'

'I'm trying!'

'Are you actually hiding in here and eating it all?' He pointed at her chin. 'Ah ha – chocolate!'

She tried to contain a smile while whisking the mixture. 'Can't a woman enjoy a guilty pleasure every now and again?'

Of course, he thought to himself, if it makes you this happy. Cara was noticeably more vibrant and this was certainly a positive. 'Yes you can but next time include me!' He cheekily dipped his finger into the bowl.

Chapter Eleven

'I'm so sorry for calling you so late last night; hope I didn't wake you?'

'You did! But I fell asleep pretty much straightaway again.' Sirena made herself comfortable in Cara's Bentley.

'OK,' Cara smiled at her. 'I was just thinking about you after a dinner with some friends and didn't . . . think.' Cara pulled away to The Connaught, excited to be back in Sirena's presence yet also slightly nervous. She was keen to impress her that evening.

Sirena glanced at Cara fleetingly as she drove. Every time Cara turned to look at her she found herself looking away quickly to face the front window, feeling a little self-conscious seeing her again after spending the night with her.

'So how are you feeling?'

'Good but just a bit all over the place. I didn't expect any of this to happen!'

'How do you mean?' Cara asked.

'Well I'd never slept with a woman before you . . . my mind just feels a bit scattered you know?'

'Oh life is about new experiences darling and you repeat the ones you like. I really did enjoy our night together, Sirena.'

'I enjoyed it all, too – just feel a bit confused that's all.'

'Oh right. Well, just think of us as friends Sirena, I really don't want you to feel confused. I enjoy your company and don't want you to feel awkward with me OK?'

'I don't feel awkward, just weird but in a good way.'

Cara nodded with hidden concern and concentrated back on the road as she drove into Mayfair.

They walked through the entrance of The Connaught after

being greeted by the doorman. Cara was two inches taller than Sirena but with her heels, which were higher than Sirena's, she stood a little taller that evening. They took their seats in the elegant and cosy Espelette dining room. Sirena looked out of the window into Mayfair; the restaurants Cara was taking her to were very different to the ones she would normally frequent with friends – and a lot more expensive – but Cara was always adamant to clear the bill. She turned back to Cara who was reading the menu.

'You look amazing tonight by the way.'

'Thank you, so do you.' Cara smiled warmly at Sirena, who was wearing a pretty drawstring dress. 'I really have been looking forward to this evening you know – hope you have?'

'Yes of course.'

Cara grinned, fleetingly adjusting her white sleeveless draped top. Sirena was looking as vibrant as ever, which was an excellent sign. She seemed to be just as happy as she was.

They ordered their starter and main courses and found themselves immersed in each other again on their third date. Cara took moments while they were eating to appreciate how enthusiastic Sirena was to meet with her again, despite the earlier talk of confusion; just one night with her would have left her in a deeper frustrated state. Treating Sirena would help to hold on to her, she assumed as she ordered the best dishes on the menu.

'So how's it been with your ex and son since they've been back? Do they know about you?'

Cara shook her head instantly. 'Gosh no they don't know darling! Only a few close friends know. What about you? Do your family know?'

'No definitely not, but you *are* the first woman I've been with.'

Cara smiled proudly within herself. 'Yes of course. Talking of family, I'm going to Cortina this Monday with relatives for over a week, so we'll have to see each other *as much as possible* before I go.' Cara paused. 'So cancel everything in your dairy, OK?'

Sirena giggled, picking up her glass of water.

'Well I don't know why you're laughing,' Cara quipped. But being with Sirena made her feel so desirous. She wanted to strip her naked and kiss her smooth body all over again. She reached out for Sirena's hand and stroked it. 'You have a great complexion you know; when you smile you just light up like the sun.'

'Thank you.' Sirena fell shy. 'Are you now cringing as much as me?'

'Yes!' Cara winced. 'I don't know what came over me,' she laughed. 'You!'

Sirena laughed. 'No it was a lovely thing to say.' She drank from her glass again. 'So are you planning to move to a place of your own soon? It must be difficult living with an ex?'

Cara withdrew her hand. 'Yes it can be complicated but we're just friends – there's no attraction there whatsoever, but I've known him for nearly twenty years so we *can* just live as friends. Obviously I'm looking forward to my own space again soon.'

Sirena raised her eyebrows. 'Twenty years is a *long* time.'

Cara nodded and put her dessert spoon down then nudged it to the side. 'Are you OK if we go back to yours later? My ex and son are both in tonight so we can't go back to mine.' She laughed lightly. 'This is one complication of living with an ex . . . I'll get my own place soon for this reason alone!'

Elle focused her eyes on the computer in her study, scanning flight times for a short trip to Courchevel for herself and her friend Valentina Lopokova.

'I feel so tired this morning,' Makram commented, walking in. He placed a smoothie for her beside the computer.

'Darling I'm going to Courchevel for five days next week,' she said airily.

'You do remember Nadine's exhibition is at the Design Centre next week, don't you?'

'Urgh Makram, I hadn't remembered – do you think she'll mind if I don't show?'

'Who knows – could be in Milan for a couple of days next week so I might not go either!'

Nadine was a very reputable interior designer who was a close friend to them both. Elle had forgotten that Makram might also be away next week. He was constantly travelling around the world, which meant she spent a lot of time on her own and with her children – when they were around. But it also meant that she could spend a lot of time with her friends and engage in activities that didn't involve her husband.

He stood behind her and gently massaged her defined shoulders. 'I'll call her at some point, Elle.'

Elle's phone started to ring. 'Oh who's this?' She saw that Lyra was calling and quickly put her phone back down.

'Someone you like, clearly.'

'A friend I can't be bothered to speak with now as I'm *trying* to organise this trip!'

Makram pulled a face. 'OK I'm going stroppy baby. Enjoy your smoothie won't you?'

'Darling thank you, I just need to get this booked otherwise Valentina will go crazy.'

'I understand – we don't want a crazy Valentina running around the streets. I'm going back to bed.'

Makram left the room. Elle took a quick sip of her smoothie and reached for her phone. She called Lyra back.

'Elle I couldn't get hold of you last night – where were you?'

'Sorry darling I was out in town with some friends.'

'Well are we meeting tonight or not?'

'Baby I can't any more, last night has exhausted me.'

'Oh right. Have you made plans with Makram instead?'

Elle huffed heavily. 'No darling, as I said, I'm just exhausted and I'll probably be getting an early night. Look, we'll meet at the end of next week – I'm going to Courchevel with a friend so I'll call you when I get back OK?'

Lyra groaned. It had been over three weeks since they had seen each other.

'Lyra I don't want this sulking business from you – you know I have commitments.'

Lyra remained silent on the other end of the phone in protest.

'I was actually going to see you a couple of days ago but some relatives made a surprise visit. I had to spend all my free time with them you know?'

'You still could have seen me for an hour or so.'

'Look, we'll meet next week,' Elle continued. She spoke closer into the phone. 'If we can't meet at my home, we'll meet at the apartment; I'm not too sure of Makram's plans yet all right?'

'OK,' Lyra sighed. 'I've just been missing you and also so stressed out with work.'

'I know my baby, I miss you too and please don't stress. Look I've got to go but lots of kisses and we'll meet next week.' She swiftly finished the call so she could proceed with booking her trip. She was eager to see Lyra but she enjoyed keeping her in suspense every now and again. It amused her.

Chapter Twelve

Sirena got into work on a rainy February Monday morning. As she sat at her desk feeling stressed over her sudden high work load, she thought about Cara's leisurely departure to Italy that day. She wished that she was going with her or on any other holiday. She sent a quick message to Cara.

Have a good flight later beautiful xx

Cara frowned slightly. She was in Paris that afternoon as she had rescheduled her trip to Cortina d'Ampezzo for Thursday morning instead, to return on the following Wednesday. David had arranged a surprise trip for them and two other friends to spend a couple of nights in Paris; they had left that morning by Eurostar and were due to return on Wednesday evening.

Cara was sitting with her close friend Helen in Les Deux Magots, Saint-Germain-des-Pres. Helen watched Cara curiously among the surrounding muffled conversations in French. Cara looked to be deep in thought more so lately.

Cara quickly snapped out of her moment of silence. 'So when are you seeing Max again?' she questioned disapprovingly.

'The next time I'm feeling lonely in my apartment all by myself, which is too frequent for my liking.'

'I'm sure you could find something else to occupy yourself with instead of him.' She looked at Helen's fair face for her alternative recommendation to one of the sexiest men in London. 'A good book perhaps?'

'A book instead of his cock?' Helen exclaimed. 'Come on now Cara darling. We both know Max is *very hard* to resist.' She pulled down the sleeves of her beige jumper, covering her paler slim wrists. 'The sex is too good.'

'Well I resisted him, thank God.'

Helen rolled her eyes. 'I don't want anything serious with him, he's just useful . . . something you should be able to understand?'

Cara gave a tight-lipped smile as she looked down at the table. 'Yes, I might.'

'So how's it been going with your younger woman?'

'She's very beautiful and sweet,' Cara replied enthusiastically, covering her mouth as she ate her Quiche Lorraine. 'She just texted me actually . . . Elle met her on Friday night.'

'Oh God, did she?! And how did Sirena cope with you both at the same time?' Cara and Elle could be quite daunting together;

both majestic with superior attitudes that they displayed when they felt like it.

'Very well,' she grinned. 'We were easy on her.'

Helen shook her head. 'Do you have a photo of her yet?'

'Not on my phone,' Cara replied, casting her eyes around the café. She looked back mischievously at Helen. 'I was tempted to take one when we were in bed together.'

'It wouldn't surprise me!'

Cara massaged her left arm over her turquoise tight-fitted sweater. 'No, I wouldn't do that. You'll meet Sirena at your party – I've invited her.'

'Oh well thank you for telling me. I look forward to meeting her then! What does she do again? I mean, what's her occupation?'

'Account executive with some agency.'

Helen raised her eyebrows. 'So she's ambitious?' She was trying to get a picture of Sirena's social standing; she didn't let just anyone into her lavish parties.

'Seems so; moved into town from Surrey to pursue her career.'

'And you said she was twenty-seven?'

'Twenty-four,' Cara grinned. Sirena was like a trophy.

'Cara,' Helen shook her head. 'She's far too close to Giles's age – what are you thinking!'

'Helen when we're together, it's like we're both the same age. It's so rare to find someone who makes me feel excited – please don't think badly of me.'

'I would never think badly of you darling, just thought she was a little older. I take it Sirena's single?'

'Yes!' Cara threw Helen a bewildered look.

'Glad to hear it! So what's she doing right now? At work?'

'Probably.'

'You should've invited her along. A romantic weekend in Paris with your girlfriend . . . ' She trailed off, teasing Cara.

'Oh so she could meet David perhaps? I'm in such an awkward situation at the moment.' Cara paused. 'She doesn't actually know that I'm here you know – I haven't told her about my change of plan.'

Helen lowered her eyebrows. 'Just make sure you treat this one better than your last,' she said earnestly, 'and I do think that you should reassess your position with David.'

'I know Helen but I treated Alessandra fine – I never *actually* promised her anything did I?'

'Just remember you're dealing with a younger woman . . . goodness knows why.' She shook her head in amusement. She was into older men and found Cara's attraction to younger women baffling.

Cara managed a small giggle and decided to change the subject. 'Isabel is skiing in Germany at the moment, wonder how it's going with her and Andrew?'

'I'm sure they're having a great time drinking glue wine in the mountains. They always just want to go skiing on their own, haven't you noticed?' Helen admired her Louis Vuitton watch, which she had bought earlier that day. 'Are they still going to Marbella after do you know?'

'Not sure.' Cara shook her head.

They both took a moment to sip their drinks. Cara glanced at Helen as she delicately ran her fingers through her shoulder-length light blonde hair. With her piercing blue eyes and delicate facial features, she was a delight to look at. She had known Helen since they were at school and she was always there to support her whenever she needed help or advice, and she provided the same in return. Their parents were also great friends so they spent a lot of time around each other growing up in Chelsea.

'So you were OK rescheduling your plans with relatives?' Helen asked.

'Yes it's fine. Ten days was going to be too long anyway, plus

David seemed so enthusiastic for us all to come out. It has been a while since we've all gone away together.'

'You know he just called me out of the blue when I was having my hair done. I thought you already knew!'

'No no no darling, he threw it all at me on Saturday,' Cara replied before taking another bite of her quiche. 'I did panic, however – thought he would have booked us into a room together like the last time.'

David suddenly appeared with another shorter man; his attractive yet monotone-speaking friend Adrian.

'We've just been into Brasserie Lipp – thought you would be there,' Adrian droned.

'Eating again?' David frowned jokingly at their table. 'I expected you two to be throwing back the vino – I was sure of it!' He glanced at Adrian who smiled cheerfully before casting a friendly gaze at Helen.

'No,' Helen replied as she exchanged a mischievous look with Cara. 'We're actually having a very private conversation, which doesn't involve the likes of you two.' She ushered them away with her hands, her ethnic bangles jangling.

'Well I'm very intrigued.' David sat down at the table and pulled a chair out for his friend. He gave Cara a gentle pinch on her waist and smiled eagerly at her.

Helen watched as Cara and David began speaking with each other at the table. They looked good together but they *weren't* good together. She had witnessed too many of their ongoing feuds and hoped that Sirena would help her to find happiness, even if it was just for a while as with Alessandra. She gave a fleeting smile to Adrian sitting beside her. David had obviously brought him along to entertain her while he tried to get back into Cara's heart once again.

Chapter Thirteen

Elle gently massaged shampoo into her hair under the water-fall, to sounds of the Amazon rainforest. She had also dimmed the lights and opted for more steam to create a perfectly choreographed showering experience that morning. After she finished leisurely shaving her slender legs, she walked out of her shower room and back into the bedroom, grabbing a white towel to wrap around her wet bronzed shoulders.

It was Saturday morning and she had returned to Chelsea from Courchevel with Valentina the evening before, where she spent the week skiing and socialising. She glanced over at a novel on the bed and groaned; Makram had left it behind for his trip to Lebanon that afternoon.

She first met Makram at a polo tournament where she had taken to him straight away. They were always very compatible in bed right from the start, but Lyra, whom she met nearly four years ago at her brother's wedding, provided her with something different. She liked to link her love for men and women with her love for money; the beautiful roughness of coins and the different, soothing smoothness of notes.

Only Cara and a few other close friends knew about this secret affair, however, and she intended it to stay that way. Her steamy marriage to Makram and their homely life with her two children were all that she had ever desired, but her extravagant affair with Lyra within her wealthy existence meant that she had something extra. She certainly did have it all in life and she wasn't going to change *anything*.

She spent the afternoon at a private art viewing in South Kensington then dashed home to inspect an old master painting, which had arrived for her earlier. She put her phone to her ear again. 'Sorry, I'm in now.'

'What was it that you were going to ask me?' Makram asked, standing in Heathrow airport with his travel bag weighing on his shoulder.

'Sorry?' She walked into the reception room, where the painting was waiting for her against the wall.

'You were going to ask me something?'

'Yes, sorry. When are you coming back and where on earth is Jasper? He said he wanted to come to the viewing with me this afternoon but I haven't heard from him all day – *most annoying.*'

'I think he told me that he would be entertaining some friends at the apartment this evening . . . but not sure where he is right now.'

Elle winced and looked at her watch. 'You mean he's going to be at the apartment all night?'

'Elle, it's the weekend – when does Jasper or Lily not stay over there?'

'I meant . . . well I thought he would . . . sorry when did you say you were going to be back from Lebanon?'

'Thursday . . . and don't cause too much mischief while I'm away – I *know* what you're like.'

Elle spent the next five minutes on the phone to her husband while inspecting her new painting. She disconnected the call and sighed in frustration. She wanted to take Lyra to the Chelsea Bridge Wharf apartment that evening but now she had to stay at Lamont Road. Jasper was in his first year at Oxford University but he came home to London every now and again, often unannounced. Her daughter Lily was staying at a friend's house in Chelsea but she wasn't sure if she was coming back to Lamont Road later that night. She knew it was always a risk taking Lyra back to her family home, but she also knew it wouldn't look particularly suspect – not to her children any-way. If they bumped into Lyra she would simply introduce her as a friend. Lyra had asked her enough times to stay over with her in Kensington but she still lived with her mother and she did *not* want to risk bumping into her.

Change of plan – meet me at Lamont rd at 8 xx

She now had just less than three hours to get ready, walk Sebastian, her West Highland white terrier, and choose a suitable location in her four-storey home for her new painting. She walked back out towards the stairs. She was looking forward to seeing Lyra; it had been a month and she usually never liked it to be more than a week. But she had been exceptionally busy and of course it made Lyra appreciate her a little more.

Just after 7.00pm, Elle finished smoothing out the white cotton bed sheets. She had slipped into her light blue cotton bathrobe, which made her feel more comfortable, particularly after a busy day. She expected a quiet night of making love to her beautiful mistress, which always left her feeling satisfied. Makram knew absolutely nothing about Lyra although Lyra knew about him, which had initially caused heated arguments, but over the years they had settled into an enjoyable routine.

Elle sat on the bed, silently stroking Sebastian while she waited eagerly for Lyra to arrive. Arousing the fairer sex made her feel empowered, and making Lyra orgasm made her mind erupt with ecstasy. Satisfying a man and woman in her life made her feel complete. After all, it took each gender to bring her into the world.

With a yawn, she wondered whether Makram was sleeping on his flight. When she first started sleeping with Lyra, she would worry excessively about Makram coming home unannounced, but after nearly four years of seeing Lyra, the concern was now almost nonexistent. The door buzzer sounded.

Elle opened the front door to Lyra, stepping aside as she

walked in with her platinum blonde hair flowing past her beautifully defined shoulders. Elle closed the door with a contented grin; Lyra was wearing a fitted jacket with tight jeans, which gave her a sexy, casual look she rather adored.

'Yes, I do remember this place.' Lyra leaned in to kiss Elle. Elle was in her bathrobe, which usually meant they were having an early night.

Elle rolled her eyes. 'How've you been my baby?' She clasped her hands gently around Lyra's slender arms. They were almost the same height, which made it easy for Elle to gaze directly into Lyra's eyes fondly. She hadn't bothered to put too much make-up on after her shower; she knew she still looked very sexy without. Lyra was also blessed with effortless beauty; prominent hazel eyes accompanied by long eyelashes and perfectly-sized full lips. Lyra was her special treat, which she constantly hoped wouldn't be taken away from her.

'You *know* how I've been,' Lyra snapped jokingly. 'I've been trying to see you.'

'And now you've got me so stop moaning.' She kissed Lyra tightly on her lips. 'I'll have to kiss you to keep you quiet.'

'You'll have to do more than that.'

'Oh so you've been terribly miserable without me, darling?' Elle grinned and turned to lead the way to the reception room of her home, in the heart of a ten-acre estate.

'*No* I've been keeping myself busy as you know!'

'So you haven't been on the lookout for a replacement? Not that one exists.'

'I've been too occupied with new projects, otherwise I just may have done,' Lyra replied softly in her typically upper English accent, which made it difficult for her to ever sound angry. 'Plus I've had three engagement parties – can you believe it?'

'Well, now that all explains how you've had the time to bombard me with texts.'

'Have you been drinking?' Lyra followed Elle into the large reception room where a crystal chandelier was hanging. Elle's new painting was still on the floor.

'Liquor chocolates.' Elle turned to smile warmly at Lyra. 'Maybe alcohol and chocolate aren't a good mix for me.' The intense excitement in the air was being contained well so far. 'Now do you like my new painting darling?'

'It's very charismatic, I love it actually.' Lyra bent down to get a closer look at the oil on canvas. Elle's home was adorned with old master paintings, notably landscapes and portraits.

'I just don't know where to put it, maybe you can suggest somewhere?' Lyra was an interior designer and Elle often liked to tap into her talents, which she ensured were used to her advantage.

'It'll go nice in here,' Lyra looked observantly around the traditionally designed room. Elle's Chelsea Bridge Wharf apartment, however, boasted a very different minimalist and contemporary style. 'Don't you think? You probably left it in here because you self-consciously think it'll go well in here.'

Elle pondered Lyra's insight but the urge between her legs was deepening in Lyra's presence. She took Lyra's hand and squeezed it tenderly. 'No darling, I quite simply put it here because it's the closest room to the front door.'

Lyra knew that, when Elle squeezed her hand, it meant she was particularly horny.

'Lyra, Jasper is at the apartment and Lily is at a friend's here in Chelsea. I don't think either will be back here tonight; I called them to check.'

'OK fine,' Lyra shrugged slightly. 'So how's everything been with you recently anyway?'

'Good, just been busy with work and so on – like you.' She leaned in to kiss Lyra gently on her lips. 'I *have been* thinking of you my baby.' She loosened her bathrobe to expose her breasts slightly and wrapped her arms around Lyra. She had prepared a light dinner but her appetite could be more than satisfied in bed. She hadn't realised just how much she had missed Lyra. 'Come on let's head upstairs,' she said sensuously. 'I can't wait a minute longer – you can give me more of your professional advice in the morning.' She gave Lyra's hand a final squeeze before leading her back out of the reception room and up the stairs excitedly.

Elle shut the door to her expansive marital bedroom on the second floor and gently took hold of Lyra's arm. She drew her in with a relieved smile and wrapped her arms around her for a hug.

'I hope you have been thinking about me,' Lyra gasped as Elle's warm lips trickled blissfully down her body.

'You know I have.' Elle kissed Lyra tightly on her blushed cheek. 'Now you need to get undressed – I'll wait for you in the bed.' She tapped Lyra's bottom playfully.

'I won't be long,' Lyra smiled benignly.

Elle slipped off her bathrobe while Lyra was in the en suite, and climbed into her king-sized bed. She was yearning for Lyra's slender and soft body to be wrapped tightly around hers; to feel her younger, full breasts in her hands. Lyra was always on her mind. With every second passing, she was becoming more impatient.

'Come on Lyra! Before we know it the night will be over!'

Lyra came out of the en suite five minutes later and walked towards the bed. She sat astride Elle, sweeping back her hair. Elle groaned in contentment with Lyra's non-faltering self-confidence in bed.

'Oh Lyra,' she gasped, 'hurry darling and take everything off.' She wasn't wearing anything and so wanted Lyra out of her lingerie so she could feel every part of her naked body against hers. She reached up to undo Lyra's bra but Lyra took her hands away and gently pushed Elle down onto her back. A look of confusion swept across Elle's face – she was the one normally in charge but tonight she found herself being submissive. The unusually long break in seeing Lyra seemed to have pacified her slightly in bed. Lyra took off her bra for Elle to enjoy her youthful breasts. Elle lay admiring and feeling around Lyra's body. She loved the way Lyra's silk-like hair flowed over her breasts and just above her endearingly tan, lean stomach.

'Why aren't you wearing your sweet little shorts tonight?' Elle asked in a playful yet stern manner, tugging longingly at Lyra's thong. She could see the tan lines as she twisted her finger around the thong; Lyra always kept her healthy tan topped up just for her.

'Why didn't you ask me to?' Lyra asked, tickling Elle's stomach lightly with her fingers. 'Although I could always go back and change . . . '

'No,' Elle groaned, stroking Lyra's thighs eagerly. 'You're not going anywhere. Darling lay down on me,' she asked imperiously, moving her hair away from her face. She breathed more heavily in anticipation. She always lay on top of Makram for an intimate cuddle, so she embraced having Lyra on top of her.

Lyra removed her thong and lay on top of Elle, leading to a shared groan of ecstasy as their bodies sunk deeply into each other. Elle heaved excitedly, pushing into Lyra as much as she could. She loosened her grip of Lyra to kiss her tenderly on the lips, becoming more aroused with the sensuous intimacy. She enjoyed Lyra's lighter weight on top of her, like the feeling of a cosy towel being laid over her on a sunlounger after a swim in her Tuscan pool. She could stay there forever.

'Oh you feel so good,' Elle breathed quickly.

Lyra started to move rhythmically against her. Elle held on to Lyra's shoulders, instructing her to keep going as she enjoyed the pleasing sensation of every inch of the female form she intrinsically desired. She then yearningly wrapped her legs around Lyra's body, tightening her hold of Lyra to push her breasts closer into hers. Although she loved Makram's muscles, the feeling of another woman's supple breasts against hers felt so gentle and special. It was a feeling she knew not all women experienced. But then again, not all women experienced such pecs as her husband's.

'Darling you feel amazing,' Elle groaned. She tenderly kissed around Lyra's neck and shoulders. She could smell the perfume she had bought her. 'I could just cuddle and kiss you every night; do you know that?'

'I could do this every night,' Lyra gasped, pushing herself into Elle while kissing her lips hungrily. She ran her hands along Elle's full breasts, down her stomach and fleetingly to her inner thighs. Elle gasped.

'Lyra, you know what I like,' Elle whispered yearningly into her ear, sweeping her fingers up and down her back in encouragement.

Lyra kissed Elle softly on the lips and around her neck to her erect nipples. Elle writhed on the bed, enjoying the feeling of Lyra's silky hair flowing onto her body. She arched her back in delight as Lyra began to trail her hands sensitively around her inner thighs, but she could only cope with this for a few seconds.

'Oh stop it,' Elle groaned pleadingly, rubbing her feet eagerly against Lyra's legs as she teasingly trailed her fingers up her inner thighs. Lyra always spent more time teasing her in bed, arousing her faster as she felt at the mercy of a beautiful younger woman.

Lyra moved to cup Elle's breasts and began kissing her parted lips. Elle faced away and stroked Lyra's back more intensely, demanding Lyra to give her what she needed. She groaned with the feel of Lyra's hand slipped between her legs where she just held her comfortably, yet knowing this quickly caused feelings of yearning frustration. Lyra knew she enjoyed the feel of her tongue on her more than she did Makram's. Hers was smaller, softer and more precise. She pushed down onto Lyra's hot shoulders, calming with the trail of Lyra's delicate kisses down her breasts to her stomach, until she disappeared under the covers where she left Elle in anticipation for too many long seconds.

Elle took a deep breath. 'Darling what are you . . . ' She groaned loudly and writhed with the sudden sensation of Lyra's tongue. She entwined her fingers around the blankets, almost begging Lyra to stop for the slick strokes of her tongue were too intense. 'Oh Lyra!' she gasped, ecstatic with what she had taught her nearly four years ago.

Chapter Fourteen

'Hi darling,' Cara called through the small gap in her car window.

Sirena vibrantly stepped into her car. Cara was driving her Peugeot family car, which momentarily confused Sirena when Cara pulled up outside her flat; she was expecting her bold black Bentley to be parked outside.

'I've missed you.'

'I've missed you, too.' Cara kissed Sirena before glancing at the back seat. 'Excuse the mess in the back. I usually use this car when I'm moving things around for properties.'

'You're moving me around for a property?'

'Why not? Thought I would plonk you in the living room of my home in Italy – we're going to Heathrow.' Cara pulled away. 'Darling I've had the most frustrating day. I have to buy some furniture but I just can't find anything I like.'

'What you looking for?'

'Dining table and chairs. I'm looking for something visually exciting you know?' Cara quickly glanced at Sirena and noticed her looking at her admiringly. Feeling a bit embarrassed, she suppressed a smile and concentrated on driving. 'I'll continue looking anyway. I just need to come across items that inspire me – maybe I should bring you along with me while I frantically run from shop to shop, so you can really see my *wild* side.'

Sirena laughed. 'How was your holiday by the way? You look really vibrant.'

'Oh do I! I had a lovely catch up with family, skiing, it was nice.'

Cara drove into Chelsea Harbour visitor's car park and into a space between a silver Rolls Royce and an elegant Porsche, to further impress Sirena. They entered The Belvedere and stepped into one of the two lifts in the twenty-storey building.

On walking out of the lifts with triple aspect views of London, Helen came out to greet them. The opened door exposed the party taking place inside, with jazz music blaring out. 'Sweetie!' she yelled with her arms reaching out to Cara.

'Hello darling, great to see you!' Cara lit up. They embraced and exchanged kisses. 'This is Sirena.' Cara gently put her hand on Sirena's shoulder.

Helen met Sirena's bright face with an approving smile. 'How lovely to meet you.' She leaned in for a quick embrace then paused for a few seconds to analyse Sirena like a brand new oil on canvas to add to her expanding impressionist art collection. 'Come in, come in!' She stepped to the side and held the door open steadily as she met Cara's proud gaze.

Sirena was immediately taken with the luxury apartment. There were floor-to-ceiling windows with a view of the Thames. A flamboyant and glamorous atmosphere was evidently present in the apartment with about forty guests standing and laughing, and sitting on sofas with glasses in their hands. A young attractive waiter was walking in and around the crowd with a silver tray of canapés and glasses, which were also neatly spread out on a long shiny black table in the kitchen.

'A handsome waiter this time?' Cara quipped, scanning the

colourful crowd. Helen's parties always drew a mixed crowd from various industries, but notably fashion.

'Hired from a model agency,' Helen smirked. 'Only the best for my dear friends – but contain yourself sweetie.' She leaned into Sirena who was also scanning the stylish and flamboyant crowd. 'Would you like a glass of champagne?' Helen beamed.

'Yes please, thank you,' Sirena beamed back into Helen's sparkling blue eyes. She loved the draped dress she was wearing and her collection of piled on bracelets, but felt a little under-dressed in her evening top and fitted jeans. Thankfully Cara was also wearing jeans and a similar draped top.

Helen signalled at the waiter to walk over to them and took a long glass from the tray, which she handed carefully to Sirena so as not to spill any of the champagne.

'Here you are sweetheart. Please do help yourself to the canapés in the kitchen.' She turned to Cara and raised her eyebrows. 'Don't let this one out of your sight tonight – there are a few predators in the room this evening.' She gave Sirena a cheeky grin as if she were a child. The buzzer sounded. 'More guests!' She hurriedly walked over towards a control panel on the wall.

'Cara!' a short man gruffly yelled, approaching her from out of nowhere.

'Charles how are you?' Cara giggled. They both embraced lightly.

'Super! Very well indeed. I heard you went to Paris last week with Helen? She was telling me all about it.'

Cara looked instantly flustered as she wasn't expecting to be thrown into an awkward moment straight away at the relaxed party. She noticed that Sirena was too busy analysing the crowd to have overheard him expose her secret.

'Oh yes, I'll call you tomorrow and we'll chat properly about it over dinner,' she said persuasively. 'Not much to tell but it was good.'

'Wonderful and I heard that Adrian went also and . . . '

'Yes we all went! So is Alice with you tonight?'

A wave of hurt swept over him. 'No . . . she moved to Florida . . . '

'Oh, sorry I completely forgot,' Cara frowned.

'So did you go to that design fair in Paris then? When I heard you were going I . . . '

'No I didn't go!' Cara intercepted. She grinned awkwardly at Sirena who still seemed to be in a world of her own, analysing the crowd.

'Oh I thought that was why . . . '

'*Anyway,*' Cara blurted as elegantly as possible, 'are you enjoying the party?'

'Why yes!' he nodded. 'Although it's only just begun.' He puffed out his chest and drank his champagne.

Sirena was now analysing Charles having assessed the other grand-looking people around her, who also all seemed to be at least ten years older than her.

'Charles, meet my good friend Sirena.' Cara lightly touched Sirena's naked shoulder. She had told Sirena that she wanted to keep their relationship hidden from people outside her main circle of friends.

'Hello there Sirena!' He turned back to Cara. 'Wish I were accompanied tonight by a beautiful young woman.'

Sirena smiled. 'That's nice of . . . '

'How old are you?' he interrupted with curiosity.

'Twenty-four . . . '

'Ah, a Thatcher child!' he boomed and met Cara's amused expression. Sirena and Charles engaged in a light conversation, although it wasn't long before both Cara and Sirena got bored of his presence as they resorted to tight-lipped smiles to feign interest. Eventually he declared that he had a weak bladder and had to use the bathroom.

Cara gently clutched Sirena's arm as she worked her way

around the room engaging in conversation with various guests and introducing Sirena as her friend, in a way that implied that they had known each other for years. She was careful not to be overly affectionate with Sirena that night. Helen was being busy as the host, greeting people and ensuring that they were all having a great time. Sirena made her way through the crowd to the open plan kitchen where Helen was standing and talking with a few guests in a corner. Sirena filled up her plate with a few canapés and returned to Cara's side, conveniently as she had just finished a conversation with a sharp-looking woman with colourful hair.

'Who was that?' Sirena asked.

'Lisa Fletcher. Owns her own fashion PR company – you should speak with her.'

'Wow I will do.' Sirena looked at her, now laughing wildly with a small group of people. She was still yet to sign up for a course at London College of Fashion – she had been too busy with work and Cara. 'Can you introduce us?'

'Yes of course but later as I doubt you'll get much from her. She's a bit of an alcoholic and she's not holding back tonight it seems.'

'Oh right,' Sirena laughed. 'Helen seems very nice by the way.'

'Yes she is.' She looked over at Helen and grinned. 'She's a very good friend.' She took a canapé from Sirena's plate.

'Does she live alone? Her apartment's *so* amazing.'

'Thank you, I designed it,' Cara smirked. 'She lives here with her eleven-year-old daughter, Annabel, who's *obviously* at her father's tonight. I don't think this party is suitable for teenyboppers, apart from you of course.' She politely smiled and nodded at familiar guests who strolled past them.

'What about her husband?'

'Lives in Pimlico – and they're divorced.'

'So she's single now then?'

'Why do you ask?'

'Just wondered,' Sirena shrugged. 'I need to introduce you to some of my friends soon.'

Cara grimaced. She had no real interest in meeting Sirena's friends and socialising with a *group* of twenty-four-year-olds. 'Yes, she is single, but dating I guess you could say.'

Cara and Sirena spent most of the time at the party together, much to Sirena's relief as she didn't know anyone – although she did meet a lot of interesting people who were all successful in their chosen fields, including international businessmen and media tycoons, some of whom Sirena found to be rather desirable. Cara was being much more flirtatious and attentive towards Sirena when she noticed men looking and then making attempts to approach her, which also drew the attention of Helen who was observing the unlikely couple. A tall and long-limbed handsome man tapped Cara on the shoulder from behind.

'Well look who it is!'

Cara turned to face the man. 'Michael! When did you get here?'

'Just now – I spotted you and *cruised* in.'

Sirena watched on as they exchanged initial words. Michael was looking very debonair in a Ralph Lauren navy shirt and cream straight-leg trousers, which showed off his narrow waist and broad shoulders.

'Michael this is Sirena – a good friend of mine.'

Michael looked down at Sirena merrily with his vibrant brown eyes. 'Well hello, do you sail at all Sirena?' he asked earnestly.

'No never sailed before . . . ' She stopped short as Michael yearningly looked Cara up and down while Cara took her phone out of her Prada bag.

His attention turned to Sirena again. 'Well Cara and I have been sailing together many times so we've had a few shenanigans out at sea.'

Cara gave him a small playful nudge before turning vibrantly to Sirena. 'He loves sailing.'

'Yes, although despite our voyages together she did trick me recently – told me she wasn't going to a friend's dinner party.' He gazed back at Cara. 'Which you knew I wanted to see you at – and then you turned up and on time for the starter, you cheeky thing.'

'But you didn't have to get *food poisoning* you idiot – you could have just cancelled.'

'You know I don't do things by half.' He turned to Sirena. 'Despite our current feud we've had many great times together.' He turned back to Cara. 'You must join Tom and I on his motor yacht during the summer, I'll probably stay with him in Poole for a week or so . . . '

'How is Tom?' Cara interrupted enthusiastically. 'I haven't heard from him in so long.'

'He's very well; just got back from Hong Kong with Yin. They're planning on having another child.'

'Oh gracious! That's wonderful news, I must see them both. I'll call them tomorrow.'

Michael nodded in agreement and finished his glass.

'By the way, this is the new property I've wanted to show you.' Cara showed him a photo from her phone, which he leaned in to see so Sirena was left standing on her own, feeling awkward. Helen suddenly approached.

'Sirena have I introduced you to Audrey yet?'

'Oh hi – no,' Sirena replied, puzzled. 'Who is she?'

'Here she is!' Helen reached for Audrey's arm. She was introducing guests to each other to keep conversations flowing. Audrey was walking by with canapés in her hand, and Helen's sudden grab of her arm resulted in one falling to the ground.

'Oh no!' Audrey cried in despair.

'Oh sweetie I'm so sorry,' Helen laughed, 'shall I get you another?'

'No because it was the last one left!'

'Audrey this is Sirena, Cara's friend.'

'Hi Sirena – good to meet you.'

'Good to meet you,' Sirena replied, unable to shake Audrey's hands, which were occupied with salmon blinis. Another guest approached Helen, leaving Sirena and Audrey while Cara and Michael giggled among themselves like naughty school-children.

The party showed no signs of trailing off fast after 2.00am despite the invitation stating from 7.30pm to midnight. Sirena watched the remaining guests in amusement. Across the living room, Charles accidently spilt his red wine over one of the expensive cream chairs as he bounced loudly on to the hard-wood flooring – he had tripped over while chasing an un-suspecting woman.

'You look cute tonight,' Cara said quietly over Sirena's shoulder, as they watched Helen run over to the chair waving her arms in panic. Helen proceeded to try to roll Charles away from the chair like a big black ball of hay, but he had firmly slumped himself on the floor with the empty glass still in hand. She pulled the glass from him and stood up to regain her composure.

'Right, party over!' she called over the crowd, but this only turned a few drunken heads. 'RIGHT!'

She stormed towards a control panel on the wall, turned off the music and clapped her hands to draw attention.

'MY SWEETIES, I'm going to round you up in herds and lead you to the front door and *you will* graciously throw yourselves into your vehicles – thank you!'

Cara and Sirena remained seated on the sofa, watching Helen encourage everyone to the front door. It took the work of three men to pull Charles to his feet. Helen shut the door after the last guest had left and flopped herself onto the sofa. She looked over at Cara and Sirena who were sitting opposite.

'Look at you two – all loved up,' she said wearily. Cara and Sirena were draped over each other and holding hands. She wished she had a man to cosy up to.

'And you look exhausted,' Cara replied humorously.

'I'm not the only one – Sirena looks like she's falling asleep. You should be taking better care of her.'

Cara sighed and looked at Sirena affectionately. 'Are you ready for bed darling?' she asked in a motherly tone.

'I am so ready to pass out . . . ' Sirena yawned.

'OK let's go and leave Helen to clean up.' Cara shuffled to take hold of her bag.

'Sweetie you're too drunk to drive Sirena home – why don't you both stay over?'

'We'll stay here if that's OK with you?' She looked at Sirena eagerly through her tired eyes.

'Just want to get into bed . . . ' Sirena yawned again, holding back her excitement for sex with Cara that night.

Chapter Fifteen

'Are you OK?' Cara yawned. 'Did you sleep all right?'

Sirena put her arm around Cara's warm back and kissed her cheek. 'So tired.'

'Me too.' Cara woke feeling satisfied yet slightly awkward as she pondered over her personal dilemmas. Her intensified feelings towards Sirena were forcing her to assess her current circumstances, which had no real degree of urgency before. Sirena was a blessing as well as a pain in this regard.

'It upsets me that you're living with your ex,' Sirena declared, now both close and confident enough to say what she really felt to Cara.

'Darling you know my situation.' She turned to face away

from Sirena. 'Urgh I don't want to get out of bed, I'm so comfortable.' She pulled the white duvet over her head.

'What does that mean?'

'Oh Sirena,' Cara groaned. She turned onto her back and took hold of Sirena's hand, placing it firmly between her legs. 'Please just massage me.'

Cara closed her eyes with a heavy sigh as Sirena started to stimulate her. She didn't like to talk about her family issues with Sirena – she was a breath of fresh air from all of that. She writhed slightly as she enjoyed the motion of a woman's hand, caressing her the way she loved. She knew it was unfair to hide anything from Sirena as she was being so honest and open with her. But she was younger and therefore had less baggage.

'Oh that feels good,' Cara groaned quietly.

She just couldn't lose Sirena. She stretched out her legs as she focused on the growing warmness and sensitivity of Sirena's hand. She loved having an orgasm in a tired, sleepy state and the feeling of calmness afterwards as she drifted in and out of sleep.

'Keep going darling,' she breathed deeply, one hand holding Sirena's arm and the other gripping the duvet, which she had pushed down to her waist from her heated chest. Sirena's slim fingers were massaging her too perfectly; her dilemma was becoming harder with every minute passing as her mind began to flutter into a universe of ecstasy. Being pleasured by the same sex aroused her faster, as the sound of a woman breathing and gasping beside her stimulated her as much as the familiar feminine touch on her body. Further tightening her leg muscles, she desperately grasped hold of Sirena's hand. 'Ooh,' she murmured, arching with her hand still gripped tightly to Sirena's. She moved Sirena's hand to rub her up and down faster, frantically pushing the duvet further down with her feet. Letting go, she arched strongly, trying to grasp the sheets around her. Like water spiralling into an open plughole, her body and mind were fast losing control. Groaning loudly she uncontrollably heaved with the sudden explosive spasm dispersing from her centre of bliss.

'Ignore the mess; my cleaner will be here soon.' Helen glanced at the time on the plasma TV. She was already having breakfast in the kitchen when Cara and Sirena emerged at just gone past 7.45am. 'What would you both like for breakfast? I have a meeting in about an hour so . . . '

'Sirena and I are going shopping before I fall into my own bed,' Cara said casually.

'I told you I've got work?'

'Can you really work with so little sleep?' Cara tightened up her thick cotton robe, with the word *Guest* flamboyantly displayed at the back.

Sirena paused as she quickly assessed how to spend her day. 'I probably would fall asleep at my desk – I can catch up on Monday.' She took out her BlackBerry and emailed Marcus.

After a breakfast of croissants and tea, Cara drove Sirena into Knightsbridge. Sirena was wearing her outfit from the party but Helen had lent her a spare pair of winter boots. Cara had brought a change of clothes with her, as if she had planned the shopping trip. Sirena gazed out of the window at all the busy people strolling up and down Brompton Road with their bags of shopping.

'Now I can't be with you for too long Sirena. After a nap I have to get a few things done by the end of the day.' Cara said this rather sternly, as if Sirena had inconveniently suggested they went shopping. Cara parked on Harriet Street and guided Sirena along Sloane Street and straight into Versace. 'I saw these beautiful heels . . . ' She trailed off as Sirena followed her through the entrance and grinned at the welcoming assistants. They walked down two short flights of black marble steps to where heels were on neat display at the end of the room. Sirena fleetingly admired a mannequin wearing the most gorgeous golden dress as she followed closely behind Cara. Cara excitedly picked up a pair of embroidered heels. 'Here they are darling,' she said brightly. She displayed the heel to Sirena in her proud hands. 'What do you think?'

'Wow they're really nice, they'll suit you.'

'Darling they're for you – they'll suit *you*! As soon as I saw them I thought of you, although I do agree that they would suit me also.' She signalled at a Mediterranean-looking assistant who was already approaching. 'Can we try these in a size . . . ' She turned to Sirena. 'What size are you?'

'Size six.' Sirena thought they were stunning but she certainly couldn't afford to purchase Versace shoes.

The assistant reappeared with the heels and Sirena proudly yet anxiously tried them on as she tried to remember her bank balance. Cara watched her admirably while the assistant stood admiring Cara.

'Darling they look just gorgeous on you. I'm tempted to get a pair myself but we don't want to turn up at a party together with the same heels, do we,' Cara quipped. She cast a small gaze at the other heels on display.

'I'll get another pair if you really like them?' Sirena suggested. Affordable shoe retailers swept through her mind.

'No no no, they look too good on you. It's a shame we're not the same size – we could have borrowed from each other,' Cara grinned.

The assistant watched on as they spoke, wondering what their relationship was; Cara was either her mother or a very generous friend, he concluded.

'Yes we'll take them,' Cara confirmed to the pondering assistant. They walked back up the marble stairs to the till.

Sirena took out her small purse but with a sudden tight grip around her wrist.

'What are you doing? I'm getting these for you!'

'Really?' Sirena felt instant relief yet slight embarrassment at Cara buying her expensive heels, which she clearly couldn't afford on her own.

'It's OK. I want to treat you.'

'That will be seven hundred and sixty-five pounds,' the assistant confirmed.

Cara casually handed over her card to the assistant behind the till, blocking out her angst. Hopefully the generous gift would divert Sirena's focus away from her circumstances. 'I need to get a quick birthday present for my niece. I'm thinking about getting her a cute bag.' She paused as she typed in her code. 'Then I'll drive you back to yours, OK? Unless there's somewhere else you need to be?'

'My place is fine, thank you. Thank you *so much* for the heels – but are you sure?'

'Yes of course. It's my pleasure.'

They entered a few more designer boutiques lining Sloane Street including Bottega Veneta, which was one of Cara's favourite stores.

'Let's go to Harrods,' Cara said, feeling some rain drops. 'It'll be easier to see a variety of bags under one roof.' They proceeded to walk back up Sloane Street to the busy Brompton Road. 'Did you enjoy the party last night then?' Cara asked as they walked in and around people walking from the other direction.

'Yes I did – I met some interesting people although missed my chance with the woman in PR,' Sirena replied, still in a daze with her new Versace heels.

'Don't worry; you'll meet her at some point. She did drink a lot last night, though.' Cara smirked to herself as she conjured up images of last night's party. She would've liked to have introduced Sirena to Lisa that night but she didn't know her that well so felt a little uncomfortable. A small group of tourists blocked their path so they had to swerve. 'Gracious, far too many people around here.'

'So when do you think you'll move into your own place?' Sirena instantly regretted asking but she wanted reassurance, which she'd failed to get earlier that morning.

Cara groaned inside as they walked through the doors of Harrods. 'Sirena I don't know. I need to find somewhere suitable.'

Her brief answer didn't inspire confidence. They walked past excited shoppers with their green Harrods bags, until they got to *Room of Luxury 1* where a variety of designer bags were on proud display.

'I do need my own space so I'll move out as soon as I can,' she continued. She inspected a classic Dior bag, under the watchful eye of an assistant who was set to pounce on them.

'Do you want anything by the way?' Sirena asked, looking around at the other bags and hoping that Cara would say no. She wasn't exactly earning enough to be on a shopping spree in designer stores.

Cara giggled appreciatively. 'No I've got everything I need.' She squeezed Sirena's hand gently.

Sirena spent the afternoon in doors, enjoying her unplanned time off work. Her shopping trip with Cara had made their relationship seem more real. She had moved to London to commence her career and ended up becoming involved with an older woman in the process. She didn't particularly care about how unconventional it was, however. She was having a great time with Cara – in bed, at the exclusive venues and being introduced to captivating characters she otherwise would have never met.

Chapter Sixteen

'I feel absolutely zonked,' Valentina giggled, sweeping back her thick blonde wavy hair. She lay draped over the antique sofa with a red Jimmy Choo hanging off her right foot.

'Well it's a good thing you live here and don't have to drive home later,' Cara smirked. She was sitting next to Valentina in a black evening dress. She was very fond of Valentina, finding her amusing even when she didn't mean to be.

'That is why I get super *super* drunk at my dinner parties, dah-ling,' Valentina laughed. She kicked off her heel, which landed on the Persian rug.

'How's your Eaton Place apartment going Cara?' Elle asked. She was sitting on an adjacent sofa, leaning casually on the sofa arm in a parallel-legs position, which showed off her majestic thighs under her draped jersey dress.

'It's going well – I'm adding more furnishings but it should be finished soon,' Cara yawned. Helen contained a grin; she knew that Cara hadn't slept last night at her apartment. 'I'm also still trying to sell my chateau in Switzerland – going there next week actually but the Eaton property is very beautiful.'

'Well done Cara.' Elle raised her glass in a tipsy manner.

'I'm tempted to move into it myself,' Cara joked, 'as I always am.'

'You'll never move away from David,' Valentina giggled. She gently nudged Cara.

Helen and Elle exchanged quick glances with each other.

'So anyway, how was your ski trip with Pavel?' Cara asked Valentina to change the subject, which she was getting tired of thinking about. Valentina supported her head with her hand to cope with her drunken state.

'Fabulous, just fantastic – food, people. Pavel lost his favourite watch but everything is his favourite when he loses something; he thinks people will look harder for him.'

'Speaking of favourites, how is Lyra?' Helen giggled towards Elle, who was sitting beside her. She wanted to liven up the conversation.

'Lyra?' Elle looked up from her glass.

'Yes your mistress – remember her?' Helen replied teasingly.

'You know I don't have favourites,' Elle replied with a hint of sarcasm. 'Lyra is very well but I think we all know I make sure of that.' She produced a mischievous grin, which created a buzz around the room. 'And Helen and I have met Cara's new girl.'

Valentina looked at Cara with surprise.

'Yes I'm seeing someone else now.' Until now, Cara had only informed Helen and Elle, to whom she was closest out of the group.

'*Who is she?*' Valentina demanded, sitting up straight on the sofa. At thirty-four, Valentina was the youngest in the room. Her soft jawline yet sharp facial features indicated her balanced nature, although she was not one to hold in her opinions, which her full and shapely lips struggled to contain.

Cara's smile lit up her face. 'Her name's Sirena, we met at the May Fair Hotel last month.'

Valentina rolled her hazel eyes. 'I thought your *fling* with Alessandra was a one-off Cara. So you're still chasing women?'

'Well I wouldn't use the word chasing!'

'Yes, *sprinting* is probably the better word.'

'Personally I'm relieved you've met Sirena. For the past three years you've been like a cat on heat. I lay in bed listening to you yowling across Chelsea,' Elle quipped.

'Oh come on Elle,' Cara blushed.

'I don't suppose David knows?' Valentina asked.

'No! And the obvious reason being that he has no idea I'm

into women and you all fully know that!' Cara paused. 'And please can we all keep this a secret?' She exchanged serious looks with all three women.

'Of course,' Valentina nodded. 'We've been telling each other our dirty little secrets for years,' she laughed. 'Or rather I've been a witness.'

Cara smiled. She knew that she could trust everyone in the room but still wanted the reassurance. Their husbands or ex-husbands weren't close friends, apart from Makram, who was good friends with David – although Elle was hardly going to share any gossip with him, given her own involvement with another woman. David knew Helen's ex, but since Helen and John divorced their friendship had drifted apart.

'How's it going between you and David now anyway?' Valentina asked. 'I can never keep up with you dah-ling.'

'Oh I don't know,' Cara replied dismissively. 'We're getting on but it's funny how one can live with someone, but not actually see much of the other, you know?'

'Yes I know what that's like.' Valentina's husband Pavel travelled extensively, given his interests in business and media, but they still had a healthy and fulfilling relationship.

'What's the sex like with Sirena?' Helen asked bluntly. She loved talking about sex despite hardly getting any in her present situation, apart from when Max was in the country.

Cara paused intently. 'Very good.' She raised an eyebrow mischievously.

Elle found herself analysing Cara affectionately. Only after four years of knowing each other did they divulge their secret desires. 'Too good to tell obviously,' Elle smirked.

'If I ever found out that my husband had a mistress I would divorce him,' remarked Valentina. She turned to look directly at Elle. 'Why do you have a woman on the side if you're so happy with your husband?'

Elle was taken aback by the sudden passive-aggressive

remark, yet was quick to answer. 'Valentina, why would one want to have their cake and eat it, when one can have their champagne and drink it?'

'Depends on the type of cake, no?'

Elle reached out for her glass on the coffee table. 'One needs variety in life, hence my properties in London, the Côte d'Azur, Tuscany . . . I couldn't live without it. In fact, I'm quite simply very lucky.' She took a contemplative sip of her champagne. 'Now someone please hand me a mirror so I can admire myself before this moment of high praise passes.'

Helen laughed. 'You would do well to hang a mirror strategically above your bed.'

'I had that idea years ago Helen and acted on it. Who else better to see first thing in the mornings?' Elle filled her glass with more champagne.

'Are you being serious?' Helen asked in amusement.

'Of course she is,' Valentina intercepted. 'Some things in life are not to be joked about – mirrors and money are two of them. How you use them both is a reflection of oneself, after all. You know I said that to Pavel when he bought the most vulgar mirror and put it in a *guest room*. I couldn't believe it – *bold* and *brash*. Our guests wouldn't have survived the night so I got rid of it. Anyway Cara, why do *you* get involved with women?' Valentina hoped for a deeper response from her.

Cara frowned slightly. 'I don't know,' she sighed contemplatively.

The room fell silent to accommodate Cara's deep thinking.

'But I do find myself yearning for Sirena like I quite often find myself yearning for a hot cup of tea on a Sunday morning.' Cara wasn't going to answer Valentina's question seriously either. The answer was obvious; she got involved with women because she was attracted to them.

'And do you think Sirena would like to hear she's been likened to a cup of tea?' Helen laughed.

'Yes, everyone likes a nice cup of tea when the situation calls for it.'

'What sort of situation then?'

Cara thought for a few seconds. 'She would be an English breakfast tea – good in bed in the mornings.'

Helen groaned. Elle sipped her champagne. 'It's also the most *common* style of tea in the UK.'

Cara shook her head in amusement.

'You would be a Twining's Selection, Cara – a woman of many tastes,' Helen joked.

'What about Valentina?' Cara asked, smiling.

'Typhoo!' Helen quipped.

'Is that a compliment? Doesn't sound like one?' Valentina questioned with concern. Having spent her early years in Russia, she was no expert on British tea. With a puzzled look, she shrugged adamantly in her seat. 'Anyway, going back to what we were talking about . . . '

Elle groaned in modest protest. Valentina ignored her.

'You cannot love two people at the same time. I find women attractive, but I would never cheat on my husband and I would expect the same of him.'

'Well congratulations darling,' Elle replied, glancing at Cara. Only Cara knew of Makram's affair four years ago with Jasmine, a young American woman he had met in a bar in Monte Carlo. 'But I know that you can love two people at once.'

Cara winced at Elle's statement in disagreement.

'You simply *can't* love two people at once – true love requires a whole heart and yours is divided,' Valentina replied. 'I'm sorry to be harsh dah-ling . . . '

'Oh I don't want to talk about this any more,' Elle groaned tiredly.

'Cara, tell us more about Sirena,' Helen asked, giving Elle a break.

'Well,' Cara smiled, 'she's twenty-four . . . '

Valentina's mouth dropped.

'She does look young for her age too,' Helen teased. Elle nodded silently; her mistress was only one year older than Sirena and she wanted to avoid the comments.

Cara laughed softly. 'Look, I just took an instant liking to her; she's very attractive and . . . well, she has something about her. I mean, I know she's very young but . . . oh I don't know, maybe I'm just losing it!' She sighed, leaning back against the sofa.

'I think you are,' Valentina joked. 'It's all very crazy!'

Cara grinned ponderously with tight lips, hurt by Valentina's response. She knew other people outside her circle of friends would judge and speak behind her back if they found out about her involvement with Sirena. And not just because of their age gap but also because Sirena was a woman. She wouldn't be able to handle that.

'I like Sirena – she came to my party,' Helen added.

'It's just that women are so different to men,' Cara said, appreciating Helen's comment. 'I mean, I would never get involved with a twenty-four-year-old guy!'

'Oh I could get with a younger guy,' Valentina grinned. 'If I wasn't married *of course.*'

'I think her age is fine sweetie,' Helen finished.

'Listen everyone, would any of you like to join me at the V&A tomorrow at about two? I need inspiration for a project, before I forget to ask,' Elle asked.

'Can't, I've got meetings all afternoon.' Cara shook her head as did the other women.

'I'm going to Dubai tomorrow for a week,' Valentina added. 'Oh, has everyone heard that Roderick is now dating Nadia?'

'Nadia? Good grief that woman gets around,' Helen laughed.

Chapter Seventeen

Elle hurried past Milesus and into Bulgari on New Bond Street. It was Monday and the four-year anniversary of her relationship with Lyra, so she had planned to buy her a special gift as last year she only had time to buy her a pashmina from duty free. After forty-five minutes she walked out with a black bag containing a beautiful white gold necklace and earring set, which was just perfect for Lyra. She walked back to her car and placed the bag carefully on the passenger seat. She had already informed Lyra about where they were meeting and what they were doing, but out of enthusiasm she thought she would remind her again.

Wyndham Grand tonight at about 7/7.15 . . . looking forward
xx

Elle returned home in the late afternoon after shopping and completing some work in one of her properties. She briskly walked up to the second floor and hid Lyra's present in a cupboard in the spare bedroom. She then walked across the corridor to her marital bedroom, where she took off her belted wool jacket and changed into airy white linen trousers and a light v-neck jumper. Sebastian suddenly ran in, making her jump.

'What are you up to?' she asked him playfully.

She strolled past him and made her way to the kitchen on the lower ground floor to make herself a quick sandwich, before joining Makram in the reception room where he was quietly reading a broadsheet newspaper. Elle took a bite of her ham salad sandwich as she lifted herself comfortably onto an adjacent sofa.

'Babe, I don't know if you remember me telling you but I'm going to see Valentina tonight – she's holding a dinner party so I'll most probably be back late, at about one or so . . . possibly a bit later.'

He turned the page. 'I'd forgotten but yes that's fine, I'm staying in so see you when you get back.' His arm reached out for his glass of water on the coffee table. 'You know I don't like it when you stay out all night. I worry.'

Elle nodded silently. She wished that she could have spent the entire night with Lyra, which would have made their special day more meaningful, but half a night was better than nothing and she didn't want to arouse any unnecessary suspicion.

At 7.00pm, Elle arrived at the Wyndham Grand at Chelsea Harbour. In a knee-length, one shoulder silk dress, she walked vibrantly through to the lounge and ordered an apple and blackberry Martini while she waited for Lyra to arrive. She lightly touched her hair, which was held up in a clip apart from a few strands either side of her face. She had made an extra special effort for Lyra that evening and she was certainly worth it. Lyra entered the lounge ten minutes later looking as gorgeous as ever in a short-sleeved dress with a sparkling sequin waist, which made Elle feel exceptionally special as people watched them embrace like two close friends. Although Lyra was fifteen years younger than her, they both looked as glamorous as each other. It was a sure sign that a relationship wasn't ideal if one party was inclined to jealousy. With Lyra, she was always proud.

They were promptly shown to their reserved table by the window in the adjacent restaurant, which showed off the beautifully lit marina.

'Happy anniversary again,' Lyra beamed at Elle. She found it very sweet that they celebrated an anniversary, seeing as they weren't exactly in a proper relationship.

'Yes you too my gorgeous baby,' Elle replied happily. She

eagerly scanned the drinks menu. 'Shall we have a glass of the Perrier-Jouet Grand Brut?'

Lyra quickly picked up the menu and hesitated.

'We'll go for that, OK darling?'

'Yes OK.' Lyra nodded brightly. She was used to Elle getting her own way so it was hardly worth her deciding otherwise.

'Now of course you know I can only be with you till about two, don't you Lyra?' Elle looked at her with a hint of concern. 'But of course you have the room all night. Makram will be expecting me back so I simply can't stay. I am upset about it but we really should have planned this better.'

Lyra looked away. She really didn't want Makram mentioned that evening. Elle was quick to pick up on her irritated mood.

'Sorry baby. I know it can be difficult but let's just make the most of the time we do have. Just wish I could make tonight more special for you.' She reached out for Lyra's hand and stroked it. 'So how was the Maldives? And your mother? How is she?'

Lyra thought it was quite humorous when Elle asked her about her mother, as she recalled her saying that it would be a nightmare if she ever bumped into her. 'It was so hot – a lot of sunbathing and snorkelling. Mother spent most of her time relaxing with spa treatments so she's returned feeling beyond rejuvenated.'

'I'm glad you had a super time.' Elle smiled at her. Lyra was certainly as tan as she'd hoped she would be and, with her platinum blonde hair flowing luxuriously around her shoulders, she was looking very sexy. 'Can you believe that we've known each other for four years? It's gone by so quickly.'

Lyra beamed back at Elle. Four years *had* gone by quickly but, despite her love for Elle, she was beginning to desire her own committed relationship again – and she had come to accept that Elle wasn't prepared to give this to her. Within the past four years she did stop seeing Elle once when she became involved in another relationship, but at the time they were both so committed to their flourishing careers that they eventually parted ways. Elle was always there to give her affection and sex when she needed it so they just carried on seeing each other, at times convenient to both.

Before their starters arrived, Elle took out a black Bulgari gift box and proudly presented it to Lyra over the table. 'Happy anniversary Lyra,' she smiled. She acknowledged that she had exquisite taste in just about everything, so she knew Lyra would naturally love the gift.

Lyra's face lit up. 'Happy anniversary to you also,' she smiled fondly and reached for her gift to Elle, which she had hidden in her bag.

'Aw thank you – I hope it's to my taste this year,' Elle joked. She opened the box to be brightened by a silver bracelet, with small round pink sapphires. 'Oh my, the bracelet really is stunning. Thank you *so much* my baby.' She leaned across the table to kiss Lyra on the cheek, but aware of the public around them. 'A necklace has come to my mind immediately, which this will match so well. Gosh it's gorgeous – so thoughtful of you Lyra.'

'I remember you wearing a very similar necklace,' Lyra smiled. She opened her gift from Elle and gasped in delight. 'Sorry it's Lily – give me a second.' Elle put her phone to her ear. 'Yes darling?' She glanced up at Lyra and shrugged – she couldn't ignore a call from her daughter. 'No Lily, I can't pick you up tonight – I'm having dinner with a friend and I'm going to be drinking. Makram is staying in tonight so call him when you need to be taken home OK?' She winced at Lyra. 'Yes I'll be back home later tonight . . . please call Makram now and call me back to confirm that he is able to collect you OK?' She smiled at Lyra. 'OK good. Don't forget to let me know. Bye darling.' Elle put her phone down and puffed out her cheeks.

'Sorry my daughter's at a party in the country, which she didn't tell me about. You know I've told her so many times that she needs to inform me early about her plans. Sorry, what were you about to say?'

Lyra brightly lifted her gift from Elle. 'I absolutely love this, thank you so much.'

'Oh I'm glad you love it – you'll have to put them on later,' Elle replied warmly. Although to see Lyra in *only* the jewellery would be a treat.

Elle took out her wallet to clear the bill at the end of their special dinner, while Lyra enjoyed finishing her dessert. Elle glanced at her watch; she only had a limited amount of time with Lyra that night and she desired to spend most of that time celebrating in bed.

From the restaurant they made their way to their marina-view suite. Elle opened the door in anticipation of the stylish and spacious suite they were to enjoy themselves in for the next few hours. Lyra dropped her bag on the sofa and wrapped her arms around Elle's waist.

'Thank you for all of this,' Lyra said happily. She kissed Elle tightly on the lips.

'Happy anniversary,' Elle replied tenderly. She began to unzip Lyra's dress.

Cara rested her elbows on the dining room table and flicked through her phone to read text messages from Sirena – she was missing her. David walked in with an apron around his white shirt.

'Dinner is ready darling,' he exclaimed. He placed the two warm plates on the table. Cara was smiling contently at her phone. 'Who are you texting now?' he asked with dipped eyebrows. He sat down opposite her.

'No one.' Cara put her phone down beside her plate. 'Just reading through some texts from Elle.' She looked admirably at the stir fry with fresh vegetables in front of her. 'This looks suspiciously good,' she complimented with a change of tone to emphasise the change of subject.

'Thank you, although I was very tempted to get a takeaway instead but as I reached for the phone I thought to myself – when was the last time I cooked for the beautiful mother of my child?' He smirked. 'I'm actually just glad that we finally managed to schedule in a suitable time.'

'I'll schedule in more dinners with you if you keep up with this standard.'

'Have you ever known me to drop my standards? I hope this has reminded you how multi-talented I am?'

'Well it has been a while since you last cooked for me, David, so what exactly has changed?'

'Because we hardly spend time together, which is something that *does* need to change, don't you think?'

'I rescheduled Italy and went to Paris with you didn't I?'

'Only when you discovered Helen was coming!'

Cara contained a smile, which would have drifted from ear to ear if she hadn't. Helen was the primary reason she agreed on going.

'Cara, I don't want us to drift apart. I've really missed you.'

'We're not drifting apart – we're sitting at the same table.'

'You know what I mean.'

'David, we're separated,' she replied with a look of concern. She couldn't help but feel guilty eating the meal, which was an obvious attempt to patch up their shaky relationship.

'We can get back on track. We don't have to end absolutely everything between us.'

Cara sighed. 'David I thought we had discussed this?' She began to play with her food on the plate to help cope with the repetitive conversation.

'I know. It's just that it's difficult when we're under the same roof you know?'

'Well maybe I should hurry up and move out soon then?' Cara said teasingly.

'I won't allow it,' David smirked. 'It's just that I'm not seeing anyone else and, well . . . '

'David no, it'll confuse me too much. We've discussed this so many times and I really don't want to go through it again OK?'

'But I'm not seeing anyone else – are you?'

'No David,' Cara frowned and continued to play with her food.

'I just think that if we spend more time with each other . . . '

'David! I'm quickly losing my appetite.' Cara dropped her fork. 'Look, spending more time together won't change anything – you know that.'

David looked despondent and fell silent.

'But the stir fry is delicious by the way.' Cara picked up her fork again.

David laughed a little. 'Thank you,' he replied with a slight smile. He knew he had to temporarily suspend his efforts to get intimate with Cara. He was sexually frustrated but no other woman could satisfy him like she could – she was so womanly and mature. He didn't care for young women, from whom he always had offers. Of course they had youthful attractiveness but often lacked sensuality and skill in the bedroom. He needed Cara back.

Sirena turned off her TV and reached for her phone before she drifted to sleep.

Hey are you free to meet on Wed or Fri? Falling asleep xx

Cara gazed at the text and didn't reply. She was finishing a quick dessert with David at the table. Sirena sent another text twenty minutes later and lay in anticipation for a response, which was keeping her awake.

*

Cara was now getting ready to leave home to quickly see a friend in Belgravia who needed her advice on a property project. She replied immediately this time, now that she wasn't in the presence of David.

Things are hectic at the moment . . . I'll let u know regarding those days. Good night to u my darling xx

She slipped her phone into her pocket. She was missing Sirena but felt that she was beginning to lose control over her emotions and the situation with David. She had always prided herself on being in control of every aspect of her life. She felt in love with Sirena but, after the initial excitement, it was beginning to dawn on her how ungraceful it was to be involved with a twenty-four-year-old; hardly the model mother she thought she was as she stepped into her Bentley. But even though she *felt* ungraceful, she had a strong connection with Sirena and enjoyed their nights together. David wasn't helping either as he was becoming more attentive towards her. She found it easy to knock him back, but he could be so charming and it was this magnetic charm that had won her over when they first met.

Elle softly kissed Lyra's shapely back, trailing her hands slowly all over her naked body. Lyra was falling asleep in the comfortable bed but she had to stay awake. She glanced at her watch; it was 2.00am and she knew she should have left the hotel by now. She thought of possible excuses to stay over but knew she ultimately couldn't. She lay on top of Lyra and swept her luxurious blonde hair to the side to kiss her neck. 'I've got to go now,' she reluctantly whispered. 'Stay here and I'll call you tomorrow.'

Lyra turned to lie on her back to face Elle and they kissed longingly on the lips. 'I want you to stay,' Lyra moaned tiredly, with her hands clasped around Elle's back to keep her in the bed.

'I can't darling, Makram is waiting for me . . . I have to get up now but you stay warm in here OK?'

She gave Lyra a kiss before getting out of bed and proceeded to change back into her dress. She put her yellow gold diamond earrings and matching necklace back on, as Lyra could only watch from under the warm covers.

'Happy anniversary, beautiful,' Elle said lovingly. She put on her sandals and gave Lyra a final kiss before leaving the room.

Chapter Eighteen

'So you're happy with it all?' Cara asked, picking up her coat collar. It was midweek on an early April afternoon. She was keen on hearing how things were going between Elle and Lyra, so she could relate to herself and Sirena.

'Very – should get a healthy return with all the improvements I've made and the master bedroom is just perfect; such a serene atmosphere with the gorgeous balcony.'

'I'll have to see it. You know, a relative has asked me to back her in her new cosmetic product. I'm quite interested. It would be good to get involved with projects other than property.'

'I think you would enjoy it,' Elle replied ponderously. Imperial Wharf was fairly quiet with a few other people walking their dogs along the river.

'How's Jasper doing at university by the way?'

'Very well – enjoying himself and things are going well with his girlfriend who's such a lovely girl.' Cara nodded.

'And how's Giles?'

'Very busy studying for exams.'

'And how are you and David these days? You haven't mentioned him in a while.'

'He's been so different lately, just really trying to make things work with me.'

Elle nodded at her, although she considered Cara's relationship with David most predictable – a series of break-ups and make-ups.

'He says he misses me but I'm just not attracted to him any more, you know?'

'Well he keeps trying to whisk you off on holidays doesn't he?'

'I know. It *is* nice for us to get away from London and as a family, but I really can't begin doing it again.' She paused. 'You know it's very annoying that, just as I meet someone else, David suddenly starts to make more effort with me.'

Elle gave Cara a sideways glance as they walked closer towards the river. 'You need to make up your mind with David and stick to it, especially now you're seeing Sirena.'

'But your relationship with Lyra works well doesn't it? It must do if it's been four years?'

'Don't remind me! Yes it works but obviously it's not ideal. I do worry for Lyra when I go back to Makram, and there's a lot of guilt.' Elle hesitated. 'But I get the impression that only seeing Sirena sporadically is not quite enough for you?'

Cara paused, pursing her full lips slightly; she didn't want to admit this. 'But do you not feel for Lyra?'

'I care about Lyra very much, as much as I do for Makram, which I know might sound silly but I can't help the way I feel – can't even understand it myself.' Their walking pace slowed down and they sat on a bench facing the Thames. Amber and Sebastian rested at their feet. 'You know, I never thought that I would be in the rather ridiculous situation that I'm in, but saying that I need both in my life is on par with the fact that I have a birthday every year,' Elle said thoughtfully. 'Well, two actually,' she smiled contently.

'A society of excess,' Cara sighed, watching Elle lean down

131

to stroke her dog. She struggled with the concept of loving two people at the same time.

'He's been playing up recently, haven't you my darling?' Elle said to Sebastian.

'Dogs can be so funny can't they?'

'They can.' Elle turned back to Sebastian. 'You are aren't you? You come out with the funniest one-liners don't you?' She turned her attention back to Cara. 'It's just that when you talk about Sirena you have a certain look, a look you get when you really like someone, which is rare.'

'I'm confused Elle. I feel so alive when I'm with Sirena and I've never really felt this way before, with either a woman or a man. Well not that I can remember anyway. I'm really not enjoying this confusion; not knowing who I am and what I want from life, or rather what I *need* from life. But it's a feeling I've always hidden away after marrying David and having Giles.'

'Why don't you just be with Sirena instead of complicating yourself with doubt about everything? Surely if you really like her, there should be no more discussion on the matter? We both know you don't love David any more.'

Cara fell silent for a few seconds. 'It's not exactly straight-forward is it?' Elle looked at her blankly, which Cara didn't respond to well. 'Well obviously she's a woman who's fourteen years younger than me. What on earth would my family and other people think? And my son – how would he feel about his mother being with another woman? And the financial difference between us is quite significant; she couldn't afford to live my lifestyle – I would have to pay for everything.'

'Yes, it is a rather unconventional situation – but you're not getting any younger . . . '

'Thanks for reminding me!'

'You should be thinking about yourself more, that's all.' Elle loosened her polo neck jumper. 'Do you want to be unhappy for the rest of your life? Before you met Sirena you were just so miserable darling.' Elle kept firing the hurtful truth. 'Of course you need to think of your family but if they see how happy you are, don't you think it'll make them happy too?'

'I just don't know Elle,' Cara shook her head ponderously.

'Before you met Sirena all you did was complain about finding someone new to love and, now that you've found someone, you doubt the whole thing. It seems silly and you're not appreciating your luck in finding her.'

'I just didn't expect it to be a twenty-four-year-old girl.'

'Really? Cara, you can't help who you fall in love with – just see how it goes and don't give yourself such a headache. Just remember how excited you were when you first met and how long you had to wait to get that feeling.'

Chapter Nineteen

Cara drove back to Sirena's flat after they had seen a show together. It had been nearly five months since they first met and she was still enjoying being with Sirena, but her growing concerns with the implications of the relationship were becoming more intense. She stepped out of her car and looked up at Sirena's flat. She preferred Sirena to stay over in Chelsea but, with David and Giles living under the same roof, it wasn't always possible. Staying at Sirena's made her feel rather uncomfortable. She was fully aware of Sirena's modest lifestyle in comparison to her own extravagant ways, and Sirena's flat, along with its contents, reflected this. Seeing Sirena within her world only made their incompatibility bolder in her mind.

She walked around the small flat as Sirena took a call from one of her friends. Cara walked into the small bedroom; it had a cosy feel to it, which was nice for their nights together. She dropped her overnight bag on the bed. She had brought a chemise with her although she knew she wouldn't have it on for long.

They had an early night after watching a classic 1980s film and fell asleep after making love. Sirena had to leave her flat at about 7.45am for work so she left Cara lying in her bed as she began to get ready. Cara lay analysing the contents of the room and grimaced at the furniture – old and with no style, although she knew Sirena was just starting out in life and thus excused her in her mind.

Cara drove back to Chelsea feeling heavy with a mixture of emotions running through her mind. She loved being with Sirena and she had many good qualities. But although she was an educated and sophisticated young woman, she wasn't wealthy – she didn't own a property or even a car, and she only holidayed once or twice a year. It was a world away from her wealthy existence, which was all she had ever known. Men who tried to date her bought her extravagant gifts and offered to take her on glamorous holidays. Sirena couldn't possibly offer her any of those things. She loved her lifestyle, which she was more than accustomed to – and she didn't know how her and Sirena could possibly work in the long term. But what was more important; Sirena and the passion she brought into her life, or being with someone more financially compatible who could live her lifestyle with her? She never really had this dilemma over Alessandra who was just as wealthy as her, but she hadn't viewed her in such a serious light. She wasn't enjoying this confusion – it was an inconvenience to her otherwise relatively carefree existence.

Elle drove out of Mayfair to South Kensington, having enjoyed a three-hour lunch with friends. She was collecting Lyra for their planned dinner at Beauchamp Place, then watching a film on Fulham Road before going back to Chelsea Bridge Wharf.

She parked outside Lyra's apartment on Onslow Square and called her from her car as usual. Lyra emerged, dressed casually in dark blue jeans and an evening coat.

'Sorry I'm a bit late darling,' Elle said fleetingly out of the window.

Lyra was about to step into Elle's car when her mother, Lizette, suddenly parked her car in front of Elle's. Elle quickly reached for her dark Prada sunglasses in the car cabinet.

'Lyra!' Lizette stepped out of her silver Mercedes and walked towards Elle's car. 'Lyra darling – just caught you! Where are you going?'

'Oh hi Mum! I'm just going for dinner with a friend.' Lyra abruptly shut the car door on Elle.

'Oh how lovely!' Lizette peered into the side window to see who was behind the wheels of the Jaguar. Elle turned to smile and wave at Lyra's mother behind her sunglasses. Lizette wasn't to know who she was and what she was doing with her daughter; all the same, she didn't want to lock eyes with her mother *at all*.

'What time will you be back tonight?'

'I'll be back tomorrow actually – we're going to be out till late so I'll just stay over with my friend.'

'Who is she? Have I met her before?' Lizette asked quietly.

'Elle. We've been friends for years but . . . don't think you have met. But anyway we're running late so I'll see you tomorrow.'

'Yes OK – have fun darling.' Lizette quickly hugged Lyra and waved fleetingly at Elle before turning to walk back to her car. Lyra stepped into Elle's car and shut the door firmly.

'That was awkward.'

'Indeed.' Elle took off her sunglasses and handed them to Lyra to place back in the cabinet. 'It would be super if we could *save* the drama for the cinema.' Elle was evidently agitated as she quickly pulled away from Onslow Square.

'I don't know why it's such a big issue, though – she's just my mother.'

'Darling if you *really* think about it you'll understand; it's like you meeting my daughter or son and lying to their faces about who you are.'

Lyra sighed and shut the cabinet door hard. 'Well you're the expert at that.'

'What?' Lyra turned to gaze out her window. 'Lyra, don't make me feel guilty when we both started this together – you're not an innocent party.' Elle glanced over at Lyra who still wasn't responding. 'Look, why don't you just get your own place? It would make things a lot easier for us don't you think?'

'I like it where I am.' Elle gave her a fleeting look of disapproval in response. She wasn't exactly putting a lot of effort into their relationship. 'I will move out soon – just need to sort a few things out.' Lyra frowned. She ideally wanted to move out with a partner but Elle was hardly going to give her the stability she needed.

'But darling why are you being negative about it? You're twenty-five years old – surely you yearn for independence?'

'Well I did live out on my own for a while, but now I would rather live with someone else Elle.'

'Lyra, I said I'll stay over with you when I can.'

Lyra shook her head in frustration. 'I just don't know how much longer we can keep this up. I need to be getting into a stable relationship soon.'

'Look, don't start this nonsense Lyra – you know it upsets me.' Elle glanced over at Lyra, who was looking ahead solemnly. 'Come on now my baby, we're supposed to be having a fun night . . . ' Elle said, disheartened.

Chapter Twenty

Cara flew Sirena to Estepona, to stay at a villa owned by one of her friends for a few days in early July. Sirena had already booked a holiday to Mallorca with friends so she had used up her work holiday entitlement and couldn't spend any more time abroad with Cara. Sirena stepped into the pool overlooking the Spanish mountains, covered in woodland and greenery.

'It's so quiet here,' Sirena commented. All she could hear were the crickets in the grass around the property.

'It's wonderful,' Cara replied from her sunlounger, taking her eyes off her novel to look around at their view. 'It's very relaxing here.'

Sirena swam to the side of the pool to reach for her glass of lemonade, which was becoming warm with the rays of the sun shining directly down on it.

'I was last here with Giles – he plays a lot of tennis here.'

'When do you think you'll tell Giles about us?'

Cara's mood instantly dropped. 'No idea.'

'It's going to be really difficult isn't it?'

'Too difficult for words so let's not talk about it.' Cara sensed Sirena's bewilderment, which angered her a little. 'Well I'm a thirty-nine-year-old woman and you're a twenty-five-year-old girl – it's not exactly the most conventional of relationships, you must agree!' Cara was still getting over becoming a year older in June, while Sirena's birthday was a week ago.

'I know but . . . '

'I care about what my family will think Sirena,' Cara interrupted. 'I have to think about Giles, you know?'

'Yes, I know,' Sirena replied sarcastically, 'I just can't believe you – *you* come on to *me* then six months later you label us as not normal! You could have warned me of your attitude before you flung me into this relationship.'

Cara rolled her eyes, hidden from Sirena's view by her summer straw hat. 'Just calm down, you know I love you darling,' she said soothingly. 'I'm just saying that it'll be difficult for me to tell family, just as I assume it will be for you.'

Sirena floated away from the poolside. 'And why haven't you moved out of your family home yet?'

'As I've told you, buying a property takes time and it shouldn't bother you anyway – David and I are not together as I've also had to tell numerous times.'

'But you buy and sell property all the time?'

Cara groaned. 'You know, the heat must be getting to your head – take a dive.'

She knew she couldn't keep up the same excuse. Although she was often tempted to buy her own place, she felt a strong connection to her family home where she felt comfortable and safe and could see three familiar faces, including Amber. Plus so far it hadn't been difficult seeing Sirena whenever she needed to. Despite her reservations with Sirena, she was finding it hard to settle on what she needed in life, although she could feel herself becoming more distant with Sirena in the process.

'You can be so annoying sometimes. If you think we're too unconventional to tell your family then I guess we'll be sleeping in different rooms tonight.'

'Stop talking nonsense.' Cara reached for her fresh fruit juice. 'I just don't think telling my son now would be a great idea, that's all. Maybe when's he's older but certainly not now.' Cara lifted her straw hat up at an angle so she could see Sirena, wishing that she wasn't having the conversation on their break together. 'Sirena you know I care for you and want us to be together but I just can't rush certain things. And of course we're not sleeping in separate bedrooms.' She turned her attention back to her novel.

During the last week of August, Cara returned from a trip to Saint-Tropez. She was feeling revitalised and looking incredibly bronzed as she sat between David and Giles watching a show at the National Theatre. This was the first time in nearly a year that they had all been to a show together as a family. After the performance, they made a short walk to a restaurant for a quiet bite before travelling home to Chelsea. Cara sent Sirena a quick text in the bathroom while David and Giles were sitting at the table, reading the menu together. She acknowledged that she had been exceptionally distant with Sirena all summer and certainly didn't want her to drift away from her, despite being unsure about their involvement. But she still wanted Sirena's attention, which made her feel valued and special. After all, Sirena was a gorgeous woman in her twenties.

Cara walked through the busy Latin restaurant and returned to the table. She was going to Monaco with Michael to attend the annual Monaco Yacht Show in September. She couldn't possibly meet Sirena before going as she had too much to catch up on, seeing as she had spent the last couple of months mainly out of town. She quickly scanned through the menu to keep up with David and Giles, who had already chosen their main dishes.

'How are your tennis lessons going?' David asked Giles inquisitively.

'OK,' he nodded.

'We played together last week and he was very good.' David raised his eyebrows at Cara. 'Almost as good as me.' Giles shook his head.

'Oh good,' Cara beamed at Giles, 'I should play a game with you soon actually.'

'But you're more of a badminton player,' Giles smirked.

David smiled teasingly at Cara.

'I *can* hit a small yellow ball you know!' She shrugged at them both.

David gently squeezed her left arm. 'You should just about be able to.'

Cara pulled a face at him as the waiter appeared to take their order. As David confirmed their choices, Cara had a deep moment's thought; she enjoyed her ad hoc family outings, which had become rarer than ever before with her separation from David. She was feeling warm inside that evening, although looked hot on the outside. She caught a waiter gazing at her across the room and flirtatiously grinned at him.

Chapter Twenty-One

Sirena arrived at a small venue in Fulham after work, where she was meeting Natalie and Chris. The two had started a serious relationship just before the summer, much to Natalie's joy. Sirena had told Natalie that she couldn't stay for long as Cara had just called to say she would be coming over later. The room was quite crowded and bright and airy with canapés and a selection of drinks on offer. She sighted Natalie with Chris in a corner and strolled briskly through the crowd.

'Hey you two.'

'Sirena, how lovely to see you,' Chris exclaimed. They kissed lightly on each cheek. 'How've you been?'

'Great – very busy with work and various other things! How have you been?'

'Good – busy with work of course and visited family in Cambridge last week. I *had* invited Natalie but unfortunately she couldn't come with me.' He turned to Natalie for her reaction.

'Yes, you know I wanted to go but I had two big family

birthdays that week. I'll definitely come with you next time. You know how much I loved meeting your mother.' She grimaced discreetly at Sirena.

Sirena giggled in amusement. They looked good together. Chris was a good-looking man with chestnut brown hair that had grown a lot since they had last met, which nicely exposed his natural waves. She left them alone while she admired the paintings of African wildlife adorning the white walls.

'Do you like big cats?' came a well-spoken voice beside her.

Sirena turned to look at the man. 'Oh, yes I do. I love them in fact.' He looked very charming in a navy pinstripe suit.

'An old friend of mine used to own a lion, many years ago of course. He used to spend so much time with her – gave her more attention than his own friends, which included me! Do you paint at all?'

'I love painting but don't have the time – your friend owned a lion?!'

'Yes – I have photos to prove it, while my friend has a scar or two!' The charming man turned back to the paintings in front of them. His hair was fair and receding and he owned a bit of a belly, but he certainly held an alluring stance that captivated Sirena. 'So would you normally use water colours when you paint?'

'I tend to use acrylics actually but sometimes mix different materials to get a better effect.'

'Yes indeed. I haven't painted for a while myself but I tended to use different types of paints, chalk and so on.' He looked Sirena up and down fleetingly as she stood beside him, about two inches shorter and in office attire.

'Isn't that painting amazing?' Sirena pointed to a painting of a charismatic-looking lion lying down.

'Yes it is very beautiful.' He paused as he admired it. 'My name's Miles by the way.' He turned to hold out his hand to her.

'Sirena.' They shook hands with equal fascination.

They continued talking to each other as Natalie walked around the room with Chris, wondering who this charming man was. She didn't want to interrupt, however, as Sirena looked to be fully engaged in conversation.

'So are you here with friends?' Miles asked.

'I'm with a friend and her boyfriend.' She located them within the crowd and pointed. 'He's also her manager actually, which is quite funny. You?'

'I'm good friends with the artist so I just came on my own for a quick look – I promised him that I would, you see. He's over there in fact.' Miles pointed in the direction of the artist who was standing in the middle of a group of people, looking very debonair. 'Listen Sirena, I'll give you my card as I'm about to head back to the office.' He took a card out of his coat pocket and handed it to her. 'Send me an email later tonight so you don't forget about me!'

He walked off leaving Sirena with his card.

MILES SPENCER
Managing Director
The London Society Magazine

She found him to be very charming and intriguing. She was certainly going to be meeting with him again, but out of curiosity for a potential new friendship. She needed to widen her social circle in London, after all, and who better than the owner of a successful magazine.

'I'm glad you enjoyed the gallery,' Cara whispered, kissing along Sirena's stomach. 'But you know I don't like you talking to strange men.' She bit her teasingly. 'You know, I'd forgotten how adorable you are.' She sat astride Sirena, and lightly tickled between her legs.

'Why have you been so quiet with me recently? I was really upset that you didn't make more of an effort to see me before you went to Monaco.' Sirena writhed slightly, trying to not react to the sensation.

'Have I been quiet?' Cara pulled a concerned expression. She lay down on top of Sirena. 'Well I've just been so busy with work darling and you know I've been travelling a lot over the past two months. I just have friends all over the place that I need to catch up with.' She couldn't bring herself to tell Sirena she had doubts about their relationship, although being with Sirena again reminded her of how much pleasure she gave her. 'Plus I have to spend time with Giles, you know?'

'Yes, I know.'

'Of course you know my darling.' She nuzzled around Sirena's neck. Her phone vibrated.

'You better ignore that,' Sirena said hazily, enjoying Cara's attentive mood, finally.

Cara reached for her phone. 'It's David.'

Sirena groaned.

'I better take it, give me a few seconds.' Cara lifted herself up from Sirena and sat on the edge of the bed to take the call. After a few minutes, she turned her focus back to Sirena. 'I'm so sorry but my son isn't feeling well. I have to go home.'

'You're joking?' Sirena turned over to look at Cara. 'We haven't spent a night together in weeks?'

'I know Sirena, I'm so sorry. David says he's really unwell. Let me go home and check and I should be able to come back all right? You know I've been longing to spend time with you.'

Sirena watched Cara put her clothes back on, annoyed that she was leaving her and going back to her home where she *still* lived with her ex-husband.

Cara knew from the tone of David's voice that he was in a mood so was bracing herself before she got out of the car. Throwing the car door shut, she walked up the short steps to the front door and turned the key. She walked through the entrance hall and into the reception room where she caught sight of David sitting down on a sofa reading a newspaper. 'David?'

'Oh there you are,' he replied sarcastically. He had returned from a business trip in Germany earlier that morning.

'Where's Giles?' she asked worriedly, standing by the door.

'He's in bed,' he replied sharply.

'I thought he was staying at a friend's tonight?'

'He was but clearly drank a little too much and couldn't make it out the front door into the great open world.' He threw his paper down.

'And where did he get the alcohol?'

'He raided the drinks cabinet with some friends when neither of us was in.'

'For goodness' sake – is he all right?' She glanced up towards the stairs.

'Yes, thanks to me.'

'Why are you in such a mood David? He's old enough to know what he should be doing – we'll both have strong words with him tomorrow.'

David raised his voice. 'Cara I'm tired of you going off into the night and not telling me about it. I wanted you to meet an important client earlier who came by but of course you were nowhere to be seen – I even checked under your bed.'

'Don't talk to me like that David. We're not even together.'

David frowned angrily.

'And you're hardly in yourself . . . '

'Because of work – I have client visits.'

'I'm sensing double standards here.'

He roughly ran his fingers through his hair. 'Us living together – it just isn't working is it? You've said it yourself enough times.'

'David I don't want to argue with you. I take it that Giles is up in his room?'

144

'Where else would he be?'

Cara glared at him.

'He's up in his room. He's feeling better now.'

'I want to check on him.' Cara walked quickly out of the reception room and up the stairs. She knocked lightly on Giles's door and slowly opened it. 'Giles are you OK darling?'

'I'm fine,' Giles murmured.

She walked over to him and gently placed her hand on his forehead. 'Are you sure you're OK?'

His reply came in the form of a mumble.

'Your father said you had too much to drink?'

He mumbled again into his pillow.

'It's *very irresponsible* of you. Just get a good night's sleep and you'll feel better in the morning OK?' She kissed his head and walked out, gently closing the door behind her. He was still her little baby. She headed downstairs to engage in a more friendly conversation with David for an amicable night.

'I never know where you are. Always so inconsiderate.'

'Look, what is up with you?'

'What the fuck do you think is up with me?'

'I'm going back to . . . to Helen's – I *really* don't need this from you.' She turned to walk away.

'Leaving us again then?'

'Just you – how do you expect me to stay under the same roof if you're going to turn into the Hulk?' He didn't answer. She left the room and walked up the stairs to collect some extra cosmetic items. She expected David to follow after her but he didn't. She headed back down the stairs. 'Call me if Giles needs me,' she said, walking past the reception room. She didn't get a response.

Cara walked hastily back into Sirena's flat and flung her shoulder bag on the bed. 'Thank you darling.' She hugged Sirena. 'Sorry to mess you around like this.'

145

'So is everything OK with Giles?'

'He just had too much to drink – not the first time and it won't be the last. He's in bed now so I'll check up on him again in the morning.'

Sirena took off her vest top and climbed back into the bed feeling relieved yet anxious about Cara's other life. 'You seem angry?'

'You know I really will be moving out soon. I'm going to speed things up for us OK?' Cara climbed back into the bed; she wanted to feel close to Sirena that night more than ever.

'I'll believe that when it happens. Why are you so upset?'

'David was in a mood for some reason. I'm so stressed myself . . . just can't handle it.' She wrapped herself around Sirena again and rested her head on Sirena's breasts for comfort.

'You should move if he's stressing you out. I don't know why you're both still living together anyway – it's not like you can't afford to get your own place.'

'You don't know the sort of pressures I have. It's easy for you to lecture me – maybe when you're older you'll have more understanding.' Cara paused awkwardly. 'Sorry for the way that came out. I'm just not thinking properly right now. I will be moving very soon – especially after tonight.'

Cara lit up in front of her laptop, as she came across an ideal three-bedroom apartment at Chelsea Harbour. She heard the front door open and close. David called out to her and she sighed heavily. She really wasn't in the mood for talking to him after the previous night. After ten minutes there was a light knock on her door. She minimised the web page before he came in.

'Hi Cara,' he said wearily, holding a Tiffany bag in his hand.

'David I'm not in the mood OK?'

'I guessed you wouldn't be but I've got something for you,' he said apologetically. 'I bought it straight after work.'

Cara frowned and huffed, remaining seated on the chair. 'David gifts don't miraculously make things better.'

'But it's a start.' He walked over to her. 'I'm so sorry about last night. I shouldn't have behaved the way I did. I was just tired and stressed.' He held the bag out to her until she reluctantly took it.

'I just can't handle you when you get into one of your moods David, whether you're tired or not. I was *so angry* with you last night.'

'I know, I'm sorry . . . was feeling emotional about things . . . about us.'

She placed the bag on the desk, not wanting to see what was inside.

'Please open it Cara. I bought it especially for you – as a white flag.'

She picked it back up and opened it to see a necklace and matching earrings. 'Gosh David these are stunning.' She paused for a few seconds. 'But as I said, this really doesn't make up for last night. Thank you for the kind thought.'

'As I said I was tired and stressed, and took it out on you and regrettably used Giles as a bit of an excuse.'

'I'm just so tired of *everything* David,' she sighed, rubbing her forehead.

'Maybe we should live apart. It would be better for your health.'

Cara looked at him with sympathy. He looked terribly upset with himself. 'I agree. Look, everyone gets emotional at times. Don't worry about it and just help me put these on.' Cara stood up and turned around so David could put her necklace on. She turned back around and admired the necklace around her neck. 'It's gorgeous – thank you David.'

Chapter Twenty-Two

Cara gazed at a text from Sirena, asking when they were going to meet again. It had been nearly two weeks since they'd last seen each other, but with David's interruption in the middle. She had successfully managed to avoid Sirena's attempts to meet with her but was also trying not to miss her – and she was doing a good job, choosing to involve herself more in her projects and social life. She had come to the firm decision to be on her own while she sorted her situation out in her head, especially as David had been away for work. Sirena was extremely sexy and she enjoyed her company but, given her position in society, she couldn't possibly be in such an unconventional relationship. She just needed to stop thinking about Sirena and then maybe she would simply forget about the past nine months.

'I've missed you darling,' Cara said, leading Sirena through her home to the drawing room. Despite her growing reservations, she'd had a moment of weakness as she yearned for another night with Sirena a few days later.

'At least say it like you mean it.'

'Sorry?'

'You hardly make an effort with me any more . . . you don't tell me anything!'

'Oh that's not true,' Cara replied dismissively.

'*It is.*' Sirena flopped down on the sofa. 'And you know it.'

'Look, my mind's just been occupied with so many things going on . . . '

'Are you sure you're just not having doubts about us? I would rather you just told me if you were.'

Cara groaned slightly, sitting down next to Sirena. 'I've been very busy that's all.'

'Well so have I but I make an effort to *try* to put time aside for you.'

'You know my delicate situation, so please can you stop going on at me.'

'I can't actually say that I do! You never really say anything about it apart from moaning about your ex every now and again. I just don't know what to think.'

'I don't wish to speak about it darling, OK?' she replied wearily. 'I'm trying to sort everything out . . . it's just all *so exhausting.*'

'Sorry if I'm being a nuisance then,' Sirena said sarcastically. She turned her focus to the TV.

Cara laughed tiredly. 'You're not a nuisance! I'm just going through some personal things, which only I can work through to make sense of it all. Don't worry my darling.' Cara noted Sirena looking despondent at the TV. 'I'm taking you to Nozomi tonight OK? You'll like it there.'

'I'm just not interested any more.'

'Oh come on now.' She nudged Sirena playfully. 'Our table is booked for nine-thirty so let's just relax together and watch crap TV till then.' She squeezed Sirena's thigh reassuringly.

They left the restaurant at 11.00pm and returned to Wellington Square. Cara snuggled up behind Sirena as soon as she got into bed with her, wearing only her lingerie. She wished she hadn't given in to her desire to see her. She kissed Sirena on her shoulder; she was feeling as luxuriously smooth as she had tried to forget.

'Shall we meet at the weekend? I don't want another long break from you.'

'I can't, have dinner plans darling.' Cara had promised David that she would stay in and join him in entertaining his brother,

Francis, on Sunday evening. She hadn't seen Francis for nearly two years. She placed her hands over Sirena's breasts and wrapped her legs around her. 'I'll be in touch to arrange something OK?'

Sirena groaned.

'Turn around,' Cara said softly, loosening her hold of Sirena. She kissed Sirena gently on her lips and then more strongly. Feeling taken over with confusion and sadness, she removed her lingerie and pressed her body closer into Sirena's. 'Sorry for the way I am.'

Cara stepped out of the shower the next morning in deep thought, but caught sight of David walking past her partially open bedroom door. She called him over as she stood with a white towel wrapped around her.

'I thought you weren't back till later?' Cara quizzed.

'Client meeting got cancelled.' He consciously avoided looking at her half-naked body by focusing on her eyes. 'I'm going to catch up on some work from home instead, then head into Mayfair.' He glanced at a framed photo on a shelf. 'Crikey that was taken a long time ago,' he said brightly. He walked over and picked up the frame, taking a closer look at Cara and Giles on a yachting holiday in Porquerolles.

'Yes I really like that one,' she said fondly. She walked back into the en suite.

'You haven't changed one bit.' He turned to leave her room but accidently stood on a patterned bra on the floor. He picked it up without thinking but was quick to notice the unfamiliar size. 'What's this?' he asked, inspecting the label.

'What?'

'Since when were you a 32B?!'

Cara felt an instant cold rush through her throat and chest, dropping her moisturising cream into the sink. She composed herself quickly and darted back out into the bedroom. She looked at the bra dangling from his finger and met his puzzled gaze. 'Well it looks like a bra David . . . '

'You're a 34C, unless you've found a way to suit every occasion!' He stared at her breasts covered by her towel, which certainly seemed to look the usual size.

Cara paused, suddenly feeling like she was in a courtroom, and ran through her mind for a response – any response that didn't involve telling him that she was sleeping with a woman. 'I don't . . . ' She curiously walked over to the bra as if she were confused herself, which bought her more time to think of something to say.

'You don't think Giles has been bringing back girls, do you? In *your bedroom!*' David's mouth dropped in disgust.

'No David!' Cara responded. She certainly didn't want her son to be accused. 'Oh, I remember . . . ' She rubbed her forehead. 'Elle and I went swimming at the Harbour Club . . . her daughter joined us and they came back here for lunch.'

'But you would normally have lunch there?'

'Yes, but we came back here and I dropped their bags off in here – I wanted to show them my new . . . top. I bought it and felt unsure about it. The bra must have fallen out from her daughter's bag.' She took the bra off him. 'I'll take it back to Elle's tonight.'

David pulled a slight face and quickly scanned the room for other unfamiliar items. 'Mystery solved then!' He walked back out into the corridor. Cara puffed her cheeks in relief but he suddenly reappeared at the door again. 'Francis and Alexia are coming this Sunday by the way. Is that still OK with you?'

'Oh . . . yes, yes of course it's fine and I'll be here.'

He smiled and walked back out again. On David leaving Cara was quick to anger. She locked herself in the en suite and called Sirena. 'You left your bra in my house – how *on earth* did you forget to put on your bra?'

'I know . . . I overslept and you saw how much of a rush I was in. I realised when . . . '

'David found it,' she interrupted bluntly. 'I stopped being a 32B when I was sixteen for goodness' sake.'

Silence engulfed them both.

'And my son doesn't exactly wear a bra! I managed to make up a convincing story but you . . . *we* need to be more careful OK?'

'Yes I'm sorry but this wouldn't have happened if you stayed around mine more often . . . or if you moved into your own place as you said you would. You know, I think you're back with your ex. Why else would you be so angry? You're not telling me the truth and it's driving me crazy – what's going on?'

Cara grimaced. 'Look, I'm not with him all right but I'm *so* angry because you put me in an awkward position – I'm not ready to come out to my family, OK? I've got to go now – bye.' She disconnected the call, surprised by her own reaction to the situation. Although she instantly regretted her coldness towards Sirena, this had made her realise what she really did have to lose if her involvement with Sirena ever got out: stability and a family home. Even though she was separated from David, he still made her feel safe in more ways than one.

Chapter Twenty-Three

'I was so pleased when you accepted my invitation to the Hurlingham,' Miles exclaimed cheerfully.

While he drove he gave Sirena his membership pad to fill in as she was visiting the club as his guest. After driving around some bends he parked his car just behind some grand gates, which secured an elegant red brick building. They walked through the entrance into a small reception area and he guided her towards the Polo Bar, pointing out numerous paintings along the way that decorated the walls. The Polo Bar was like a large yet very warm and elegant living room, with a dozen or so people seated on sofas and standing by the bar. Miles proceeded to order them a drink before finding a quiet area in the conservatory to sit down.

'Isn't it beautiful here?' he commented, sitting down on a cane chair with a red squab.

'Yes I love it here already!' Sirena replied brightly, admiring the plantation all around the bright room.

'I come here often.' He waved at a very stylish woman who walked past in the distance. 'That was a dear friend of mine – we spoke earlier. I had lunch with her husband yesterday at the House of Commons.'

'Really?'

'Yes, super chap. I left my pass in his car, which is rather annoying, but hopefully his wife will remind him to give it back.' He blew his high bridge nose into a handkerchief from his top jacket pocket. 'So, were you inspired by my dear artist friend and have you painted at all since we met?'

'No I don't actually have any paints.' Sirena gave a tight-lipped smile. The past few weeks had been filled with project deadlines, out of office client dinners and heart-numbing angst. 'I will paint again soon, though.'

By the time their food arrived in the restaurant, the conversation was in full flow – although it was Miles who was doing most of the talking.

'Have you heard of my magazine then?'

Sirena hadn't until she met him and was reluctant to say so, considering its prestige. 'It rings a bell but I haven't actually read a copy. I don't think so anyway!'

'It's about people and life in London, published quarterly. It covers travel and the arts with inside information on trends and superb photographs. It really is a great read. I'll give you a few copies when we meet again – I started it up when I was in my mid-twenties you know?' Miles analysed Sirena with intrigue. He was certainly attracted to her and loved that she was willing to sit and listen to him all evening, although he knew he was exceptionally interesting to the everyday person.

'Wish I could achieve as much as you had done then. Sometimes I feel so bored at work. I would rather have my own independence.'

'Yes, freedom was always a top priority for me. Why don't you start up your own company? In fact I have a dear friend who could be useful for you to meet. Her name's Lizette – used to own a very successful PR firm. I'll arrange for you to meet.'

Cara glanced at her watch; it was 5.15pm. David's brother and his wife were due to arrive any minute from Guildford. She checked her appearance in the mirror in her en suite; she had changed into a short pearly tunic dress and put her hair up with her fringe swept just above her eyebrows.

The entry phone rang and David brightly ran to let Francis and Alexia in. Cara gave herself a final check in the mirror before walking down to greet them. She'd always had good relations with them seeing as they'd known each other for years.

'Francis how are you?' Cara beamed. Francis was looking very well; he had clearly been to the gym more frequently since they last met. He was five years younger than David and looked very different with a fairer complexion. His wife Alexia was slightly taller than him and with curves in all the right places.

'You're looking very well Cara,' Francis said admirably to her. 'David giving you a break from his foolery?' Francis was used to his brother moaning about his relations with Cara but he knew they would always live together; they suited each other despite the quarrels.

Cara and David laughed. Cara turned to welcome Alexia who was dressed in a beautiful white silk kaftan.

After the initial welcome in the reception room they moved into the dining room, with Giles in tow.

'Cara you must come over more often again for my dinner parties – it's been so long since all us girls have got together.' Alexia looked at Cara hopefully across the table.

'I know I've been so all over the place. You'll have to let me know when the next one is and I'll come over.'

Francis laughed. 'Cara, don't let Alexia here pressurise you – we know you have a busy life here so just be stern with her.'

Alexia playfully pushed Francis.

'I do miss our get-togethers Alexia.' Cara's phone vibrated; it was a text from Sirena. She turned her phone off.

Two hours later and Francis was more than a bit tipsy. Luckily Alexia stayed composed to drive them home.

'I remember when Cara and David came with us to Barbados and I can't remember how, but David ended up falling into the pool!' Francis put his hand over his face to contain his escalating laughter. 'All I could hear after the huge splash was him screaming, *My watch! My new watch!*" '

David gave a tight-lipped smile at everyone around the table as they laughed at him.

'You had bought me that watch darling.' David jutted out his bottom lip at Cara. She echoed the expression as she contained her laughter. David composed himself. 'Well Francis, I remember when I was at yours and you spent absolutely *ages* in the kitchen making fish linguine – you were singing with joy. Then I watched you as you walked into the living room. You were so happy holding your dish in your hand – then suddenly you dropped it and it splattered all over your floor!'

Francis hid behind his hand to control his laughter and embarrassment.

'And then . . . ' David continued, 'and then you bent down and started eating it off the floor!'

Cara and Alexia grimaced at each other.

'I was eating the top layer – not the part on the actual floor!' Francis laughed. 'I was just so hungry and I spent so long making that damn thing!'

Cara took a moment to examine how she was feeling. She was having a splendid time eating, drinking and laughing with warm and familiar faces she had known for many years at the table. As they spoke and laughed, she looked at each of them carefully and pondered what it would be like if she were to move out and leave David completely. She felt secure and enjoyed recalling memories over the years that they all shared together. She couldn't do this with Sirena and her family, she thought as she took out a couple of empty plates at the end of the evening. In fact, she had no real desire to meet Sirena's family and experience the awkwardness it would entail. If anything, the evening had served to remind her how fortunate she *actually* was, and that maybe she was being ungrateful and flippant about what she had with David. And if she were to find a new man, she would have to build up friendships with his family and start all over again. At her age, she didn't think she could be bothered with all of that. So if Sirena couldn't make her happy and if she couldn't build new relations with another man, it was David she would return to and never leave again.

Chapter Twenty-Four

Are you having doubts?

Cara grimaced at the text as she prepared for an evening at the Opera with David. She had to be stronger within herself to not give in to her temptation and see Sirena at all until she was out of her system. She couldn't deal with the situation now in any other way – she didn't want to hurt her with words so she hoped she would just get the hint, especially as Christmas was drawing closer.

Are we over or what? I would rather you just told me than ignore me like I mean nothing.

She had hardly seen Sirena throughout most of October and November, and her contact was certainly less frequent than ever before. She felt bad but there was no other way. Sirena began to call her continuously.

Cara put her eye shadow down with a groan and picked up her vibrating phone from the marble shelf. 'Have you completely lost it or what?'

'YES – because of you.'

'What do you mean?'

'Look, why have you become distant? Why aren't you being direct with me?'

'This really isn't attractive . . . '

'And your behaviour is?'

'Sirena, I'm just so busy and . . . '

'Are you back with your ex?' Sirena interrupted. 'You can tell me – it's been nearly a year since we met and you're still living together. I can just move on if you are . . . I need to know OK?'

Cara paused awkwardly.

'Clearly you are.'

'Sirena, I'm not back with David, as I've told you two, three . . . ten times before. I just have a lot going on and a lot to think about.'

'Such as? I just don't understand you Cara – are you worried about us as a couple?'

Cara sighed. 'It's not you, OK? You know I think a lot of you but the whole thing between us is getting a bit heavy . . . '

'So that's why you haven't been in touch?'

'I already have a lot to deal with you know?'

'No, I don't know.'

'Look, I'm sorry for the way I am. You know I care about you but I just need a break Sirena.'

Sirena paused. 'Cara, can we please just meet and talk about things properly? We haven't seen each other for ages and I really miss you. Please?'

'Yes, we'll meet soon.' Cara sighed heavily, suppressing her guilt. She just couldn't let Sirena down with words.

'That was amazing,' Cara said, tightening her arm around David's. She had more than enjoyed their evening at the Royal Opera House, although she still felt a little dazed after her conversation with Sirena earlier that evening. She strolled straight to the kitchen on the lower ground floor to make tea. David quickly walked into the reception room where he put on 'Let's Dance' by David Bowie, which played loudly into every room on the lower floors. Cara grinned as David danced into the kitchen. He had taken off his tie and used it as a prop in his eighties style dance moves. Cara leaned against the kitchen table and watched him, mildly amused.

'Care to join me?' He held out his hand.

'Not particularly!'

He pulled her close towards him and she playfully danced with him for a few seconds.

'You haven't lost your moves,' he laughed.

'But you've lost your mind!'

'Would you rather I put on Duran Duran?'

Laughing, she pulled away from his grip. 'No David! I'm off to bed now to leave you twirling on your own – just don't break anything!' Cara picked up her cup of tea and left the kitchen to head to her bedroom.

She lay in bed thinking; she'd had such a great night with David, just like they used to. He was making such an effort and things began to feel like the way they once were. Maybe

David was right – all they needed was to spend more time together. When they both made a special effort with each other, there was always a warm, familiar feeling in the air, which she just could not get from anyone else.

Elle got into bed with a glass of water at 11.30pm. She had left the launch party earlier than planned. She glanced at her phone. Lyra still hadn't contacted her, even though she should have arrived at 10.30pm. She called Lyra for the sixth time but there was no answer so, with frustration, she turned off her lights.

She hadn't seen Lyra for two weeks and was looking forward to making love that night but, surprisingly, Lyra seemed to have changed her mind. There were times when she worried about Lyra finding someone else as she did two years ago, although it only lasted for eleven months before she then returned back to her. She knew that it was only a matter of time now before Lyra found someone who she really liked and who could offer her a proper relationship. Lyra was stunning but her strong ambition had always kept her away from relationships. Elle wrapped her duvet around her tightly. She certainly didn't want Lyra to phase out of her life but she couldn't offer her anything more to keep her in.

Cara tried to drift off to sleep but she was still wide wake at 1.30am. She gave Amber an affectionate smile and climbed over the warm covers – it was winter but she was feeling so hot inside that it was like trying to sleep during a hot and sticky summer. She flung back her tousled hair from her face, pulled off her pyjama top and sat on the edge of the bed. She was feeling desirous but, instead of yearning for Sirena, she was yearning for David across the hall. She shook off her pyjama trousers and walked over to her wardrobe to put on her oyster-coloured silk chemise. She quickly freshened up in the en suite and then walked quietly across the hallway feeling mischievous.

She slowly opened his partially closed bedroom door so as not to startle him.

'Cara?' he tiredly murmured.

'Yes it's me,' she whispered.

'What's happened?' He lifted his head from the pillow.

She walked to the bed without replying and took off her robe to reveal her lingerie, which she had initially bought for a night with Sirena. David sat up speechless. He didn't know whether he was actually awake or dreaming as she pulled over the duvet and lay beside him. She placed her hand gently around his face and kissed him softly on the lips. He placed his hand around her face and she kissed him more intensely.

'Cara, what are you . . . '

'Shh,' she whispered, and kissed him passionately again, breathing more heavily as she rubbed herself against him under the covers. She climbed on top of him and continued to kiss him on his lips and around his face as he moaned in pleasure and frantically ran his hands all over her familiar body. She pulled off her chemise to reveal her breasts, which made him gasp in delight. He put his hands out to feel her breasts and stomach.

'Cara I've missed you so much,' he groaned with a mixture of pent-up frustration and excitement; no other woman turned him on more than she did. She didn't respond as she stroked his chest in return and started to rub herself against his boxer shorts, forcing any images of Sirena to the back of her mind. He leaned towards her to take his shorts off but she moved his hands away then bent down to kiss his chest. She took her time kissing him, adjusting to his body again after so many nights with Sirena. But with every touch of her lips on his chest, she struggled to feel the intense emotion for him, which she thought would arise in the intimacy. She slowly ran her hands along his inner thighs and up his shorts, making him groan in anticipation. His erection was clear to see under his shorts and she couldn't contain her patience any longer. She sat up and pulled off his shorts eagerly.

'Oh Cara,' he gasped as she began to massage him with her beautifully manicured hands. She enjoyed watching him writhe around on the bed; she knew *exactly* what he liked.

'How much have you missed me darling?' she asked seductively.

He struggled to reply with the sensation of Cara's sensuous hand's moving up and down. She carried on stimulating him but stopped before he was about to climax.

'Let me remind you.' She took off her knickers, embracing the moment, which was filling her with warmth and comfort. She slowly mounted him, gasping loudly. She trailed her fingers around his stomach and moved down to kiss him on the lips, but he could barely kiss her back with the pleasure she was giving him. She giggled affectionately and stroked his face. She arched back to give him a sensuous ride, which made David groan excitedly. She wanted their making up session to last for the rest of the night.

'I just don't believe this,' Elle murmured.

Lyra was calling her phone repeatedly. She answered angrily to listen to Lyra desperately informing her that she was freezing outside her front door. Elle threw the bed covers off and got out of bed, putting on her blue bathrobe. It was impossible to ever fake an orgasm during sex with another woman – that was the only time she had slapped Lyra. Lyra had never faked one since but she was now feeling just as furious as she was that night. She quickly put on some eye make-up in the bathroom and tided up her hair; Lyra could wait outside for a few more minutes for being late, she thought, trying to calm herself. Although she was tired and agitated she was also excited, but she was going to hide the fact given her rude awakening. After five minutes, she walked down to the front door.

'*Lyra,* it's *two in the morning* – where on earth have you been?' she asked sternly, holding the door open. She closed the door behind Lyra quickly. 'I came back early from the launch party for you and now you've just woken me up!'

'I told you I was going to be out tonight,' Lyra exclaimed. She stumbled down on the chair in the entrance hall to eagerly take off her new heels, which were more than hurting. 'Why did you take so long?'

'You waited for five minutes – I waited for hours and you're drunk for goodness' sake?'

'How *very* observant of you . . . ' She certainly wasn't appreciating the frosty reception after she had finally come in from the cold.

Elle bypassed her catty remark. 'Let's just get to bed because I'll need you to be out of here by ten at the latest, OK? You know I have *a lot* on tomorrow Lyra.'

'I'm not that drunk you know,' Lyra replied in delayed defence. 'It was a friend's birthday so I *had* to go out tonight, and I did tell you I was probably going to be late so I don't know why you're acting the way you are.'

'Whatever, I don't want to argue about it – you can damn well make me feel like it's my birthday now so get upstairs, get undressed and get into my bed,' Elle ordered. She walked back up the stairs for Lyra to follow. Lyra pulled herself to her feet and followed to the second floor.

With a yawn, Lyra turned over and picked up her watch. It was 6.00am. She had to meet a client at Earls Court at 8.30am. Lyra rolled back over to Elle and kissed her shoulder before climbing out of the bed to the en suite. While Lyra was out of the bed, Elle lay alone feeling guilty for the way she initially spoke to her, and for making her wait outside in the cold. She watched Lyra affectionately as she walked back to her bed.

'I must apologise for how I was with you last night when you came in. I forget you're still young and of course you need to go out and enjoy yourself.' She looked at Lyra fondly as she got back into the bed. 'Thank you for last night.' She drew herself into Lyra as soon as she lay back down beside her.

'I am sorry for being so late, but glad I managed to come over,' Lyra replied tiredly, stroking Elle's arm.

'Indeed,' Elle groaned contently. 'So did you have a good time at your friend's party? The restaurant launch was so packed . . . was glad to have left early, I have to say.'

'It was a little messy to say the least,' Lyra smirked. 'My friend's house is going to be in such a state this morning.'

Elle giggled and climbed on top of Lyra. Lyra groaned in delight when Elle began to wriggle about on top of her. Elle licked her nipples lightly and grinned inside with Lyra's excitable reaction. 'You're far too sexy,' Elle said proudly. She ran her hand along Lyra's breasts.

'I think that about you,' Lyra smiled happily, stroking Elle's back.

'Let's go on holiday together soon – somewhere remote and sunny?'

'I would love to.'

A sudden bang made them jump. It sounded like a bedroom door – their bedroom door.

Elle turned around and met Makram's infuriated eyes.

Chapter Twenty-Five

Cara woke on one side of the bed with David sprawled out on the other. She moved in to put her arms around him and stroked his chest sensuously. She was more than tired of the confusion that she had endured with Sirena. She could grow to love David again, especially after last night. Her phone vibrated, which woke David. She reached for her phone to see who it was but David reached out and threw his arms around her to draw her back into him.

'Morning beautiful.' He kissed her back then her shoulder.

'Morning.' She turned around to kiss him on the lips and unwrapped his arms around her so she could reach for her phone again. There were three text messages, including one from Sirena at 8.45pm.

Cara it would be really good to meet soon so we can talk properly. Please let me know when you're free. I can't lose you – I need you. I just feel so upset.

She groaned inside, frozen with guilt. She didn't know how she was going to tell Sirena about David. She couldn't hurt her. David suddenly glanced at her phone.

'Anything I should know about?' He gave her a playful kiss on the cheek. She quickly put her phone down and kissed him back.

'No just missed text messages.' She clasped her hand around his face and kissed him tenderly. 'You OK, darling?'

'Yes of course,' he grinned. He placed his hand between her legs, feeling how aroused she was. This was the Cara he knew, passionate and warm, and he was glad to have her back in his arms. He kissed her firmly on the cheek. 'Hang on beautiful, I just need to go quickly.'

Cara took the moment on her own to send Sirena a text to keep her quiet for the timebeing.

Darling please don't be upset, we'll catch up soon xx

She put her phone under the pillow and stretched her whole body under the comfortable covers. What a mess, she moaned to herself. She listened to David fumbling about in the en suite while waiting patiently for him to climb back under the covers. The video entry-phone began ringing. 'David!' Cara called. 'Someone's at the door – it's seven in the morning for goodness' sake.'

David emerged from the en suite with a toothbrush in hand and walked over to the entry-phone monitor on the other side of the bedroom to see Elle standing at the door.

'It's Elle,' he exclaimed. 'Have you forgotten about an arrangement with her or something?'

Cara sat up in bed, puzzled. 'No . . . I don't recall arranging anything . . . let her in . . . '

David spoke into the monitor. 'Morning Elle, this is an early visit . . . are you all right?'

'Yes I just need to speak with Cara,' came a weak voice.

David turned to Cara. 'She needs to speak to you?'

Cara looked bemused. 'Let her in . . . I'll get changed quickly.'

David buzzed her in and quickly swung on his bathrobe. He walked down the stairs to the front door in controlled anticipation. Cara quickly walked back to her own bedroom and pulled on a pair of linen trousers and a vest top.

Elle was trembling with Sebastian in her arms. 'Has something happened?' David asked.

Cara emerged slowly down the stairs. 'Elle what are you doing here so early?' But as she walked closer, she saw that Elle was in clear distress. 'Elle what's . . . '

'Cara I need to speak to you about something,' Elle said, as calmly as she could.

David placed his hand on her shaking shoulder. 'What's happened?'

'David do you mind if I speak with Elle in the reception room?' Cara interrupted.

'No not at all, I'll just be upstairs,' David replied with dipped eyebrows. 'I do hope you're all right Elle.' He placed his hand gently on her shoulder before walking back up the stairs.

'Come on.' Cara led Elle away to the privacy of another room.

'I just need to talk to you,' Elle trembled. She followed Cara to a sofa.

'Darling what's happened?' Cara asked with concern. She had never seen Elle in such distress before.

'Makram . . . Makram came back this morning . . . '

'Darling, calm yourself. Take your time.'

'We had an argument,' Elle managed to continue before tears appeared.

'Aw darling.' Cara leaned in and put her arms around her. 'You'll be OK . . . '

'We had an argument,' Elle sobbed, 'because he *should* have been back on Sunday night but I had no idea . . . he didn't tell me . . . usually . . . ' She put her hand to her face in an attempt to contain her tears.

Cara's face slowly dropped as a dreaded thought came to her mind. 'Darling hang on.' She got up from the sofa to close the doors properly. She sat back down and looked directly at Elle with concern. 'Was Lyra with you last night?'

Elle avoided looking at her as she crumpled a tissue in her hand. She held the tissue to her eyes as she tried to steady herself.

'Elle take your time,' Cara said soothingly. 'Darling, did Makram . . . '

'Yes he caught us in bed together,' Elle replied angrily through her tears. 'He walked in on us . . . together . . . ' Elle covered her face with her hands.

'What?! Elle darling – what on earth did he say? What happened?'

'I was with Lyra . . . we were in bed and he just appeared. He screamed at me . . . his trip was cancelled – he had stayed with his business partner . . . '

'Elle – what did Makram say?'

'Cara what do you think he said? What on earth would you say? I do hope Lyra's OK.' She glanced sadly at Sebastian who had followed her as she left the house. 'He asked me very calmly what I was doing – he seemed to be in a trance but then he just went crazy and started shouting. It was just awful . . . just awful! Cara what am I going to do now?'

Cara put her hand to her forehead; this was simply something she didn't want to hear and for a whole host of reasons.

'He tried dragging me out of bed but then he just walked out and slammed the door,' Elle continued as Cara sat in shocked silence.

'I'm assuming Lily and Jasper weren't at home?'

'No of course not – thank goodness Cara. Jasper's at university and Lily's with her boyfriend.' She sighed deeply.

'OK, so where's Lyra now?' Cara quizzed.

'I told her to get changed and leave – she clearly didn't need to be told. When Makram heard the door shut he came back into the bedroom and just started shouting at me again, calling me vulgar things. What am I going to do now?' Tears fell from Elle's swollen eyes.

Cara rubbed Elle's back. 'Darling please calm down, you must. Does he know you're here?'

'I don't know.' She put her tissue on her lap and stroked Sebastian for comfort.

Cara felt dazed. 'Darling the most ironic thing is that he put you through the exact same thing with that American woman – so you have nothing to feel guilty for, OK?'

Elle ignored her statement as of course she had something to feel guilty for – two wrongs don't make a right, after all. 'He said he didn't want to see me – that I was a disgrace among other things. But he's right. I've been cheating on my husband for goodness' sake. I just couldn't stop with Lyra – *I couldn't end it.*'

'Darling we'll sort this out together. You can stay at mine OK?'

There was a knock on the reception room door, making them both jump.

'David?' Cara called.

The door slowly opened. Cara and Elle stared in anticipation.

'Sorry, I don't mean to interrupt, but I was wondering if you would both like a cup of tea?'

Elle nodded at David as he stood in the doorway.

'Yes please darling,' Cara replied as collectively as she could.

'OK.' He smiled passively at Elle and gently closed the door.

Elle's phone began to ring. 'It's Helen. I called her while I was on my way to you but she didn't answer.'

'You better pick up,' Cara replied, preferring someone else from their close circle to be also drawn into the messy situation, which had already given her a very unwelcomed headache. She walked to the kitchen to help David with the tea, while Elle spoke to Helen.

'Elle looks so broken,' David commented. 'What's happened?'

'She's had an argument with Makram.'

She avoided looking at him in the eyes – she couldn't tell him the reason for their argument despite the risk that Makram may tell him anyway. She rubbed her forehead wearily. If Makram was now going to tell David about Elle, then would David question her and her own sexuality? She didn't want even a *hint* of suspicion about her involvement with other women. She stirred the tea, around and around in circles, until she could hear echoes of David's voice.

'What about Cara?'

'Hmm? Sorry David?' She snapped out of her deep thoughts.

'Are you OK darling?' David asked for the fourth time as he observed her in a mesmerised state.

'Yes . . . sorry I was just thinking about something. I need to get back to Elle.' She put the spoon on the table and picked up the two cups.

'Cara what was her argument with Makram about?'

She hesitated. 'About . . . David, I don't think she wants me to disclose that. I need to talk more with her and I'll speak to you later.'

'OK . . . maybe I should call Makram?' he asked reflectively.

'No don't do that – he doesn't know she's here so we don't want him coming around do we? We'll have a drama on our doorstep as well as in the house.' She rolled her eyes to play down the seriousness of the situation.

David wrinkled his mouth. 'OK – call me if you need any-thing then.' He opened the door for Cara to walk back up to the reception room. 'I'm so hard for you by the way . . . '

'Just wait for me in the bedroom,' Cara grinned, playfully brushing past.

'Helen said I could stay at hers.' Elle felt instant relief with Cara's company again as she sat back down beside her.

'But you can stay here if you like?'

'It'll be better if I stay at Helen's. She's on her own as her daughter is with her ex . . . and Makram is friends with David – it's best if I stay with Helen.'

'Sure but what about your apartment? Isn't that empty?'

'I can't go there,' Elle frowned. 'And anyway, Helen is going to buy some food for Sebastian now for our stay.' She picked Sebastian up and cuddled him.

Cara nodded. 'I'll come with you to Helen's. When do you want to leave?'

Cara didn't know whether to feel terribly sorry for Elle or annoyed – how could she have been so careless? But then Sirena had often gone back to hers, as had Alessandra, so she was treading thin ice. Unfortunately for Elle, she fell through.

Chapter Twenty-Six

Elle woke the next morning in Helen's guest room at Chelsea Harbour. She lay in bed listening to the sound of the harsh wind hitting the windows as if it were trying to reinforce her memory of the storm conjured up yesterday. Yesterday wasn't a bad dream; her husband catching her in bed with another woman was reality. She knew she had to see Makram later that day to face up to it all. She had tried calling him several times the previous day but he didn't answer. She desperately wanted to speak with him, to explain herself but without having to look him in the eyes. She was deeply ashamed and the fact that it was just a few weeks before Christmas wasn't going to make it any easier. She couldn't suddenly go on a month's break to escape on her own or with her children; she had to be at home with her family.

Jasper was due back from university in a week and she had called Lily yesterday to let her know that she wouldn't be back until the next day with some rushed excuse, but thankfully Lily had spent the night at her boyfriend's so she wouldn't have crossed paths with Makram since he'd caught her. She knew, but deeply prayed that he wouldn't now tell her children about what he had seen as she had kept quiet over his affair. She used all her energy to lift her head from her pillow and climbed out of the bed; she needed to see him urgently to prevent any further damage and to explain herself to save her marriage, which she just couldn't lose.

Elle returned to Lamont Road before midday but the house was empty. Their marital bed looked as if it hadn't been touched and their en suite shower hadn't been used. She tidied up her appearance and got changed, tearful and trembling with guilt. She knocked on Lily's bedroom door on the first floor but of course she was at college.

Elle spent the majority of the day in bed, waiting for Makram to return. In the late evening, she was lying down, listening to the sound of her phone as various friends asked her to come out for dinner or to go to bars, not knowing what she was going through. She still hadn't heard from Makram and not knowing his whereabouts was emotional agony.

She had only told Cara and Helen about Makram catching her and they both kept calling to check up on her, but she just couldn't face them. They offered for her to stay at theirs or to stay with her at her Chelsea home, but she needed to be on her own with Lily who was downstairs watching TV, blissfully unaware of events.

She sat up and brushed strands of her hair away, which had stuck to her wet cheeks from the tears. She reached for another tissue to wipe her cheeks dry. She had never felt so guilty, upset and angry with herself but she couldn't blame Lyra – she only had herself to blame. A light knock on the door made her jump.

'Mum are you in there?' Lily called. The door handle turned.

Elle composed herself quickly. 'Yes but don't come in – I'm not feeling too well darling. What is it?'

'Nothing, just wondered where everyone had got to. Is Makram around? Someone called for him earlier but I haven't been able to get through to his mobile. I thought he was going to be in Bahrain till Sunday?'

Elle put her hand to her face to try to hold back the tears. 'He's out with friends – not sure if he'll be back tonight,' she managed to reply clearly.

'OK, thanks. Are you all right?'

'Yes, just need to rest.' Elle lay back down on her stomach and sunk her face into the pillow, listening to Lily walk back down the corridor. She knew she couldn't hide away in the bedroom all night.

Cara smiled inside as she put up decorations in the drawing room with David and Giles. Christmas songs were playing. All of a sudden they were a family again and it felt good. No more confusion, no more uncertainty – just a feeling of being at peace.

'Guess what I've got you for Christmas?' David prodded Giles.

'A new iPad? I've asked you for it about six times!'

'Well you'll just have to wait and see. I may have decided to surprise you this year.'

'And what have you got me?' Cara asked merrily.

'Nothing – couldn't be bothered,' he replied dismissively.

Cara laughed, throwing a bauble at him. Although behind her laughter was a deep concern for Elle. She was aware that Makram had disappeared.

Hi Cara can we please meet soon? I can't take not knowing what you're thinking. I love you OK? xx

Cara sent a quiet reply to Sirena.

Darling you know I care about you. We could meet tomorrow . . . let me confirm OK xx

She knew it wasn't a good idea to see Sirena after she had now begun to get her relationship back on track with David, but it was Christmas. She swiftly put Sirena to the back of her mind again when David came up behind her and wrapped his arms around her waist.

'How's Elle?' David asked, placing the bauble on the tree. He kissed her cheek and walked away to hand Giles some holly leaves to put by the marble fire place.

'She's a bit better. Have you heard from Makram at all?'

'No, I tried calling him earlier actually but he didn't answer.'

'Oh.' Elle wasn't answering her calls either. 'I'm actually just going to see Elle quickly. I won't be long.' Helen had informed her earlier that Elle had returned home and she thought this was surely a mistake. She grabbed her white winter coat and left her house.

Lily happily opened the door to Cara. 'Hey Cara, how are you?'

'Hi Lily, I'm well thank you – enjoying the build up to Christmas?'

'Yes as always!'

Cara smiled in response. 'Is your mother in at all?'

'Yes but she's in bed resting at the moment.' She moved to the side so Cara could enter the house, adorned with Christmas decorations. 'Not sure if she'll be awake but you can see.' She shut the door and walked off, leaving Cara to find her mother.

'Elle are you in there?' Cara could vaguely hear Elle crying inside the master bedroom. She opened the door slowly to see Elle with her back to the door, lying curled up on the bed. 'Elle it's me.' She sat down beside her on the bed and rubbed her back over her camisole. 'Darling come here.'

Elle moved on to Cara's lap and hugged her waist without saying anything. Cara stroked her hair and back soothingly in the silence.

Chapter Twenty-Seven

Elle solemnly put up additional Christmas decorations in the drawing room. No one had heard anything from Makram in two days and he hadn't returned any of her calls or messages, but she was reluctant to contact his family or friends due to the nature of the situation. She also hadn't seen Lyra since. Her daughter was out with friends and she was looking forward to surprising her with the extra decorations when she returned, although she was hardly in the mood for Christmas celebrations.

She would keep her spirits up for the sake of her children. She put up the last piece of tinsel and sat back down on the sofa to watch some festive TV but the sound of the front door opening and closing interrupted her. She listened to the sound of footsteps going up the stairs, but she remained seated in the drawing room feeling anxious for a further five minutes, before investigating who had walked in. She walked up into her marital bedroom and her eyes locked with Makram's across the room. Elle felt her eyes swell up with tears. 'Where have you been?' she asked shakily.

He ignored her as he continued packing clothes roughly into his bag.

'We need to talk about this Makram – where have you been? I've been so worried.'

'Start talking then . . . ' he replied, quietly but angrily.

Elle shut the door in case her children returned and paused, trying to compose herself. She had no idea what to say. The shock of seeing Makram again had just engulfed her. She tried to speak after ten seconds of silence. Makram angrily walked to the wardrobe to take more of his clothes.

'I find my wife cheating on me with *another woman* . . . why Elle? You're a disgusting disgrace to yourself and your family.'

'Makram, I'm sorry I . . . '

'Sorry?' he yelled. 'What overcame you? I don't know you – I thought you loved me?' He punched the wardrobe hard and glared at her. 'What the fuck do you have to say for yourself?'

Elle was unable to answer him as she began crying.

'You have nothing to say?' he yelled with his palms laid out to her.

'I . . . I don't know . . . it just happened . . . I was drunk . . . '

Makram took a framed photo of them off the wall and threw it on the floor. The glass smashing made Elle jump and she fell weakly against the wall to steady herself.

'Drunk? Is that what I should expect from my wife when she's drunk? To sleep around like a disgusting whore? Get out!'

'Stop it Makram, please! It's nearly Christmas – we need to talk things through for us and the children!'

'There is no us and there is no Christmas,' Makram yelled. 'How could we possibly . . . '

'I love you!' Elle cried. 'You know I need you Makram! I'm

174

so sorry . . . we need to talk about this!' She knelt down on the floor, unable to stand as she watched him furiously stuff his belongings into bags. 'Where are you going?'

He zipped his last bag up and without a reply walked past her and left the house.

Sirena raced back to her flat after spending the day shopping and stepped into a warm bath. She was bursting to see Cara who had confirmed that they would be meeting. After drying herself she walked into her bedroom to put on her outfit. She had an unread text message – it was from Cara.

> Sorry darling but I'm not feeling great to go out tonight. Let's reschedule . . . sorry xx

Sirena threw her phone back down and brushed the Christmas present she had bought for Cara aside. With a yearning sigh she tried calling Cara for a better explanation but she didn't answer.

Meanwhile, Cara frowned at her phone. She just *couldn't* tell Sirena that she was back with David and didn't want to lose their friendship, which she knew would be at risk. She still loved Sirena but just couldn't see how a relationship with her could possibly work out. She sent her a text from her Sussex home, where she had arrived earlier that day with Giles and David for an unplanned family weekend away.

> Darling I really just need a break from everything. You know I care about u but I'm just all over the place at the moment. I'm truly sorry for the way I am. We'll meet in the New Year when I'll be in a better frame of mind after a break OK x

Elle lay in bed crying. It was January and a New Year but she would have preferred a different start. Her eyes felt puffy and her cheeks were beginning to burn with the tears. She had a quiet Christmas and New Year with her children. Makram had called just before Christmas to speak with Jasper and Lily and gave them an excuse as to why he had to be in Lebanon all of a sudden, when he had planned to stay with them in London. She was immensely grateful that he kept quiet about her secret, but she hadn't spoken to him now for weeks and she had no idea when, or if, he was coming back to her. She lifted her head from her pillow to prepare to get up to face the world. She had to see her mother and father in Dorking, Surrey, for a New Year lunch with her children.

'So when will Makram be back?' Lily asked curiously. She shut the car door and Elle pulled away from Lamont Road.

'Soon Lily, he just has a few things to do in Lebanon. He doesn't see his son an awful lot so it's good for them to spend time together, especially at this time of year.'

'It's just all a bit strange. He said he would be with us for Christmas and New Year so don't you find it a bit rude of him? I sure do.'

Elle paused awkwardly, feeling trapped into a corner of her car. 'We had an argument as well,' she sighed. 'That's why he suddenly took off. I just haven't wanted to talk about it. I've been getting over the whole thing.'

Lily gazed at her mother with concern but Elle remained focused on the road ahead. 'What was the argument about? Must have been serious for him to leave us at Christmas and New Year?'

'Oh it was about various things – we had a disagreement darling. It'll all be fine.' She glanced at Jasper through the rear-view mirror. 'Now I hope you two remember that your father is coming to visit you tomorrow and please remind your grandparents also. I know he's bringing New Year gifts for you all.'

Lily nodded. 'Why don't you stay the night with us? You can drive back in the morning?'

'I can't. I have a dinner tonight with close friends Lily. But I'll come down again early on Sunday all right?' Elle had told her friends that she would be joining Valentina's party, but she knew she would probably cancel as she needed time on her own.

'I knew Elle would cancel . . . I spoke to her after David dropped me off.'

'I just cannot believe you two are back together,' Valentina said with a look of surprise. 'It's so soon after your separation, no?'

'We're making another go of things.' Cara lifted her multi-coloured pearl necklace away from her neck and fiddled idly with it, meeting her friend's intrigued faces.

'And thank goodness. You do not realise how much this is music to my ears.'

'Huh?'

Valentina closed her eyes dreamily. 'Clair De Lune – Debussy.'

'Do you think this time things will be different?' Helen intercepted, although she already knew the answer to her question.

'Yes, I do,' Cara replied defiantly, knowing what Helen was thinking.

'And you told Sirena why you both couldn't go on?' Valentina asked.

Cara hesitated. 'Yes – we haven't seen each other for a while now anyway.' She knew she would have to sit through unwanted lectures if she told her friends that she hadn't told Sirena.

'And how did she take it?' Helen added.

'Not too well.' She received a text from Sirena.

Hi Cara, LET ME KNOW when you are free to meet. You said we would be meeting in the New Year?!

'I'm very happy for you and David,' Valentina said. 'You can concentrate on being a family again – a New Year and a new start.' She held up her glass of champagne.

Michael walked into the room and sat down on an antique armchair.

'We just raised our glasses to Cara being back with David – again.'

Michael raised his eyebrows at her and locked eyes with Cara, who smiled at him. He forced a smile back.

Cara took a sip of her champagne as her thoughts turned to Elle. She certainly hadn't been her usual self over Christmas and the New Year. Another text arrived from Sirena.

Clearly we're not going to be meeting. Just tell me what's going on so this whole thing can end now.

Cara knew she had to stop treating Sirena selfishly to suit her needs. While her friends chatted, she deeply considered suggesting a date to meet with her in person to discuss her situation, but decided to just send a clear-cut text instead. She felt terrible but could see no other way.

Sirena, I just can't be in a relationship at this stage in my life. I hope you understand. I'm sorry that I've been off with you for the past few months. I've been thinking things through with my life, which hasn't been easy. I need to just focus on my work right now. I hope that we can stay friends. You know I think a lot of you x

*

178

At Lamont Road, Elle packed her laptop away in the bedroom. She had returned back to London an hour earlier, leaving Jasper and Lily to stay over with their grandparents for two nights unil Sunday. She had just booked herself into a day spa in Chelsea – she needed a complete mind, body and soul detox but couldn't find the energy to go further afield for a programme to follow in the Far East. She tied up her hair lazily and sunk into a cashmere sweater. She needed to get some air so she put on her warm boots and headed towards the entrance hall with Sebastian. 'Makram?' she exclaimed, standing by her open front door. He had just stepped out of his car in front of the house.

'Hi,' he murmured.

'Makram, what are you . . . '

He walked towards her with his luggage. 'I need to unpack,' he mumbled.

'I've missed you so much darling, we need to talk,' she said shakily.

'Later, I need to unpack and sleep – it was a long flight.'

Elle stood aside from the door and he walked into the house without a further word. She got into her car and sat shaking with nerves and delight. She got back out and walked into the house. He was standing in the entrance hall. 'Makram I'm so sorry – please forgive me,' she pleaded. 'I've been frightfully upset and so ashamed of myself – you must believe me?'

He gave her a blank look and walked along the corridor to the stairs, leaving his luggage in the hall. Elle sighed in frustration and followed him up to their bedroom.

'Makram, are you all right?' She closed the bedroom door gently.

'I just don't know what to say to you right now – coming back is hard enough,' he shrugged without looking at her. He sat down on the edge of the bed and rubbed his eyes tiredly. 'I need to think things over so just leave me alone for a while Elle.'

'But we haven't spoken for weeks! I can't just walk away now that you're back? I need to know what you're thinking and to know that we're going to be OK – the whole thing has been driving me completely crazy!'

Makram groaned angrily and raised his voice. 'I can't even look at you right now let alone speak to you! Just go away . . . '

'But we need to . . . '

'Leave me alone Elle.'

She gazed sadly at him, before reaching for the door and walking back out without saying a word.

Elle woke in the morning in the spare bedroom. She hadn't heard from Makram at all since last night but she didn't want to disturb his time to calm down now that he had chosen to return. She got out of bed to face whatever the day was going to throw at her. After brushing her teeth, she opened her bedroom door but jumped with surprise; Makram was walking towards her like a ball whizzing through the air in a furious polo match.

'Darling, are you ready to talk?' she asked softly, as he drew closer.

'Yes.' He stopped just a short distance from her. 'We need to talk about us,' he said calmly.

'Are you all right?'

He shook his head. 'It's been a long month. Elle, why did you cheat on me? Why were you in bed with another woman? Can you understand how I'm feeling? I'm confused, angry and . . . I thought I knew you!'

'You do know me – Makram, this is so hard for me to explain. I don't know why I . . . you know how much I love you, I just met her and we . . . '

'Had sex in our bed?'

'Makram please can we just talk about this properly?'

'We are Elle; we've established that you love me, but you met this other woman and had sex with her.'

Elle sighed heavily and shook her head. 'I just want us to get back to normal – the way things were between us – and I know you do too.'

'You know I do but it's going to take a while Elle.' He rubbed his forehead and winced. 'I've missed you but . . . '

Elle reached out to hug him but he drew away.

'Don't Elle. You've got some serious explaining to do.'

Chapter Twenty-Nine

'It's funny how things work out, isn't it?' Helen said thoughtfully. 'But I guess mistakes are there to be learnt from.'

Cara lowered her eyebrows and gazed out the window of Helen's apartment at the cloudy sky. It had been three weeks since she had ignored Sirena's plea to talk. Sirena certainly wasn't a mistake but she did learn from the episode. She realised that she valued her family life and her social position more than anything else. 'Elle loves Lyra. The whole situation is very difficult for her, you know? I hope she's feeling better.'

Helen gazed at Cara – it was interesting for her to comment on Lyra rather than Makram. 'Yes of course. I wonder how Elle is getting on with Makram now – she hasn't answered my calls for the past couple of days.'

'I expect they're working things out.'

Helen nodded in agreement and reached for another slice of the Fiorentina pizza.

Elle and Makram sat on separate armchairs in the drawing room. An atmosphere of awkwardness swirled around the room as they read with the occasional cough from Makram behind his broadsheet newspaper. In the past three weeks, Elle had devoted all her time to Makram, attempting to explain why she was in bed with another woman – but he seemed to have forgiven her.

'So what are your plans for tomorrow?' Makram broke the silence.

'I'm going to the gym in the morning. I have to buy Lauren and Ben a wedding gift so I'll probably go to Harrods then . . . '

'I've booked us all some theatre tickets,' he interrupted. Since his return, he had been rather cold despite seemingly forgiving her.

'Jasper and Lily also?'

He nodded quietly behind his newspaper. 'Yes.' He reached his arm out to take hold of his cup on the marble side table.

'What show?' Elle rested her book about European interior design on the sofa arm.

'*Mamma Mia.*'

'How wonderful – thank you darling.' Elle shuffled about in her armchair. 'I'm just going to the loo. Talk about it when I get back.' She stood up and left the room.

On her way to the bathroom, she checked her phone in the bedroom. She had received a text from Cara.

Hey darling hope you're OK . . . please let me know x

Hey babe I'm fine, I'll call you tomorrow x

She dropped the phone on the bed and turned to head back out. 'Oh!'

'I thought you were going to the bathroom? But instead I see you in here on your phone.' Makram paused. 'Don't you think you've lied enough to me lately?'

'I think it's a bit extreme for you to classify my detour to the bedroom as a lie Makram.' Elle looked at him, baffled.

'Who were you texting?'

'A friend.'

182

'Which friend would that be? A girlfriend you sleep with or one that you don't?'

'Yes, here it is – I thought you were a little too calm.' Elle stormed straight past Makram and into the corridor.

'Why a woman?' he yelled after her.

'You can give my ticket to Jasmine – I take it you still have her number?' she shouted.

'I should give her number to you!'

Elle stopped in her stormy tracks and turned to face him. 'I'm delighted we've discovered something else we have in common. The list just keeps getting bigger, doesn't it?' She thundered into the bathroom and slammed the door. She leaned against the door and wiped away a tear. She couldn't help but get emotional as she publicly confirmed her affair and his, but she was also missing Lyra.

'Are you a lesbian?'

Elle sighed loudly. 'Am I a what?'

'Are you a . . . '

'Yes yes I heard you Makram . . . no I'm not. Look, I don't want to keep talking about it so please can we just leave it and try to start the New Year afresh?'

'You can't expect me to just leave it! I caught you in bed with another woman for fuck's sake! It's clearly going to raise a question or two in my head don't you think?'

'I'm not a lesbian, all right? It was . . . I don't know what it was but I don't want to talk about it . . . I feel embarrassed.' Elle frowned.

'Then why were you having an affair with a woman and not another man?'

'I really don't know Makram. I . . . I met her and . . . '

'When did you meet her? And who is she exactly?'

'I've told you all this.' She couldn't remember what she had told him. 'I can't think about it now, OK? I really am exhausted.'

183

'How many times did you sleep with her?'

'Not many Makram.' She sighed and opened the door to him. 'It's over now anyway.'

Chapter Thirty

Cara and Helen emerged from their separate shower cubicles at KX and into the large changing room, where they took their positions on high stools facing a large mirror against the wall. Elle tightened the white towel around her and sat down on the third stool to put her make-up on and dry her hair, after her sauna and plunge pool session. She was still feeling upset with her conversation with Makram the previous day and hoped it would be the last time he questioned her sexuality.

'Oh I forgot to ask, how is Tom doing?' Helen asked, inspecting the hair drier in front of her. 'I drove past his wife walking along Ixworth Place earlier today when I was on my way here.'

'He's very well – his Mayfair bar is launching next week,' Cara replied. 'May see him later actually for more details. I keep rescheduling on him.' She adjusted the white towel wrapped around her, which nearly unravelled.

Elle combed through her wet hair in the mirror. 'I'm seeing *Mamma Mia* with Makram and the children.'

'I saw that with my mother,' Helen responded. 'Great if you like Abba, of course.'

'*Mamma Mia* Makram,' Cara quipped jokingly in an Italian accent.

'Makram isn't even an Abba fan so I don't know why he chose it,' Elle said. 'And he rarely ever goes to the theatre.'

'But things with Makram are obviously getting better,

regardless of his sudden love for Abba and the theatre?'
Cara asked, applying moisturising cream to her face in the
mirror.

'Yes and no,' Elle groaned. 'Of course he has every right to
still be angry and upset with me but I just wish things would
get back to normal.'

'And things will Elle. It'll just take time. How is Lyra,
though?' Helen asked.

'She's all right. We've spoken on the phone but we're going
to meet for a proper chat in a few weeks.'

Cara gazed at her in shock through the mirror. 'What?'

'Lyra and I have been friends for nearly five years now –
we can't just end *everything*. And I've been so worried about
her.'

'Does Makram know about this?' Cara quizzed.

'No, don't be ridiculous darling.'

Helen met Cara's shocked gaze. 'Elle, what if he finds out?'

Elle threw her hairbrush down roughly. 'I'll be meeting her
at a hotel . . . he won't find out. I just need to see her, to see how
she is after everything you know?'

Cara and Helen looked directly at her in confusion.

'Not to stay the night you fools – we're just meeting for a
completely innocent drink. We just need to speak OK? One
doesn't suddenly stop caring.'

'So you're staying faithful to Makram now I take it?' Helen
asked in a concerned tone.

'Yes.' Elle looked down.

Cara noted Elle's despondent expression.

'I'll stay in touch with Lyra but . . . ' she hesitated. 'I really
am going to miss her but friendship is better than nothing
at all.'

Cara rubbed Elle's back tenderly. 'Of course you'll miss her
darling, but it's for the best that you just be friends – the whole
thing wasn't going to last forever.'

Elle felt her heart sink at Cara's comment; she knew she was right but it was painful to hear.

'What does Lyra think about the whole thing now, though?' Helen asked.

'She misses me – understandably, of course. The thing is, Lyra was good for me you know? When Makram is away for long periods of time on business, sometimes a week to a month, I get quite lonely. The children are always out here and there and I'm often alone.'

'But you have us?' Cara applied her lip gloss and pouted slightly.

'When I say lonely I mean lonely in bed darling.'

'Well I wouldn't be able to help you there,' Cara grinned ruefully in the mirror at Elle.

'Sirena darling – please do come in,' Lizette said eagerly. 'Miles has told me a lot about you!'

Sirena walked in from the cold evening air and followed the slim graceful woman into the open plan reception and dining room, amused by how enthusiastic she was towards her visit. When she entered the room she immediately noticed a large black statue of a majestic bull by the front-facing windows and a framed picture of Frank Sinatra.

'I was just on the phone to one of my daughters who lives in New York,' Lizette said in her soothing voice.

'Wow, I would love to live there for a while. What's she doing over there?'

'Acting, she's a very talented actress – do please take a seat sweetie.' She guided Sirena to a cream and gold patterned sofa with two large burgundy silk cushions. 'Do you like cats?' she asked as she remained standing with her delicate hands clasped together.

'Yes – love them.'

Lizette excitedly vanished from the room to return with a

chocolate-coloured Persian cat. 'Isn't she gorgeous?' She sat down and brightly held her cat close to her high cheek. 'Her name's Lia.'

Sirena reached out to stroke her. 'Wow she's beautiful!'

'She *loves* being told that.' She carefully put Lia down. 'So I hear you're interested in PR?'

'Yes, I work for an agency at the moment but want to be on a faster track!'

'There's no magic wand Sirena but I can surely give you advice. I have been out of the game for a while now you know . . . ' she trailed off. 'I could get in touch with friends who are still in the business, though.'

'That would be great,' Sirena replied eagerly.

Lizette glanced at the silver-framed clock on the white wall, which was adjacent to a framed picture of Marlon Brando. 'Well I'll go through the PR industry and tell you who's who over dinner, which I actually need to finish preparing. I do hope you approve of my chicken salad. I'll just get us a couple of drinks. I won't be a second.'

Sirena was left looking around the captivating and dramatic room before Lizette returned in haste to lead Sirena to the dining area.

'I'm glad we've been able to meet Sirena.' Lizette smiled at her with her friendly brown eyes. She put Sirena's plate down in front of her on the table. 'Miles is the perfect gentleman. He said you met at an art gallery in Fulham?'

'Yes we did, I was with a couple of friends and we just got talking.'

'He loves art; post-impressionism mainly. Has he taken you to Chelsea Art Club yet? He loves it there as do I, I must say.'

'No he hasn't – what's it like?'

'Fantastic atmosphere with a lot of interesting characters. Good place to go to meet friends. He bought a few paintings when we were last there together. They weren't exactly to my taste but each to their own as they say.'

An hour passed and Sirena had spoken mainly about her career and how Lizette could possibly help her, which involved introducing her to more friends and acquaintances within the industry. As with Miles, she also listened to her stories of those she rubbed shoulders with during her whirlwind career and what they were all up to now. They moved back into the reception room area after dinner and Sirena took her seat again on the sofa. Lizette sat down on a modern white armchair in a parallel-legs position, which showed off her lean frame.

'Miles did tell me a bit about you. I hope you don't mind me mentioning this but he said you were seeing an older woman?'

'Oh yes, well, I was seeing her . . . but it's over now.' Sirena tried to hide her anguish and surprise at Lizette suddenly bringing up the sensitive subject. She had told Miles about her sexuality and was feeling rather irritated that he would disclose it to someone else.

'Oh?'

'She just changed towards me,' Sirena said dismissively, trying to avoid getting upset about the whole thing.

'Really?'

'Well she became quite aloof and we just weren't meeting . . . she said she couldn't be in a relationship right now, which is a lame excuse.' She groaned excessively. 'I don't even want to talk about her.' Cara had caused her enough upset.

'Well I'm sorry to hear that Sirena. I do find this very interesting, which is why I've brought it up with you . . . '

A young woman with the same platinum blonde hair as Lizette suddenly entered the room. She jumped slightly when she saw Lizette and Sirena on the other side of the large room – she didn't realise her mother was entertaining.

'Oh Lyra darling, where have you been?'

'Just at a friend's in Fulham.' She walked over to Lizette with her car keys in hand. She glanced at Sirena and gave a tight smile; her heart skipped a beat, but she wasn't in the mood for meeting and greeting.

'Where were you last night darling?' Lizette asked. Her eyes followed her daughter's movements. 'I called but you didn't answer.'

'I was just at a friend's.'

'Darling this is Sirena; Sirena this is my youngest daughter Lyra.' Lizette looked back at Sirena with a warm smile. Sirena and Lyra shook hands. 'Sirena is a friend of Miles,' Lizette continued.

'OK. Mother I need my passport but I *can't remember* where I've put it.' She walked over to a line of cupboards on the other side of the room. 'I don't suppose you've seen it anywhere?'

'No – are you going somewhere? If you're going to New York to visit Emma I'll come with you darling?'

'No . . . just going to Florence for the weekend.'

'Oh with whom?'

'Going on my own for a project I'm working on,' Lyra replied distractedly as she searched through the drawers. 'It's not here either,' she groaned. She fleetingly said goodbye to her mother and Sirena before leaving the room.

'So that was my daughter,' Lizette grinned. She took out a cigarette. 'She's a very bright girl, my Lyra; she's an interior designer.' She walked over to one of the large windows by the bull statue and opened it. 'And Sirena – you're a very beautiful and intelligent girl. You should forget about this woman. I know I don't know her, but for her to just change towards you and mess you around . . . well, she sounds utterly selfish.'

'I have a feeling that she's back with her ex-husband,' Sirena sighed, trying to block images in her mind of Cara with someone else.

'So you only like women or men as well?' Lizette exhaled

outside the window. 'Sorry you're not too cold with this open window are you?'

'No I'm fine.' Sirena crossed her arms as the chilly February wind gently blew into the room. 'I guess I like both but being with Cara . . . I had never felt so in love before.' She didn't particularly want to discuss her sexuality so she changed it around. 'What about you?'

'Do I like women?' Lizette asked quizzically before being quick to answer again. 'Well I've wondered about being with a woman but don't worry, I'm not going to pounce on you,' she grinned at Sirena. 'For one I'm old enough to be your mother – *most inappropriate*! I don't think I could ever be intimate with another woman. Gosh it's windy today . . . ' She closed the window. 'What's the name of the woman you were seeing?'

'Oh, no one.' Sirena was reluctant to divulge details.

'And what does *oh no one* do?'

Sirena grinned. 'She's a property developer.'

'I know quite a few property developers in this area . . . well, I call them dealers and dealerettes,' she smirked. 'You know, you're a young and attractive woman so you should just enjoy yourself Sirena.' She looked at Sirena with sudden curiosity. 'I have a friend who I would actually like to introduce you to. His name is James Halpern, a very good friend of mine – and Miles actually. I know he's in town this weekend so let me arrange a meeting for tomorrow. I think you'll like him.'

Chapter Thirty-One

Sirena waited in anticipation for James to arrive. He sounded perfect from what Lizette and Miles had been telling her. He was thirty-seven, looking for a stable relationship and the founder of a high profile property company. She didn't feel ready to start dating again but, as Natalie advised, it would probably be for the best.

Fifteen minutes had passed and Lizette stood to excitedly greet James at the door. Miles and Sirena remained seated with each other. Sirena watched the reception door open slowly as James emerged into the room, wearing a crisp white shirt with rolled up sleeves and dark blue jeans. She was very pleasantly surprised. He had a very sophisticated look, with short, tidy brown hair and a slim physique. He locked eyes with Sirena and his lips parted perfectly to produce a confident smile, which she returned. All of a sudden she felt self-conscious as he walked over to greet her and Miles.

'You must be Sirena?' He held out his hand to her.

'Yes I am,' she smiled rather shyly. She met Lizette's excited gaze when James turned to greet with Miles.

Sirena couldn't help but feel quite awkward over lunch as Lizette, Miles and James did most of the talking, although this also meant she was able to analyse James properly. She liked his low-set eyebrows, which made him look quite intellectual, and his well-shaped lips were particularly inviting, although very different to Cara's.

She glanced away from him as she felt her heart recoil with sadness.

'I spoke with Lance recently,' Miles said.

Lizette pulled a slight face. 'Yes and how is dear Lance?'

'He's well but he does voice his concern over not hearing from you in a while.'

She pursed her lips excessively to display her contempt. 'I will get in touch with him again at some point Miles, but he did behave rather inappropriately at my charity party. My youngest daughter was least impressed as you can imagine.' She changed the subject quickly. 'James you went to Royal Ascot last year didn't you? It was a shame I wasn't in the country but I will certainly make sure that I go every day this year to make up for it. I spoke with a friend yesterday who promised to make me an exquisite hat!'

James smirked. 'Yes, I only went for one day but bumped into so many friends.'

Miles laughed. 'Including Jane and her usual entourage?'

James laughed to mirror Miles's amusement. 'Of course! I have a photograph of us together.' He gave a fleeting look at Sirena who was sitting opposite him at the table.

'I went every day apart from Saturday,' Miles said. 'I had a lovely picnic in car park one in my usual bay with Richard.'

Lizette turned to Sirena. 'Sirena did you go to Ascot last year?'

'No, I've never been actually.'

'I'll take you there,' James jumped in. 'You will love it – I promise.'

Sirena smiled at him, trying to appear happy.

'I have a friend in Chelsea who makes hats especially for Ascot and other special occasions so I'll introduce you,' Lizette added.

'That'll be great, thank you,' Sirena beamed, feeling warm surrounded by people who all seemed to be making such an effort with her.

James raised his eyebrows at her and smiled warmly. Miles noticed the exchange between Sirena and James. He was aware of Lizette's intentions to pair them up and spoke well of James but still felt jealous. Even so he appreciated that James was better suited to Sirena than he was – James had never been married and had no children.

As the afternoon carried on into the early evening, Sirena began to feel a bit drained but didn't quite know how to make her exit. She felt jealous of Miles when he managed to get away.

'I'm looking forward to your *extra special party* this year.' Lizette raised her eyebrows at James.

'The tenth anniversary – can you believe it?'

'Where do the years go?' Lizette shrugged. 'Lyra is most excited about going by the way – it'll be such a great opportunity for her. I told her that she couldn't miss out this year. If she can't go on the tenth anniversary then when will she go?'

'Indeed.' James looked directly at Sirena. 'Sirena, I hold an annual dinner party at my home – would you like to come? I invite only my friends within the property field but perhaps it will inspire you to get involved one day?'

'Maybe . . . when is it?' Sirena replied with enthusiasm, instantly feeling more alive with the topic of property, which Cara was so passionate about.

'November – I usually have it early in the year but I'll be in Monaco next month.' He could see that Sirena was looking tired. 'Where do you live by the way?'

'Putney.'

'Oh great, so you can get to my party easily! I actually have to leave soon myself . . . I can drive you back if you want?'

She suddenly liked James a lot more for his ability to read her mind. 'That would be great if that's OK with you?'

'Of course. I live just by Sloane Square so it's not too far.'

James promptly drove Sirena back to her place in his BMW – he was infatuated with her. 'Sirena I would love to see you again . . . maybe next week if you're not busy?'

'Oh, that should be fine. I've enjoyed meeting you also . . . bit of a random arrangement wasn't it!'

'I know – Lizette told me about you and I must say I was intrigued and now I'm very glad I satisfied my curiosity. You're more delightful than I was informed, Sirena. I'm going to call Lizette to tell her that I don't like being lied to!'

'Oh!' Sirena laughed.

'Let's arrange to meet again next week?'

'That's good with me,' Sirena smiled.

Chapter Thirty-Two

Elle arrived at Chelsea Harbour on Tuesday evening as planned, having ignored the advice from her close friends. She looked up at the Wyndham Grand with a deep breath, then walked through the entrance and headed straight for the bar. Her eyes darted around the lounge for Lyra; she didn't seem to be there.

She didn't realise how nervous she would actually feel seeing Lyra again. She turned to walk back out of the lounge with strangers glancing up at her from their tables, but looked twice at a woman in the far corner of the room wearing big black sunglasses. Lyra? She walked over and sat down opposite her. 'I don't think we need to meet in disguise,' she retorted. She rested her shoulder bag on the table, suppressing her delight in seeing her again.

Lyra took off her Dior glasses. 'I'm not hiding – just feeling a bit uncomfortable, which I think is understandable.'

Elle groaned. 'I'm glad we're able to meet face to face Lyra after so long. I simply feel awful for what happened. You must have been terrified my darling?' She refrained from reaching out to hug her.

'You could say that but I've been so worried about you . . . it really is good to see you again.' Lyra stopped herself from reaching out for Elle's hands. 'It hasn't been the easiest of times for you has it?'

'It's been hard to say the very least.' Elle gazed away, overwhelmed at being in Lyra's presence again.

'So what happens now? Can we be friends?'

'I've been doing a lot of thinking and I honestly don't know what to do,' Elle frowned. 'Yes Makram caught us and now knows about me. Yes I feel incredibly guilty for the whole thing but . . . urgh, I just don't know what to do.' Elle rested her forehead on her hand to make her anguish clear.

Lyra sat back and looked out into the marina. She didn't know how to respond to Elle's confused answer.

Elle looked deeply at Lyra. Her hair was looking more wavy than usual and it suited her high cheekbones and angular chin as it flowed intimately around her face. She couldn't possibly give her up. Her hazel eyes were not as bright as usual, but all she surely needed was someone to put the sparkle back.

'It's difficult,' Elle continued.

'Look, if you think it's best to finish things completely I'll understand. It's too risky; you have your family to think about and I need to be in a relationship myself now as well, so the distance would be good.' Elle was instantly thrown into disarray on hearing Lyra's quick defeat but before she could reply Lyra threw in a question. 'How's Makram been by the way?'

'It's been very awkward but we're making progress,' Elle replied awkwardly. She felt strange discussing Makram with her so kept her answer brief. She was even a little surprised that Lyra would ask about his feelings at that moment. A waiter came over to take their drink order and Lyra automatically reached for her Dior glasses, exposing her nervousness. She needed to take care of Lyra. It was clear she was as distraught about their overturned relationship as she was. But Lyra was better at hiding it. As usual, she needed to take charge. 'Darling I think we should have a break from each other but I don't think I can finish what we have – do you?'

'What do you mean?'

'We can't just throw everything away can we?'

'I still don't . . . '

'Lyra I need you and not just your friendship for goodness' sake,' Elle interrupted. She sat back heavily against her chair. 'Gosh, this is far more difficult than I imagined it would be.'

'I would love to keep seeing you but you risk your marriage.'

Elle puffed out her cheeks and glanced away in clear frustration. 'This is just not a situation I ever imagined I would be in.' She turned back to Lyra. 'My family mean a lot to me but so do you. It's like you're a part of my family. I feel like losing what I have with you is ending a significant part of me. I know I must sound terribly selfish and an irresponsible mother, but I'm telling you how I truly feel about all of this.'

'It's going to feel too different and I can't be responsible for the break-up of your family if we're caught again Elle.'

'Lyra you wouldn't be . . . and we won't get caught together again. I can promise you this. We were complacent before.' Elle trembled slightly, fighting back her desperation for a positive response from Lyra. 'I'm sorry for all this, OK. For everything.'

Lyra gazed sadly at her. 'What happened made me think about things a lot more. I'm twenty-six now – I need to start looking for a stable relationship and you know I feel down when you go back to Makram. All my friends are getting engaged or married and . . . '

'Oh you're still very young Lyra. You *don't* need to be in a stable relationship – and what do you mean about feeling different?' Elle was almost angry at Lyra for the way she made her feel. 'And I'm sorry that you get upset about my marriage – I really am.'

'I do need to be in a proper relationship now and as soon as I meet someone I like I will start one. And of course what we have is going to feel different – your husband saw us.'

'OK Lyra, please just stop this. I'm finding this very difficult and I'm really not going through a great time right now because of you – I mean, the whole thing. I just need you in my life.' Elle glanced around to make sure no one in the lounge was listening.

'Elle I'm never going to any of your places again and I don't think what we have is healthy. You need to focus on your family.'

'Lyra you know I love my family more than anything but I love you, too. And please stop going on about a proper relationship. It really upsets me – you know I would like to give you one but I just can't.'

'Well then there's no point in . . . '

'Lyra please,' Elle intercepted, 'I have tried *so* hard to not think about you, about us . . . about everything for goodness' sake. It's impossible and seeing you just makes me . . . Lyra I can't explain.'

Lyra sighed deeply.

'I need you.'

Lyra could see Elle's eyes beginning to swell up. 'Look, if we're going to continue to see each other, it'll be best if you stay with me. My mother travels every now and again so I have the place to myself.'

'Darling you know what my response is to that so it's pointless even mentioning. Can you imagine if your mother ever caught us? Because I can – it would be most dreadful. I think from now on, we'll stick to hotels – like the one we're in now.' Elle shrugged her shoulders and looked admirably around at the decor and the other people. 'But I do wish you would hurry up and get your own place. I thought you said you were going to think about it?'

'I have been thinking about it and I will buy soon,' Lyra

reassured her with a heavy sigh. Elle had pulled her back in and, despite wanting her own stable relationship, she couldn't resist.

Cara finished her cup of coffee and reached for her phone. Gosh, she exclaimed with surprise at a message from Sirena.

> I'm going on a date with someone else now . . . James. Thinking of you, though.

> Hi Sirena, I'm truly sorry for the way I've been with u. I hope you're OK.

Goodness, Cara sighed heavily. She felt saddened and didn't like the idea of Sirena with someone else. She expected Sirena to be back with a man as she had hardly been a great first experience for her, having just ended their relationship without giving her a proper and truthful explanation. She focused back on her project and paperwork, which lay in front of her in the study of an apartment she was developing in South Kensington. A new en suite was being built but she was also redesigning the interior. She looked at her watch; it was late but she was being constructive so she carried on working through the night, although her thoughts kept diverting to Sirena.

Her phone started to vibrate on the desk. She answered quickly so she could return to her work. David was quick to speak. 'Cara where are you?'

'I'm working on a project, just sorting through some paper-work.'

'It's nearly two – come home!'

'I'll be home later. I have a meeting tomorrow with the structural engineer to go through the full survey and then I'm meeting some friends, so if I'm not prepared for tomorrow everyone will be set back darling.'

'Well can't you do it at ours?'

'No – I need to measure up later for a few items. David, I'm fine. Don't worry and I'll see you later all right?'

David hung up. She put her phone down angrily and glared at it for a few seconds. She picked it back up and called him back.

'David what is wrong with you? I never hassle you when you're working late and you're usually fine when I do – so what is up with you tonight?'

'Cara, we have a very important client dinner tomorrow. I know what you're like, you'll hardly get any sleep tonight and then moan all evening and ruin the dinner. You know this is one of my important clients.' Cara was speechless. 'So if you're not back within an hour I'm arranging to attend with someone else OK?'

'Well that's fine with me!' Cara hung up and threw her phone down on the desk.

Elle rested her head on a cushion, making herself comfortable on the sofa in her reception room. Makram was out of the country on business and her children were away with friends. Listening to ballads on her own was making her emotional, but she needed to let her tears out. She gazed around the room at the photos of her family; they meant the world to her but life would be incomplete without Lyra. She was never willing to deny it to herself but she was coming to terms with it now in a way she hadn't needed to before. She knew what it would do to her family if she was caught again but she had discovered how much of a risk she was willing to take. She reached for a tissue and wiped a heavy tear away before picking up her phone.

Hi babe, it was so lovely seeing you earlier. Let's meet again tomorrow – 8pm? x

Chapter Thirty-Three

Easter arrived two months later. Cara had returned from a week's break in Barcelona with David and Giles two nights ago and was at a dinner party. She wondered what Sirena was up to in Rome with her new boyfriend as she played with the sushi on her plate. She loved Rome.

'Cara are you OK?' an intrigued male friend asked.

'Oh yes – sorry,' she giggled. 'I was completely elsewhere.'

'No kidding – thought you were trying to communicate telepathically with the sushi. It might be raw but that's it, Cara. Are you up for a visit to see Will's new place in Hampstead? He called while you were in a trance.'

Cara smiled at the other four guests around the table who were beaming back at her. 'No I'll head back home soon – not feeling too great tonight.' She wasn't in the mood for a trip that would prolong the night, preferring to head back to hers to get under covers. She was feeling concerned for Sirena now that she was in a relationship with someone else after she had seemingly fallen in love with her. Of course, with Sirena's looks and confidence she was never going to stay single for long – but she wished that she had.

Cara returned home at 9.00pm and climbed into bed alone. David was abroad for meetings. Two hours later, Cara was still awake with Amber sleeping by her feet. She couldn't sleep after getting into bed so early and with Sirena on her mind. With a deep breath, she called her.

Sirena's vibrating phone startled her as she lay in bed at Eaton Terrace. Cara's name was showing and she disconnected her by mistake in the panic.

Feeling confused as to why Cara wanted to speak after so

long, she called her back instantly before James came back up to the bedroom.

'Hi,' Sirena said, as flatly as possible.

'So what's he like?'

'Who?'

'Your new boyfriend!'

Sirena pulled a face at Cara's directness. 'He's good-looking, intelligent, *reliable* . . . we've just come back from Rome.'

'Really?'

'I told you I was coming back today.'

'Oh yes, you did. I came back from Barcelona a couple of days ago with . . . ' Cara hesitated. 'Giles.'

'So have you moved into your own place now then?'

'Yes, at last.' Cara winced uncomfortably. 'So you're happy with James?'

'I wouldn't be with him if I wasn't,' Sirena replied firmly, trying to fight back her old feelings for Cara.

'As long as you're happy, that's the main thing.'

'Since when did you care for my happiness?'

'That's a silly thing to say Sirena.'

'Well what do you expect?'

'You know I've always liked you, I just couldn't see how things would work for us both – and I still can't! I know I must sound weak but I really did give us a lot of thought. I've hardly been in touch because I need the space to sort things out in my mind. I do still think about you, though. You must know that I do?'

Sirena rolled her eyes. 'Well there's no point saying that to me is there? I'm in another relationship now so I guess we'll just be friends from now on?'

'Yes of course, I would like that.'

'So are you seeing anyone now?'

'No,' Cara winced again. She still couldn't bring herself to tell Sirena that she was back with David, let alone that she hadn't moved out. 'I'm very busy you know? But glad to hear that things are working out well for you – you deserve it.'

Chapter Thirty-Four

Cara stood among friends at Chelsea Manor during a warm June evening. The past two months since she last spoke with Sirena had been busy, but being at the party reminded her of when she used to have special birthday celebrations with Giles. She once organised a party for Giles at the Chelsea Manor and she missed all the fun childish activities.

She sipped her glass and beamed brightly around the hall at the familiar faces. David was in Paris and Giles in Marbella, enjoying his freedom before the start of his first university term. She was trying to ignore the fact that she was feeling dreary all over again with her life when she had resolved so much conflict in her mind to be happy with David. To live together as a family. But it was all very much the same without Sirena giving her full attention as she once did, and she missed her. Hearing that Sirena had moved in with James had also been a big blow.

'So how long have you known him?' Sirena asked. James had just asked one of his friends, a TV personality, to come over and greet her so she was feeling rather overwhelmed at the table.

'Years – he bought a property off me. I often see him in here actually.' James opened one of his top buttons. Sirena was looking exceptional that night, which was making him aroused with thoughts of making love to her after dinner. 'Now my princess, what would you like to eat?'

Sirena picked up the dark green menu. Going for dinner in glamorous venues used to be exciting, but it was becoming plain and the high prices were now just random figures to her. Still, she acknowledged that she was very lucky to be in such places. 'I think I'll start with the peppered Scottish beef carpaccio.' Sirena felt her phone vibrate in her bag. She'd received a text and gazed at her phone. It was from Cara.

Hey Sirena, been thinking about you. Hope you are well. Are you around at all to meet later? x

Sirena was puzzled – she hadn't seen Cara for seven months and all of a sudden she wanted to see her, although confusion quickly turned into excitement as all her feelings rushed back. Even though she hadn't seen Cara for months, and despite being angry with Cara's behaviour, she still thought about her every day.

'I would love an early night in,' James smiled sweetly at her.

Sirena glanced up from her phone. 'I would, too,' she smiled back.

As the minutes passed and James spoke to her about his day, she drifted off, deciding on whether to meet with Cara that night. She couldn't help it; despite the times she let her down, the thought of seeing Cara again was exciting. But she had no idea what excuse she could possibly have to leave James that night, apart from that she needed to see a friend, which would actually be true anyway.

I'm having dinner with James at the Dorchester – I can meet you at about 10.30pm?

Sirena looked up at James. 'James, I hope you don't mind but I need to see a friend after dinner.' She winced.

'Oh . . . that's a bit sudden!'

'I know, she just sent me a text. I haven't seen her for so long and she's in town. It'll only be for a couple of hours to catch up.'

'Sirena it's fine. If you haven't seen each other for a long time then have fun and enjoy the night. I'll be waiting for you at home, needless to say . . . '

Sirena texted Cara just after 9.15pm and asked where she was going to be later. Cara replied straight away.

Nozomi I think . . . I'll confirm with u x

Great, Sirena thought. She loved that restaurant. She quickly responded to confirm what time she was going to meet her but after twenty minutes she still hadn't received a response. She sent another text at 10.00pm with no response. She began to lose her collected state at the table with James as she tried to fume in silence. 'Sorry James, I'm not sure if I am meeting my friend now. Let's stay here for another ten minutes and if I haven't heard anything I'll just go home with you.' She glared at her phone, hoping Cara wasn't going to mess her around – again.

Cara frantically rummaged through her bag at Nozomi – she couldn't find her phone. She walked back to her car but she couldn't find it in there either. She must have left it at Valentina's where she took a quick detour before heading out. She walked back in to persuade Valentina to take her back to hers but she was occupied. Cara huffed in frustration. She really wanted to see Sirena that night but the opportunity was slipping away.

It was 10.30pm and Sirena resigned herself to the fact that Cara was not going to meet with her. She had messed her around yet again. 'OK let's head back,' Sirena said to James weakly.

Sirena got into bed reminded of Cara's old ways and turned her phone off. She certainly never wanted to hear from Cara again – apart from an apology. She couldn't take the excitement at the prospect of meeting and then the let-down when she cancelled. She moved closer to James and kissed him passionately. She wasn't going to think about Cara for the rest of the night.

Chapter Thirty-Five

'Does that feel good?' Elle smiled tenderly, pushing her fingers inside Lyra, the way she liked it. She kissed Lyra's face, licking the water droplets as they fell.

'Yes it does,' Lyra breathed, grasping her hands around Elle's shoulders. The warm droplets of water trickled down Elle's back as Lyra leaned against the shower wall.

'Good,' Elle gasped. She increased the water temperature as she moved inside Lyra more intensely. Her arms strengthened with Lyra's tighter grip around her, but as she drifted into a further state of arousal Makram came to mind. Since being caught she had felt more guilt while with Lyra. Lyra pulled her closer in, resting her chin on Elle's wet shoulder as she focused on Elle's movements inside her. Any guilt had to be washed away.

'Just leave the towel!' Elle laughed. They climbed under the covers of the double bed feeling refreshed. Elle was feeling more desirous after the shower. Within the past five months, her relationship with Lyra had returned to the normal routine. As a film started, she leaned in to kiss her. 'I love you more than I should.' She ran her hands around Lyra's soft naked body and entwined their legs. Resting her head on Lyra's breasts gave her the feeling of being wrapped in protective cotton wool.

'Come here.' Lyra clasped her hand around Elle's face and kissed her on the lips. 'Now's probably a good time to tell you my big news . . . I've found a one bedroom apartment in Onslow Gardens, which I'm going to put in an offer for.'

Elle leaned up quickly. 'Lyra – that's *wonderful news*, congratulations my darling! Gosh that's made me so happy.' Elle turned down the light beside her. 'Come here my baby and let me reward you properly.'

Cara finished styling her hair in front of the dressing table mirror and put on her favourite pearl earrings. Sirena had agreed to meet with her and was most grateful, considering the previous night. She was excited about seeing Sirena again but also nervous; she hadn't seen her in a long time and wondered if she had changed. She was also worried she would fall for her again on seeing her after so long, recalling the confusion Sirena had caused her. Although she was with David now so she wouldn't let that happen again. She reached for her make-up bag to add the finishing touches.

'Cara?'

'David?'

'Hello . . . it's me,' David called out, walking towards the bedroom.

Cara frowned and stood up from the chair just as David entered.

'David? What are you doing back? I thought you were in France till tomorrow?'

'Wow, what a lovely welcome.' He dropped his travel bag on the parquet floor with relief.

'It's just a surprise to see you.'

'I would have called but had a few other calls to make as soon as I got into London. It was all a bit frantic. Anyway, you remember I told you about the party I wanted to attend tonight? Well now we can go! Harry and Kristin said they would meet us there . . . and you're all dressed and ready.' David walked past Cara and quickly took off his shirt by the wardrobe.

'But I've already made plans for tonight David – I can't go.'

'Where are you going?'

'I'm meeting a dear friend.' She gazed away from him.

'Darling you know I was keen to go to this – I've returned from Paris early especially. You said last night you would go if I came back.' He looked at her with his shirt in hand. She gazed back at him through the dressing table mirror reflection.

'Can't you just go with Harry and Kristin?'

'Cara . . .'

Cara's heart sank. 'It's just that I'm supposed to be meeting my friend at eight and if I cancel now it'll be so last minute . . .'

'Cara I've come in from Paris and you said last night you would come. You can't cancel on me now.'

'David you should have called me this morning to confirm. I had no idea you were coming back tonight.' Cara groaned. 'OK I'll call my friend and cancel.' She walked sulkily out of the room.

So sorry darling but have to cancel tonight . . . explain later OK? We'll rearrange . . . I really am sorry xx

Cara closed her eyes, breathing in and out deeply to relieve the sudden pain in her heart. A friendship with Sirena just wasn't meant to be. She needed to stop contacting Sirena and forget about her. She needed to set her mind straight once and for all.

Chapter Thirty-Six

James Halpern's annual dinner party arrived in early November, which had been marked boldly in all calendars. Lizette took the invitation off the board in the entrance hall and placed it neatly in her clutch bag. She gave herself a final look in the long gold-framed mirror; her ivory sequined gown glistening in the light. 'Lyra, are you ready?'

Lyra walked down the stairs. 'I'm ready – wow you look stunning!'

'Thank you my darling and you look very glamorous in your dress. I don't think I've seen it before have I?'

'No, it's new.' Lyra smoothed her long Grecian slinky dress down and, like her mother, took a final glance at herself in the gold-framed mirror. She walked through the door, which her mother proudly and excitedly held open for her.

Sirena watched in excitement as the caterers rushed between the kitchen and the double reception room. James was spending time speaking to *Living the Desire* on the phone in the study. The prospect of sitting at a dining table engaging in conversation with his friends and business contacts was quite daunting and she had rather hoped that Lizette would be sitting next to her. But the seating plan was already in place.

From 7.30pm, Sirena watched as elegant couple after couple walked through the front door, where they were greeted by a pretty waitress with a silver tray of champagne. Classical music was playing throughout the property, from the London Symphony and Philharmonic Orchestra. James was now greeting friends and engaging in quick *how are yous* and *you're looking younger than evers*. The cosy yet expansive double reception room where all the guests congregated was filled with long tables of champagne, soft drinks and creative-looking canapés.

Sirena took a quick look around at the crowd of about thirty guests. They were admiring James's beautifully crafted antique furnishings as well as his new contemporary sculptures, which created a theme of nature throughout. She sighted Lizette and Lyra walking through the room and on to the large and central Oriental rug. Lizette called out joyfully to one of the guests and Lyra looked over at Sirena, giving her an acknowledging smile. Lyra clung to her clutch bag, fully aware that this was one of her mother's key social events of the year. She was yet to decide whether it would become one of hers.

James loitered rather anxiously around the entrance hall after an hour had passed. He exchanged quiet words with a caterer who came up to see him from the kitchen.

'Are you all right?' Sirena asked, on finding him.

'Yes, I'm just expecting a few more guests to arrive before we can all sit down for dinner. Oh well.' He glanced at his watch. 'Are you having fun tonight darling?'

'It's been great so far – spoken to a few of your friends . . . they're all really nice.'

'Good, that's good to hear.' He fiddled with his cufflinks distractedly. 'I think we should all go into the dining room now – we can't wait any longer.' He spoke again with the caterer who then dashed away to the kitchen on the lower ground floor. James walked off to speak with another guest.

'Sirena,' Lizette called. She walked briskly over to her with a wide smile. 'Sirena I've been meaning to ask you how your interview went for the PR role?'

'It was OK . . . I never know how interviews have gone, you know?'

'Well I hope you get it. It's such a good company.'

'I know. James doesn't want me to return to work, though. He won't tell me why, which is rather disconcerting!'

'Sirena princess, dinner is about to be served.' James suddenly appeared back beside her. The doors of the adjacent dining room were opened and James proudly took Sirena's hand to lead her in. James heard the sound of voices in the entrance hall. 'Ah, I'll see who that is.' James promptly walked back out.

Sirena stood by the table of canapés to finish her champagne before walking towards the dining room. Lizette had walked off to find Lyra. As she put her empty glass down, she could hear a familiar voice nearing the room. She glanced over at the door to see Cara emerge with a man – a man who looked familiar from a portrait she recalled seeing in Cara's house. Her ex? Overwhelmed with sudden joy at seeing Cara after so long, she wanted to call out to her – but confusion and panic took over and her eyes darted around the room for an exit, which she headed straight for. Cara and David walked confidently into the centre of the room to the other guests and they were closely followed by Elle and Makram.

'I've just spotted an old friend,' Makram remarked to Elle. 'We'll have to speak to him later.' He put his arm proudly around her waist.

'Yes fine,' Elle replied, happy that she had chosen to wear her backless Yves Saint Laurent evening dress.

James walked back over to them for a brief and lively conversation before they took a seat around the table. 'Makram, Elle, I was just saying to Cara that I'm so glad you could both make it this year. Cara speaks very highly of you both – hope it's all true.'

'I really can't comment James,' Elle quipped. 'But what I can comment on is your home – it's so beautiful.'

'Yes I know, but everything in my life is beautiful, which certainly includes you right now Elle.'

Makram laughed along with James and Elle, although a little irritably.

'I'm sure Cara will show you around my home tonight – she's been here many times.' He motioned at Cara who stood smiling in her long sequined dress, with David beside her in his bespoke dinner suit.

'Yes and I must say that his tastes are almost as good as mine,' Cara remarked.

'As is your arrogance darling.' James reached his arms out to embrace lightly with her. 'Now I want to introduce you all to my gorgeous new girlfriend, but she seems to have disappeared . . . ' he said, looking around the room.

Cara raised her eyebrows cheekily at Elle, hoping she

remembered their previous conversation about his dozy girlfriends. James left the foursome together in the room to find Sirena, after spending some time with them.

'Well I'm glad you've finally met James,' Cara said to Elle and Makram.

'He seems very nice,' Elle smiled. 'Doesn't he darling?' She nudged Makram and he nodded in agreement.

'Pleasant. Let's see who else is here . . . ' Elle followed Makram across the room.

'Oh I love this piece by Holst – it just makes me feel so grand!' Lizette gasped. One of her favourite classical pieces, 'Jupiter' from *The Planets*, had started playing. She began to sway but, in doing so, accidently knocked into a woman walking past her.

'Oh sorry dear,' she said quickly.

Elle glanced at the woman to offer a friendly exchange. 'That's quite . . . ' She paused momentarily as she found her eyes meeting directly with the mother of her mistress for the first time. Her friendly expression quickly turned to that of a stunned panther caught in safari car headlights. 'Oh! Hi . . . that's quite all right,' she replied collectively with a forced smile. She quickly turned away to follow after Makram but he had stopped in his tracks to speak with a familiar face. She turned back to check that it was Lizette, Lyra's mother, as she had only seen her a few fleeting times unexpectedly, but they had never locked eyes or spoken. It *was* Lizette.

'Come on darling.' Lizette turned to Lyra, who'd just finished a conversation with a guest. 'We best head to the dining room now.'

Lyra appeared from behind her mother and sighted Elle cautiously looking around the room next to Makram. Lyra's face dropped – as did her glass of champagne. Elle looked over as the sound of smashing glass diverted her panicked thoughts and, with stunned eyes, saw that Lyra was also at the party.

'Oh Lyra!' Lizette stepped away from the broken glass, suddenly flustered.

'*Fuck,*' Elle muttered under her breath. She immersed herself in conversation with Makram and his friend to distract him from looking around and seeing Lyra. She knew that if she now fainted, which felt imminent, then at least she would have given herself an efficient escape route.

'How did you drop your glass?' Lizette asked as calmly as she could. The guests had made a small clearing around the scene and one of the staff rushed to clear it up. Her daughter stood staring at the broken glass. 'Darling are you OK?'

'Sorry?'

'You've gone whiter than white?'

'Have I? Sorry, I'm OK – I think I've had a little too much to drink already.'

'If champagne doesn't go down well with you then you shouldn't drink it, Lyra.'

Elle and Makram started to walk into the dining room. Elle lightly took hold of Cara's hand and whispered into her ear, 'Lyra is here and with her mother – *I need to get out of here.*'

Cara looked at her with bewilderment and turned to locate Lyra among the other moving guests. She sighted her speaking with an older woman; she had only met Lyra a few times before but had never seen her mother. 'Gosh I had no idea that was Lyra's mother – how bizarre!'

'You knew they were going to be here?' Elle asked with more force.

'No, of course not. I didn't even realise that was Lyra's mother but she always makes an appearance at this party. I've spoken to her briefly a good few times but I've never seen Lyra here with her.' She winced. 'Did you not mention you were coming to this party to her?'

Elle groaned in response and stopped walking. She pulled

Makram's arm so he came to a halt. 'Makram stop – I'm not feeling very well.'

'You're not feeling well?'

'No, I think I'm going to be sick actually.'

'Really? Well let's rush to the bathroom then!'

'No I think we should go home – please take me home darling?'

'Home? We've only just arrived!'

David placed his hand on Makram's shoulder. 'Come on you two, you can talk at the table . . . '

Makram smiled at David then grimaced back at Elle. 'Are you really going to be sick?'

Elle couldn't take any more of the awkward conversation and turned to just walk out, hoping Makram would follow, but she sighted a pale-faced Lyra and her mother walking straight towards them. She turned back to Makram to block them from his view. 'You know what, I'm fine – I probably just need to sit down and eat something. Come on, let's just get our seats.' She nudged Makram towards the dining room. If Lyra used the left side of her brain and sat at the other end of the table, then she hoped Makram wouldn't notice her there at all. She was now relying on Lyra.

The caterers stood by the double doors to James's grand dining room and smiled lightly at Elle and Makram as they walked through. Cara turned to give Elle a sympathetic look as David led her by the hand to the dining table.

James finished his conversation with a friend by the dining room door and then looked around for Sirena among his pride of guests. She still hadn't come down. He made a final check that all was in order with the caterers before walking off to find Sirena again in haste. Cara and David took their seats at the long deep brown table, which took up nearly half the space of the large traditional room. The spiral white walls were adorned with paintings of James and members of his prestigious family.

James often joked that he liked his late relatives to watch him eat the fruits of their labour. Cara gazed around the romantically lit room by the chandelier centred above the table and motioned at Elle and Makram to come over. Their seats were towards the opposite end of the dining table from where James was going to sit and close to dramatic patterned drapes, which covered a floor-to-ceiling window. Elle and Makram pulled out the antique dining chairs next to them.

'Are you enjoying it so far?' David asked Elle and Makram. 'You should receive an invitation every year now, which is fantastic.'

'Well I understand from Elle that your poor wife has been trying to take us for a quite a few years now,' Makram motioned at Cara who fleetingly grinned.

Elle nodded as brightly as she could at Makram and David. Makram put his hand on hers lovingly as soon as she had sat down beside him.

'So far so great – we'll have to come to this every year.'

'Yes indeed,' Elle replied in a daze. She glanced at the entrance.

'Are you sure you're all right Elle?'

'I'm fine – probably just need to eat something then go to bed.'

Lizette entered the dining room and walked eagerly to the table to find her seat. When she spoke to James about the seating plan, she was thinking strategically as this was a great business opportunity for Lyra – an interior designer among high-end property developers was *more than* ideal. He had thus promised to seat her next to one of his new guests. She walked towards her place at the table, catching sight of the woman whom she had accidently knocked into earlier. Thankfully she was sitting next to her; she felt inclined to apologise and then she could engage in conversation, especially as she had never been to James's party before. She delighted in her initiative and pulled out the chair next to the woman who was busy speaking with the dark-featured man beside her – presumably her husband. She sat down with delight on seeing the vast array of beautifully designed silver cutlery and glassware across the table, and signalled for Lyra to sit opposite. She had ensured that Lyra didn't sit beside her as she wanted her to speak with as many guests as possible at the party. 'Take your seat darling!' Lizette demanded calmly, feeling agitated with her daughter's uncharacteristically cautious movements.

Makram became engaged in conversation with David so Elle turned her attention away to see who was sitting next to her. She locked shocked eyes with Lyra opposite who momentarily posed in a half-seated position in mid-air. Lizette looked at Lyra and then Elle in confusion.

'Oh do you two know each other?'

'Sorry?' Elle turned to Lyra's mother sitting beside her. 'Oh!' With a forced expression masking her sudden disarray, she looked back at Lyra. 'Sorry I thought I recognised you for a moment – you look a lot like someone I used to know,' Elle giggled, dipping her eyebrows uncomfortably at Lyra.

'Yes you look like someone I used to know, too.' Lyra shuffled in her seat, focusing on the silverware in front of her to try to settle herself.

'You must have met each other before at a party or some-thing,' Lizette said brightly, puzzled by the curious connection. 'Very intriguing – I'm sure it'll come back to you both at some point tonight!' She turned to speak to a friend at her side.

Makram glanced back over at Elle and smiled happily before turning back to speak with David, but in doing so caught sight of a rather familiar face adjacent to him. He joined in with Cara and David's conversation but had to take another look at the young woman as flashbacks of her in his marital bed hit him hard.

215

'Oh my,' Elle winced, noticing the shocked and unfriendly look between Makram and Lyra. She covered her face with her hand, begging the heavens to float her out of the wretched party. Lyra partially covered her face in despair and looked away, forcing a grin at the random guest next to her.

'*Take your hand away from your face,*' Makram whispered into Elle's ear. He was just as mortified as she was, if not more so, but certainly not willing to be humiliated at the party. The last thing he wanted was for David or anyone else to find out that his wife had been sleeping with another woman – and one who appeared half her age. '*That's the girl I caught you in bed with, isn't it?*'

Elle nodded silently, avoiding looking at him and Lyra.

'*Why is she here? What is this?*'

'*I don't know . . . I didn't realise she was going to be here – how would I?*'

The 'March' from *The Nutcracker* came on, which would have usually lifted her mood.

Lyra turned to her mother, interrupting her conversation. 'Mother – can we sit further up the table?'

'The seats are already taken Lyra. Do you want to ask them to get up?'

'No I was just . . . I just thought it might be nice to sit closer to James?'

'We're fine where we are. Lyra darling, we'll speak to James after the dinner.'

Sirena remained hidden on the second floor, discussing with Natalie on the phone possible reasons for her not being able to participate in her boyfriend's biggest party of the year.

'Maybe if you say you have stomach cramps he'll . . . '

'Sirena?' James asked at the door. 'Dinner is ready, my princess – are you coming?'

'Sorry – just on the phone!'

'Yes I can see that but you shouldn't be away from the party. Dinner is about to be served and we're *all* waiting for you.'

'Right OK, yes . . . I'm coming.' She disconnected the call amid Natalie's giggling and joined James, who gently held her arm as they walked towards the stairs.

'You look stunning tonight by the way. I picked the perfect size for you.'

But she suddenly found it very hard to breathe in her silk bronze evening dress.

Sirena's position at the head of the table was next to James, which she had ensured. She smiled at some of the guests who had stopped their conversations to see who James's new girl-friend was. After a swift gaze, she kept her head lowered till she reached the safety of her seat. She glanced across the table for the whereabouts of Cara and spotted her towards the other end in relief. She looked as alluring as when she last saw her a year ago. But the sight of her ex sitting comfortably beside her explained everything in a second.

'So that's James's new girlfriend,' David said quietly to Cara. 'He told me she was special and he wasn't wrong.'

Cara glanced over to where David was looking, lifting her head – then quickly lowered it again. Sirena? She panicked. She was thrown into a state of disarray, which was rapidly replaced by the shock of Sirena being with James; a man from *her* social circle and a *good friend* of David's. Not knowing if Sirena had already seen her at the party, she would try to remain hidden. She sent Elle a discreet text from inside her clutch bag.

SIRENA'S HERE WITH JAMES???!!!

Elle gave her a sideways stare to acknowledge her text and slowly turned to look over at Sirena then back at Cara again, locking eyes with Lyra by mistake. She gave her a cold look, which Lyra only had the delight of seeing when Elle was seriously angry. But Elle was feeling very uncomfortable in the extremely precarious situation and dizzy with the fumes Makram was giving off beside her.

The waiters emerged with the starters and James stood up to make a short speech, meeting the happy gaze of everyone at the table. 'Hello ladies and gentleman! Well here we are again after ten years. Thank you all for coming. You really are all looking exceptionally stunning this evening – but after ten years you all know not to turn up looking otherwise!'

The guests started to laugh and talk fleetingly among themselves. The mood in the dining room was high and bright, which James always ensured.

'Now I'm sure we have all fully embraced the extraordinary year we have had, with the stronger market driven by overseas purchasers as well as the rising local demand. The early quarter of last year was a particularly uncertain time for all those within the market but we stood strong and so here we are this evening, enjoying a revitalised market together. The rise in buyers competing for every property in London's finest addresses has resulted in tremendous returns so let's raise our glasses to congratulate ourselves on our hard work, and the valued contributions we have made to the magnificent market of property. May we carry on creating diversity, to meet the desires of buyers both abroad and at home. Cheers everyone!' He raised his glass as did all the other beaming guests around the table. 'Now I have my very tolerant girlfriend, Sirena, who is sitting here beside me this evening.'

Sirena knew this was her cue to stand up but she found herself stuck to her chair and smiling warmly at everyone instead. She looked up at James and saw the disappointed look in his eyes because she was not standing to introduce herself. With a deep breath she stood up, in full view of everyone sitting around the table. She looked over at Cara quickly, who was staring at her in contained shock.

'Hi everyone . . . I've spoken to a few of you already this evening – so hi again! James and I had a lot of fun organising this tenth anniversary so I'm happy that I met James – but for various other reasons also!' There was light laughter around the table. 'It's great to see you all and hopefully I'll speak with more of you after the dinner . . . thank you all for coming.' She sat down again, relieved.

'She really is stunning,' David remarked.

Cara nodded silently and exchanged another awkward look with Elle. But she couldn't have agreed more with her husband. She was jealous of James.

Everyone began to eat their starters and the conversations around the table were in full flow as James proudly looked on.

Lizette was aching to know more about the mysterious woman beside her as so far they hadn't spoken much to each other. 'So Elle, this is your first time at James's party?'

Elle turned and met the eyes of the mother of her mistress. 'Yes, I'm fairly new to property development you see . . . just a few years . . . '

'Oh really? How splendid – what drew you to property?'

'My husband Makram – he's been in property for many years and he taught me a lot about the industry, as well as inspired me of course . . . '

'That's lovely! What were you doing before if you don't mind me asking?'

'No it's fine. Well I spent my twenties bringing up my two children and then I ran a fitness business – just a small one. I like to keep healthy so I enjoyed it and the experience of running a business has been very good for me.'

'Well variety in life is beneficial and one must enjoy what one does otherwise nothing great would be accomplished. Passion and dedication are needed to achieve great things.'

'Yes of course,' Elle replied, silently trying to keep herself together.

'So with your property projects, do you do all the work yourself or do you use a team of designers?'

'I actually tend to do most of the design myself as . . . '

'Because my daughter could be very useful for you – she's an interior designer.'

'Oh?'

'Lyra darling,' Lizette called to her across the table. 'This is Elle – not the person you thought she was, and Elle this is Lyra my daughter – not the person you thought she was!' She laughed.

'Quite,' Elle replied. She and Lyra both forced smiles at each other while Lyra avoided the gaze of Makram, who had one angry eye on her and one on his food.

'Lyra has an extensive client base already, mostly here in London – don't you?'

'Yes,' she nodded.

Makram broke his angry silence. 'I can imagine she is very good – do you think she could help you darling?'

Elle fleetingly glared at Makram for getting involved in the already awkward conversation. 'Yes, what sort of design work do you do?' She tried not to stammer at Lyra.

'Various – depends on the client's requirements.'

'Yes I bet,' Makram remarked.

Lizette looked at Lyra brightly yet was frustrated by her vagueness. This was her opportunity and she was making nothing of it so she felt inclined to help. 'She really is fabulous with design, great within all spaces of a property – kitchens . . . bedrooms . . . drawing rooms . . . aren't you?'

Sirena dug her fork into the starter of smoked salmon, quietly wondering how on earth James knew Cara. She looked over at Lizette. Her head was feeling heavy with the stampede of questions in her mind – did Lizette know Elle *and* Cara? James nudged and smiled contently at her, intervening with her confused thoughts.

David turned to Cara after speaking to a guest opposite him. 'Have I told you that you look absolutely divine tonight?'

'Yes, but keep saying it anyway,' she grinned as she multi-tasked by listening in on Elle's conversation with Lizette and Lyra. She was feeling immensely sorry for her having to sit through a meal right in front of Lyra, with Makram clinging on to every word exchanged between the pair. Elle reached for her glass.

'Oh I love your bracelet,' Lizette complimented. 'Where did you find it?'

'In Istanbul actually.' Elle blushed as Makram put his hand out to touch her bracelet. She could feel his anger and was waiting for him to explode at the table. She felt helpless.

'Oh I love it there!' Lizette replied dramatically.

'Do you really?' Elle asked, forcing herself to look into Lizette's eyes, so as not to appear unfriendly.

'Yes – why, don't you?' Lizette quizzed with intrigue.

'Oh I love it, truly.'

Lizette nodded radiantly. 'So do you live close by? Here in London, I mean?'

'Yes . . . Lamont Road.'

'Oh wonderful, I know it – I live in Onslow Square,' she beamed.

The mains were served and the conversation between Elle and Lizette showed no sign of abating. David had got involved, much to the annoyance of Makram.

'Lizette your daughter looks very much like you,' David complimented, although he noticed Lyra looking despondent. 'Don't you think Makram?'

Makram looked at Lizette and instantly felt greater concern over his wife talking with her. For all he knew, they could be flirting with each other at the table. 'Yes,' he said succinctly.

'Do we?' Lizette asked. 'We do get that quite often actually don't we darling?' She turned to Lyra.

'You could easily be sisters!' David further complimented, to the joy of Lizette and embarrassment of Elle. Cara contained herself from kicking David under the table.

'My eldest daughter, Emma, looks very much like me also. She actually lives in New York – a very talented actress, as Lyra is talented at design.'

Lyra grinned and took a bite of her medium rare steak.

'So what else do you like to do when you're not being a design extraordinaire Lyra?' David asked. Makram flinched.

'Gym, travel, bars . . . '

'All with your boyfriend, I assume?'

'I'm single at the moment actually, but *definitely* looking.'

Elle hid her dissatisfaction with Lyra's response and kept her eyes focused on her food in front of her. Maybe if she finished her dinner early, she could leave the table before everyone else had finished as her mother sometimes used to allow.

'Have you just come out of a relationship then?' Makram asked calmly, but with intent.

'My darling's been single for quite some time now – haven't you?' Lizette cut in. 'I know it can be difficult to combine work with relationships, though.'

'Well my work is always so hectic with my various clients and I have to travel . . . '

Elle continued to look down at her food solemnly. Cara watched on with concern.

'But can you not fit a boyfriend in – maybe a part-time one?' Makram asked. 'Whatever is most convenient for you?'

Lyra looked at him bravely while Lizette felt slightly puzzled by his odd questioning.

'I just don't have the time.' She fleetingly locked eyes with Elle who held an expression of helplessness. Elle was silently bracing herself for their outing, which Makram only moments ago seemed desperate to avoid but was now engineering.

'Yes, of course it's understandable, having to travel and not having the time. I travel a lot – have *no idea* how Elle copes when I'm not in town.' Makram gave Elle a playful nudge. Elle looked up to give Lyra a rueful smile.

'Us women have our secret ways of keeping ourselves entertained, don't we Elle?' Lizette giggled.

Elle nodded weakly and smiled at her.

'Disclose one of those secrets,' Makram asked fiercely. He sipped his wine and thumped the glass heavily on the table.

'Makram . . . ' Elle tried to intercept in heightened panic.

'A woman never tells her secrets . . . do we?' Lizette exchanged a cheeky look with Elle.

'No.' Elle shook her head slightly. 'Gosh, I am hungry – you know I do tend to eat a lot these days.'

'But what sort of secrets are we talking about here?'

'You are curious aren't you?' Lizette giggled, although she felt there was no need to keep the subject of conversation going as it was just a joke. 'You know Elle, I do love my food as well! This food is just delicious.'

Elle grinned and looked across the table at the other guests, all with happy and content expressions as they enjoyed the company of those around them, eating their food merrily. She could just walk out but she didn't want to raise any eyebrows, which her exit surely would. She was stuck to her chair – forced to endure the rest of dinner.

James had been admiring Cara and David sitting next to each other at his table. 'So Cara, David, when are you renewing your vows?' he yelled over at them.

The table fell silent. Cara looked down, feeling her face turning as red as the glass of wine in front of her. The evening was going from bad to worse; she had never been in such a situation. She waited for David to respond. Sirena lifted her head to check that it was the Cara she knew who was 'divorced'. Cara glanced up and saw Sirena looking at her, but all she could do was look away.

David laughed. 'I don't think we need to renew our vows. We're the tightest couple around regardless, aren't we darling?' He beamed at Cara lovingly and rubbed her shoulder.

'Yes we are,' Cara grinned back at him.

David hid his dissatisfaction with her unenthusiastic response.

'I can see!' James quipped with a wink. 'Carry on!'

Sirena tried to remain collective at the table as James and his surrounding friends continued to talk to her.

'That was unexpected,' David laughed quietly.

Cara smiled weakly at him and gazed back down at her plate. 'Yes it was rather.'

'But it's best to be spoken about than not at all!'

'Yes, even if it is right across a crowded dinner table.'

David placed his hand tenderly on Cara's and she withdrew after giving him a fleeting grin.

After dinner, the photographer from *Living the Desire* arrived with two assistants and a mass of photography equipment. James ushered everyone to the expansive and traditional drawing room for the best setting.

'OK everyone, it's time for photographs. Can we all group together?'

All the guests grouped together closely for the photos with James proudly looking on with Sirena at his side until they were to take their central position. Cara was in the middle of the group with David; she avoided catching eyes with Sirena – she knew she was watching with James. Makram found himself standing next to Lizette with Elle on his other side. Lyra stood beside her mother closely so Makram wouldn't be able to see her. James and Sirena joined the group and the photographer began to take photographs until he was happy he had a big enough collection to choose from.

As the group dispersed, James enthusiastically walked over to the photographer to take a peek at the photos to ensure he looked presentable for publication. 'Gosh we all look so happy,' he beamed. 'Let's all have one more photo and squeeze in tighter together!'

Sirena silently moaned as did Cara, Elle, Makram and Lyra. The guests all re-grouped but to Elle's dismay she was pulled in towards Lizette who looked at her brightly. 'This will be a super shot!' She hugged Lyra who stood to her other side. Sirena positioned herself again with James and looked around to see where Cara was. She noticed a ring on her wedding finger, which was resting on David's shoulder. She had never seen her wearing it before. She forced a smile as the flash went off.

The photographer continued to take photos around the drawing room as the guests dispersed to enjoy each other's company before the party was to come to an end. Cara eventually sighted Sirena standing alone in a corner and excused herself from a group conversation. She approached her quickly, her heart beating faster than each foot step towards her.

'Sirena we really need to talk,' she said quietly, reaching for Sirena's hand desperately. 'It isn't what it looks like . . . '

'It's exactly what it looks like,' Sirena intercepted, moving her hand away abruptly from Cara's. She put her glass down on the side table and walked away for safety by James's side for the rest of the evening.

To Elle's relief, Lizette and Lyra didn't approach her and Makram for the rest of the evening, instead speaking with the other guests. She was even more relieved to see them leave earlier than most of the other guests.

'Sirena I want to introduce you to more of my friends,' James said, casting his eyes around the room for Cara and David. He remembered saying he would introduce her to them.

Sirena sighed. She'd had enough for one night.

'Oh there they are! Come on princess, I want you to meet my friend David and his wife.' He took her by the hand and marched her over to his friends. 'David, Cara – here is my beautiful girlfriend, Sirena.'

Cara turned around to see Sirena beside her. She glanced away, feeling her whole body weaken.

'Hello Sirena,' David kissed her lightly on each cheek. 'Well what a delight to meet you; we were all saying at dinner how stunning you look this evening, weren't we Cara?'

'Yes we were,' Cara said as enthusiastically as possible. She locked her apologetic eyes on Sirena; to her dismay, she could clearly see how disappointed she was with her.

'That's very nice of you,' Sirena said as brightly as she could, trying to avoid looking directly at Cara. 'I hope you liked my brief speech?'

'Loved it – with speeches, the briefer the better,' David quipped. 'Particularly yours James . . . '

'Yes we all know you have a short attention span David.' James turned to Sirena. 'I could listen to your voice all day and night,' he said flirtatiously into her ear, embracing her proudly. He could sense David's jealousy with his new girl.

Cara's stomach turned at the sight of James's hands wrapped around Sirena – hands which were just so different to hers. She refrained from pushing him off Sirena, suddenly overcome with anger. David put his arm around her, agitating her even more; she wanted Sirena's arms around her more than anyone else's.

'Sorry I have to make a quick call – can I come and find you all in a couple of minutes?' Sirena said, unable to cope with Cara's presence.

'You and your phone tonight . . . ' James grimaced at her lightly.

At 1.40am, the majority of guests gradually began to leave and go their separate ways. Makram kept Elle close by his side as they prepared to leave the party with Cara and David. David assisted Cara with her coat as Sirena watched on from

226

a distance. David pulled in Cara and gave her a playful kiss on her forehead.

'I'm getting you out of that dress and straight into bed,' he whispered into her ear.

Cara smiled silently at him; she wasn't in the mood for sex at all.

Elle held on to Makram. 'Let's just go,' she said quietly.

James walked up to the group of four. 'Thank you all for coming . . . I hope you all had a fabulous time?'

'We had a bloody awful time.' David put on his coat dramatically. 'So awful we were all trying to sneak off home but now you've caught us.'

'Well you know I only invite you because you bring along such exquisite women,' James quipped back, glancing at Cara and Elle. 'You're all invited to my gin palace this summer by the way, although I can't guarantee it'll be as entertaining as tonight!'

'James we had a wonderful time tonight,' Cara added politely. She wanted to cut the idle chat and head home to sleep the whole messy night off without having to endure more time with her ex's new man.

'Well then why don't you all stay over?'

David paused to consider the usual offer; James always knew how to have a good time and clearly he didn't want the night to be over yet. 'Well we *were* heading back . . . Cara what do you think?'

Cara fell silent and glanced at Elle, who looked exhausted. 'Elle what do you think?' she asked, knowing her answer. She didn't want to appear anti-social herself.

'Whatever. I'm not doing anything tomorrow.'

Cara panicked. 'I actually need to see my personal trainer early in the morning – gosh I've just remembered!'

'Listen, you all think about it. I'm just going to have a quick word with a friend. I need to catch her before she leaves.'

'David I think we should just go home – I'm so tired,' Cara insisted, leaning on his shoulder.

David looked over at Makram.

'I'm ready for bed,' Makram responded. David turned back to Cara. 'OK, we'll head home.'

Cara nodded tiredly, yet felt great relief inside.

Chapter Thirty-Seven

'Last night was a success!' James congratulated himself. 'A great turnout. I'm looking forward to seeing the photos in print.'

'So how do you know Cara and David?' Sirena asked, suppressing her sadness. She was getting changed in the bedroom into jeans and a jumper. So far she had done well to hide her anguish over finding out Cara was still married.

'Oh, I've known them for years.' He put on his cufflinks. 'Don't keep in touch a lot but they're such a lovely couple and Cara's a golden one. You know when he first introduced me to her, I was so jealous of him,' he smirked. 'Although of course you outshine her by a million stars.'

Sirena forced an appreciative smile. James walked into the en suite but Sirena wanted to find out more. She joined him and began to put on her make-up. 'I spoke to quite a few of your friends last night actually. So how long have Cara and David been married?'

'About twenty years I think and still going strong. Well, they've had their ups and downs like any married couple but, from what I saw last night, they seem to be very happy now.' He adjusted his tie in the mirror. 'Although who knows what happens behind closed doors?'

*

Lizette handed Lyra a glass of fresh orange. 'I expect you're very glad you came to the party with me?' Lizette asked, sitting down beside her at the breakfast bar. 'You managed to make some great contacts.'

Lyra nodded with widened eyes, wishing she had gone straight back to her apartment at Onslow Gardens after the party. 'Yes I did, it was good.'

'And Elle was just delightful. I simply must invite her and her husband over.'

Lyra chewed her toast slowly, feeling all the muscles in her face fail with trauma.

'We spoke for most of the night but that's why I love James's annual party. I always meet someone interesting who becomes a delightful friend. Although having said that, I met Lance at James's party and what a mistake that was . . . '

Lyra nodded and ate her breakfast while listening to her mother's overly positive analysis of the party.

'Now, Elle gave me her card, which I can't seem to find.' Lizette frowned. She got up to retrieve her bag and brought it back to the breakfast bar.

Lyra momentarily felt slight relief before a smile graced her mother's face again. 'Ah, here it is. I'll call her this evening. She did express some interest in your work also, which is promising.' She looked at Lyra optimistically with Elle's card in her hand.

Cara lay in bed, listening to David getting ready to venture outside. She couldn't quite find the energy to move; the party had drained her of her physical abilities yet caused an emotional upheaval.

'Cara, are you all right?' David asked, walking to the bedroom door.

'Yes I'm fine . . . drank a little too much last night that's all,' she murmured softly.

'Oh my beautiful . . . just stay in bed, I take it you'll be in when I get back this evening at about 7.00pm?'

'Yes I should be. What would you like for dinner?' She swept back her hair from her face and turned to face him by the door.

'Darling we have an awards ceremony to attend – you've been looking forward to it all week!'

Cara's face went blank momentarily. 'Oh yes of course, I remember. Have a good day, kiss kiss.'

She turned back over when David closed the door. She lay still recalling everything that happened at the party; what was said and the face expressions exchanged. Seeing Sirena again after so long had brought back deep feelings, which she had until then managed to block out. She looked so beautiful and so elegantly mature. Seeing her in the arms of someone else had hit her harder than she had ever imagined. She so wished that it was *her* sitting next to Sirena at that table instead of James. But she couldn't believe that she was also going out with James Halpern – a man she had known for years. She suddenly panicked; what if Sirena had told James about her? Then he would tell David. Surely she wouldn't have, she calmed herself. She continued to lie in bed, unable to lift her heavy head up, which was filled with questions and thoughts.

Elle was alone in her house. Makram had left for work an hour ago. She was in her bathrobe sitting in the kitchen with a bowl of muesli, playing with her phone. She contemplated contacting Lyra but quickly decided that she needed to just sit quietly to collect her thoughts. She turned off her phone and sat eating in silence.

*

Cara called Sirena for the tenth time that day, but she still didn't answer. She sent her another text in the evening.

OK I'm married but we had separated. I didn't want to tell you before cos I knew it would put u off me. I was going to get a divorce but I got scared ☹ I've always loved u but u know I've found it difficult to come to terms with everything. This is silly! Please can we talk? U haven't told James about us have u?

No of course I haven't told James!!! I don't want to hear from you ever again – you've only ever just thought of yourself. Goodbye Cara and good luck with everything.

Cara felt her already broken heart smash into tinier pieces. She heard David walking along the corridor. He knocked lightly on the bedroom door.

'Cara darling, are you ready?'

'Yes I'm coming, just a few more minutes.'

The last thing she wanted was to go to an awards ceremony and have to put on a happy façade. She had spent the whole day indoors to recuperate. She wasn't in the mood for seeing anyone and had even turned down Elle, who wanted to meet to discuss her sudden awkward situation with both Lyra and Makram. She tidied her stray golden brown strands of hair, which had fallen from her clip, and looked at herself from all angles in the dressing table mirror. She was looking vibrant that evening in her light printed evening dress but her feelings certainly didn't match. She didn't want Sirena to be with someone else; she *needed* her back to herself. She picked up her heels and left the room to join David and Giles, who were waiting patiently in the entrance hall.

'Sorry I was having trouble putting my dress on,' she said, walking towards them barefooted.

'It's all right,' David said proudly, casting his eyes from her head to her toes.

She bent over to put her heels on and forced a happy grin when she stood straight again. 'You look very smart Giles,' she said to him warmly. Looking into her son's eyes somehow made her feel instantly better.

At Eaton Terrace, Sirena got into bed and turned off the lights. Tears started to roll down her face; she was so hurt by everything and regretted ever meeting Cara. James was returning home that night after a late meeting, which meant she had time on her own to let out her tears. She certainly didn't want James to ever know of her past, which Lizette and Miles had promised not to inform him of.

Elle anxiously watched her home phone ring. Jasper walked into the room to answer it, bemused as to why his mother was just staring at it from the sofa on the other side of the room.

'Mum it's for you,' he said, holding out the phone to her.

'Who is it dear?'

'Lizette?'

Elle winced inside and tried to signal at Jasper to make an excuse but he just looked at her, confused. She stood up and walked over to take the handset. 'Hello, Elle speaking.'

'Elle, it's Lizette! We met at James's party last night?'

'Oh . . . oh yes – how delightful for you to call. How are you?'

'Very well thank you. I had such a super time last night. Did you enjoy yourself?'

'Yes I really did . . . '

'Fabulous,' Lizette intercepted excitedly. 'Well I woke this morning feeling very pleased that we met. I often hold parties and charity events and so on myself, you know – I'll have to add you to my invitation list – but Elle darling, I'd like to invite you and your husband over for dinner at my place next week. I must say that I really enjoyed your company last night – a lot of mutual interests!'

'Quite . . . '

'Now I don't know what day is good for you . . . '

'I'll need to check my diary Lizette – '

'I was thinking next Thursday?' Lizette replied, pushing the conversation in the direction she desired. She had friends arriving at any moment.

'Oh sorry I actually can't meet that day . . . '

'Well what about Friday? I was going to be flying that day but I've cancelled.'

'Friday . . . '

'Elle, tell me, when is good for *you*?'

'Oh dear, I can't think right now! Actually Thursday is fine.' Elle caved in, just wanting the call to end. 'Sorry Lizette I'm really just feeling all over the place today.'

'I am too actually! Well Elle I look forward to seeing you on Thursday.'

Elle got off the phone as soon as she could and fell down on to the nearest armchair. She retraced every single step that had led her to this desperate moment in her life. She had dreaded bumping into Lyra's mother and now she'd just agreed to have dinner with her – at her place. She couldn't see a way out, unless she cancelled – but to do such a thing would be very unsociable. Still, she couldn't possibly sit through another evening with the mother of her mistress. She wasn't going to ask Makram to join her for dinner with Lizette either; she wasn't even going to mention it to him. If she had to go, she would go alone.

Chapter Thirty-Eight

Sirena sat down with James at the dinner table after he returned just before 10.00pm. She had made herself look presentable again although her eyes still looked a little puffy, which she blamed on tiredness.

'Sirena, there's something that I've been meaning to tell you.'

'Yes?'

'I'm opening an office in Monaco next year, which was all confirmed today. To ensure it runs smoothly, I will need to be in Monaco for a while . . . in fact, I would like to move there. You do remember me telling you about my thoughts on the move?'

She stared blankly at him. 'I can't remember right now. But you need to *move* there?'

'Yes, I know – it's all very exciting! I was going to mention it at my party as part of the speech but for some reason it just didn't feel right – plus I was waiting on a few things, which were clarified today. In fact, I'll still hold my annual party here in town so we'll be back for those. It's so exciting!'

'We?'

'Of course – you're coming with me! We would be back in the UK every now and again as our friends and family are here but I thought that this would also be really great for us?' He looked at her hopefully in anticipation for her enthusiastic response.

'Erm . . . well I need to think about it. It sounds amazing but will I be able to find work out there?'

'Princess you don't need to work – I'll take care of you. You'll love your new lifestyle in Monaco; you could go skiing in the morning and be back on a beach or shopping in the afternoon! Plus the weather will be perfect for you – you always complain about the lack of sunshine in England. In Monaco you'll be a different person.'

'Oh thanks.'

'No no no, I mean you'll feel different – you'll really feel alive and, as I said, we'll be back in London every now and again, although we may have to cancel our gym memberships here and so on – but that's something to look into nearer the time. Look princess, please just say you'll come with me?'

Sirena thought quickly in her dazzled state. A move abroad would be hugely exciting and certainly mean putting her messy past with Cara firmly behind her. 'Yes! OK, yes I'll come! Although I've never been to Monaco . . . '

'I'll take you in a couple of weeks but I have plenty of literature in the study so you can read about the area. Or just take a day trip – I've been too many times to count myself!'

Sirena grinned with excitement. She suddenly felt relieved and revitalised; James was giving her an emotional escape route from Cara.

'You'll really love it – it'll be a new life for us.'

Elle walked briskly into the study and closed the door firmly behind her. Pulling out her phone from her pocket, she called Lyra. Lyra picked up straight away but took a few seconds to speak while she walked quickly through the crowd in Mahiki, where she was having cocktails with friends. Elle began speaking again as the noise of the club trailed off in exchange for the wind outside.

'Lyra, first of all I'm sorry for earlier – my battery died and I just couldn't move from the sofa. Now listen my baby, your mother has just invited me over for dinner on Thursday and I had no choice but to accept. I can't begin to tell you how I'm feeling . . . are you going to be there at all?'

'Elle, are you serious? You're coming over for dinner?'

Lyra walked further away so she couldn't be overheard by the doormen at the club entrance on Dover Street. 'I don't believe you.'

'Darling it was her idea – not mine,' Elle replied angrily at Lyra's annoyed tone towards her. 'You know very well that this is putting me in a *very* precarious position. I just can't believe that we finally solved our privacy problem with your new place, and now I'm going to end up at your mother's anyway – and by bloody invitation. Why didn't you stop her from calling me? Or get rid of my card – you saw her ask me for it?'

'But you don't have to meet with her!' Lyra paused. 'Please don't say Makram is coming with you?'

'Oh that fucking party . . . ' Elle groaned.

'Well?'

'No of course Makram's not coming! I don't want him involved *at all* in this. I'll meet with your mother just the once to be polite and that'll be it, OK? If I cancel now she'll just reschedule, which will only prolong all this.'

'Elle, what if Makram finds out?'

'Oh don't make me feel more stressed about this Lyra. Look, I'll just meet her for dinner and that's it. I'll put us to the back of my mind the whole evening. It'll be fine . . . just a little odd for me, that's all.'

'I really can't believe what's happening.' Lyra groaned loudly. 'Mention *absolutely nothing* about me. She cannot find out about us, she simply can't. Look, I have to go – it's freezing. Just don't make things worse all right?'

Lyra disconnected and left Elle rather surprised. Usually it was her telling Lyra what to do. With raised eyebrows she walked back out of the study.

'Good grief! What are you doing?'

'Just came back,' Makram sighed, leaning against the wall opposite the study. 'Need to spend an hour or so in the study . . . '

'I was just on my phone.'

'I don't know about you, but I'm still getting my head around last night.' He rubbed his forehead wearily. 'How are you feeling?'

'Not great at all – it was just all so unexpected,' Elle sighed. Guilt swept over her as she examined Makram's tired face. His dark eyebrows were slumped over his sad eyes. 'Come here darling.' She squeezed him tightly, wishing she were a better wife who had inherited her mother's morals. 'I'm so sorry for everything.' She couldn't possibly tell him that she was going to have dinner with Lizette.

James sat close to Sirena in Nobu on Berkeley Street the next evening. He wanted to celebrate their move to Monaco but he was also making an extra effort to serenade her in case she had any doubts about the move. Being in Nobu was making Sirena feel sad as fond memories came back from when she was last there with Cara nearly two years earlier. She received another text from Cara as she and James waited for their sushi.

I know I've really hurt you and can't apologise enough. We really need to talk . . . please meet with me? I've got to explain everything to you – please?

Sirena deleted the text straightaway.

As the night grew on, Cara became more frustrated with Sirena. She had sent her three more texts and not one reply. At 11.30pm, she was reading in bed with David beside her, typing on his laptop. He glanced at her as she read; she looked cute immersed in her book. He packed up his laptop and rested his head on the pillow, facing Cara. He teasingly caressed her stomach inside her pyjamas.

'David that tickles,' she giggled.

He laughed and gently stroked her inner thigh as she continued to read quietly. She really wasn't in the mood to speak to him, let alone be intimate. All she could think about was Sirena with James as her brown eyes moved from one random word to another on each page. 'David stop it. I'm trying to read my book, OK?' She moved her leg away.

'Can't you read the book tomorrow?'

'No I really want to finish it tonight,' she said imperiously.

He reached out and squeezed the remaining two hundred unread pages together. 'You're going to read all that tonight?'

'Yes.'

'Darling we haven't made love for nearly a month now . . . ' He hesitated. 'What's wrong?'

She put the book down flat on the bed and rubbed her forehead. 'I'm just not in the mood tonight. Let's just sleep all right?'

'I thought you were finishing your book?'

'I can't when you keep pestering me.'

'Pestering?'

With a huff she reached her arm out to turn off the light, then snuggled under the covers.

'Cara if you think I'm pestering you . . . '

'I'm just not in the mood David!' She got up angrily to use the en suite.

'I know when something is up with you,' he said, standing outside the door. 'You're not telling me something – what is it?'

'It's nothing.' In her emotional state, she couldn't cope with an argument of any sort with David. She walked back out after four silent minutes. 'Just stressed with work and tired, OK.'

David had done nothing wrong but she knew she had to make big changes, which weren't going to be easy for anyone.

Chapter Thirty-Nine

Thursday arrived too fast for Elle when she found herself parked outside Onslow Square. She gazed up at Lyra's family home, fraught with nerves. She groaned harshly; she needed to compose herself and get the evening done with. It was just Lyra's mother for goodness' sake. She stepped out of her Jaguar and walked past the two white pillars on either side of the building. With a deep breath in the icy November air, she pressed the buzzer. Lizette was quick to greet her at the front door.

'Hello Elle! Come in!' Lizette beamed. 'It's lovely to see you again.'

'Thank you Lizette.' Lizette embraced Elle fondly by the top of the steps. 'It's lovely to see you, too.'

'My, you're looking splendid – where's the outfit from?' Lizette asked before she led the way to the open plan reception room.

'Oh thank you, it's from Peter Jones actually.'

'Gosh it's beautiful. Come into the reception room where all the action in my home takes place . . . ' She turned to look at Elle who was following close behind. 'Would you like something hot to drink Elle?'

'I don't mind – maybe just an orange juice for now?'

'Super, I'll get one for you. Do make yourself comfortable.'

Elle sat down and assessed her surroundings while Lizette quickly walked to the adjoining kitchen. She noticed photos of Lyra in her school days and her graduation photos in prime spots around the room alongside black and white prints of iconic movie stars and singers.

'Doesn't Lyra look glamorous in that one?' Lizette asked, walking back into the room. 'Friends *always* comment on that photo.'

'Yes she's very beautiful,' Elle replied collectively. She looked away from the large framed photo of Lyra on a beach, wearing a sarong she had borrowed from her.

'So you enjoyed James's party? They're always such great fun.' She handed Elle her drink and sat down beside her.

'I did enjoy myself, very much.' Elle gave a tight-lipped grin.

'You live quite close on Lamont Road with your family, as I recall you saying?'

'Yes, well my two children are both at university now but my son comes back every now and again. We also have an apartment by the Thames, which the children normally cause mischief in.' She grimaced.

'Yes I know how mischievous children can be and that's actually what I miss now that my two are grown up,' Lizette laughed. 'Your apartment must have amazing views?'

'Yes of course. I should spend more time there really.' Elle gazed away to grasp a few seconds and steady herself. Lizette was quick to speak again.

'Lyra recently bought her own place.' Lizette sighed. 'Rather selfishly I kept telling her that I didn't want her to move out and leave me.'

'Well they do have to fly the nest at some point don't they?'

'Yes of course,' Lizette frowned slightly. 'I would rather she find a lovely boyfriend first, though. I don't want her to live on her own as I have done since my husband passed away.'

'Oh I'm sorry to hear that,' Elle replied awkwardly.

'It's OK. But Lyra still comes back here – she's left a lot of her things here actually. Do you miss your children while they're away at university?'

'Yes I do but my daughter only started last month. My son comes back often; he can't keep away from London you know?'

'Well if they have a lovely apartment overlooking the river to play in it's understandable! It must be lovely to entertain – do you hold dinner parties there often?'

Elle raised her eyebrows as she sipped her orange. Fond memories of her playful times with Lyra in the apartment flashed back.

'Elle darling,' Lizette laughed. 'You look so serious – I think we both need a stiff drink – hurry up with your orange!'

Evening turned to night. Elle received a blunt text from Lyra.

Have you gone yet?

She received another text shortly after from Makram, asking where she was. She stuffed her phone back into her bag and retreated back with Lizette to the flamboyant reception room area after their dinner. Elle was now rather enjoying Lizette's company as she made her laugh throughout the evening. She had even momentarily forgotten she was the mother of her mistress.

'Well it's a shame Makram couldn't come,' Lizette giggled.

'Yes I thought so,' Elle sighed lightly. Lizette made similar expressions to Lyra, which was captivating. She was careful not to display any familiar fondness in her eyes, however, and diverted her thoughts from her beautiful mistress.

'Well maybe next time if he can handle our conversations on the male anatomy! So how come this year was your first time at James's party? I can't remember now if you told me.'

'Well I only got into the business a few years ago and Makram was always too busy to attend,' Elle shrugged. 'He travels a lot.'

'Oh, well James invites me because we're such good friends – I was in PR you see. The party is very useful for my daughter, however, so I'll be taking her to it every year now that her career is flourishing.' Lizette took a sip of her coffee.

Elle drove leisurely out of South Kensington at around 10.30pm. Spending the evening with Lizette was a pleasant surprise. She took a keen liking to her. She also felt even closer to Lyra as a result – like Lyra really was part of her family.

*

241

Cara reached for her phone. She had firmly made her decision and was prepared to carry it through this time.

> I know you're ignoring me but I've made an important decision which involves you.

> I'm so confused by everything. Why were you not honest with me?

> It was difficult . . . was just so afraid. Please meet me tomorrow evening at my place?

> Don't know, need to think about it.

Chapter Forty

Elle stood in her entrance hall in disbelief that she had just accepted Lizette's invitation of a shopping trip. Lizette sounded so enthusiastic and she did enjoy her company over dinner but she didn't want her to actively pursue a friendship with her. She was reluctant to inform Lyra of their arrangement – so she simply wouldn't. She picked up her gym bag to head out of the front door for her morning workout.

Sirena jogged along Chelsea Embankment, thinking about Cara. She *needed* to see her to find out why she had lied. She sat down on a bench to make contact.

> Meet tonight?

Cara was more than relieved and agreed. She looked back at Helen's disapproving expression.

'Darling you need a long holiday – maybe a mind body and soul detox in the Far East?'

'No, I know what I want now Helen – I've made my choice.'

'But can you really go through a divorce? I know you darling, you won't leave David.' Helen glanced across the reception room at one of Cara's family portraits.

'Yes I can go through a divorce and I should have done so years ago . . . you should be supporting me Helen.' Cara paused thoughtfully. 'I haven't been able to stop thinking about Sirena – just seeing her again was so . . . '

'I'm just so worried,' Helen pushed in. 'Are you sure you can be in a relationship with Sirena?' Helen looked into Cara's eyes. 'I don't want you to make the wrong decision for yourself, David and Giles – your *family*.'

'Yes I'm sure now,' Cara replied adamantly. 'After everything that's happened, I know what I want. I just hope Giles will understand . . . I never wanted to leave David while he was so young, you know?'

'But I thought you said you couldn't be with another woman for his sake?'

'Gosh Helen I know. This is what stresses me the most but he's older plus he's now at university. He should understand – his generation should be more understanding, don't you think?'

'I really couldn't say how your son would react,' Helen said earnestly.

Cara nodded a little, knowing she would come up against difficulties by being with Sirena and she really didn't know how she would tell Giles. But Sirena was who she wanted to be with, the one person who had been on her mind every day since they met. She couldn't continue to lead a life where material possessions and the opinions of others were more important than love and her own happiness.

At 8.00pm, Cara opened the door to Sirena at one of her property projects in Belgravia. 'Hi,' she said softly, feeling her heart beating faster now that she was in the private presence of Sirena once again.

'I'm only meeting because I want to know why you lied to me,' Sirena said coldly.

'Yes of course,' Cara said, rubbing her weary forehead. 'Come.' She led Sirena to the nearest reception room.

'Why did you treat me like I meant nothing?' Sirena took a fleeting glance at Cara's unfamiliar wedding ring, which was now on full display. She sat down on a sofa. 'You were married the *whole time*?'

'Oh Sirena, I just couldn't tell you. I met you and *really* liked you, but I was so confused as well. I began trying *not* to like you because I just couldn't handle the stress it was causing me.'

'You did a good job leaving me confused. You were just using me all along. I'm so angry with you. I knew something was going on with your ex – I mean, your *husband* – when you hadn't moved and started to ignore me. But I just didn't want to believe it – I thought so much of you.'

'I never wanted to upset you,' Cara replied quickly. 'I'm not in my twenties like you – I have responsibilities. My decisions aren't easy, you must understand that?'

Sirena puffed out her cheeks in frustration, but her anger was being clouded with her affections for Cara. Not one day had passed since they'd met when she didn't think about her, and sitting so close to her again was annoyingly exhilarating. 'So you must have been sleeping with David all along. When you cancelled nights out with me, you were staying in with him? You just threw me aside when it suited you?'

'No I didn't, it wasn't like that *at all*. David and I were *not* together, we were separated – hardly saw each other. We slept in different bedrooms for goodness' sake! When we were together, I was with you *only* and my marriage to David was just a piece of paper. We were going to divorce but the pressure of everything just made me panic. As time went by I just couldn't see us working for various reasons – what people would think, you know?'

'But who cares what other people think? And why didn't you just tell me you were having doubts?'

'I should have but I was just so all over the place. Sirena, David and I only became intimate when our relationship ended. It felt like the best thing for everyone at the time but . . . it's all made me realise a lot . . . about myself.'

Sirena sat back on the sofa to take everything in. She didn't know what to believe. She loved Cara, more so than anyone she had ever met, but she had also hurt her in a way no one else ever had.

'Why were you not honest with me?'

Cara glanced away solemnly before looking back at Sirena with tired eyes.

'I just don't know what to think any more.' Sirena gazed into Cara's warm yet tired brown eyes, uncomfortably relieved with Cara's desire for her again. 'When you finished it with me by *text* I didn't want to see you again because it would have hurt me so much to see you with someone else. When I saw you with David at the party, do you have any idea how that made me feel?'

'I'm so sorry but it was a shock for me to see you with James as well. Sirena, when we were together David and I were separated – we weren't living as a couple.' Cara took hold of Sirena's hands tightly. 'I'm going to get my own place and make everything up to you.'

'I thought you already had moved?'

Cara groaned. 'I just couldn't tell you that also. Again I was so afraid that I would lose you completely. Look, I never stopped thinking about you – I tried to see you remember? Nozomi and the night after? I was missing you and wanted to talk things through properly but it just didn't work out . . . '

'It doesn't matter. I'm moving to Monaco with James now anyway.' Sirena withdrew her hands from Cara.

'What?'

245

'Early next year – he's opening a new office there.'

'Oh, so it's really serious between you two?'

'Why wouldn't it be?'

'You told him you would go?'

'I'm young so it'll be a good opportunity, don't you think? I'm in my twenties so my decisions are easy after all.'

Cara groaned. 'James has a playboy reputation. He's had a new girl on his arm every year at his party.'

'I'd rather you didn't criticise James.'

'I'm just saying what you should know – James was with a tall blonde last year and this year you were the trophy of the night.'

'You're a fine one to talk. I don't know why you're appearing to be so upset when all you've done is mess me around – doesn't make any sense.'

'I've been trying to figure things out.' Cara leaned back on the sofa in exhaustion. 'I haven't known what I've wanted but I do now Sirena.'

Sirena sighed heavily, unconvinced by Cara's excuses. Cara suddenly took hold of her hands again.

'Darling please come back to me?'

'But what about your marriage?'

'I'll get a divorce.'

'You said you were moving out of your house when I first met you and you're still living there . . . do you really think I'm going to believe in anything you say now?'

'Oh *shh* darling and come here.' Cara clasped her hand around Sirena's familiar face and leaned in to kiss her. Sirena couldn't control herself as she felt Cara's familiar lips against hers.

Sirena broke away from her. 'I should go. I really can't do this – you're just confusing me. You'll have changed your mind again tomorrow anyway, if not by later tonight.' She stood up quickly.

'Sirena sit back down . . . ' But Sirena was quick to leave.

Cara huffed loudly, wanting the sofa to swallow her up.

'How's your work?' Lizette asked enthusiastically. 'Or do you like to call it a hobby?'

Elle smiled while trying to hide her nerves on Saturday afternoon. 'Very well and yes, it is more like a hobby!' She was worried about being seen with Lizette on the open King's Road. She led her into the safety of Calvin Klein.

'My youngest daughter Lyra loves this store,' Lizette said brightly.

'I know,' Elle laughed. Despite her nerves, she was enjoying Lizette's company again.

'Oh, really?'

'Oh . . . I mean my daughter loves this store also.'

'Does she? Oh we must buy them something from here, don't you think? And we should also treat ourselves, not that I have anyone to dress for in the bedroom these days.' She glanced around the store. 'Do you come in here for Makram?' she asked playfully.

'Gosh, I have enough lingerie to put on a twelve-hour fashion show,' Elle grinned. She spotted a silk bra and brief set, which Lyra was wearing the last time they slept together. Lizette honed in on it.

'This is gorgeous Elle. I wonder if Lyra would like it?'

'I can't see what woman wouldn't.' She was desperate to tell her that her daughter already had it but couldn't. She watched as Lizette rummaged through the lingerie set for the correct size in frustration. She looked away and gazed at the neatly presented lingerie, wondering what else she would love to see Lyra in. 'Lizette – she would adore this,' Elle said, fondly taking hold of a floral chemise.

'Gosh, that really is beautiful Elle. I'll get her that instead.'

'Super – she'll love it.'

Chapter Forty-One

You can't leave with James . . . I'm getting a divorce and moving out. I'm going to tell David OK? I really mean it . . . I love you x

Cara sent the text then rested her heavy head in her hands. She had confirmed her decision in writing to Sirena to finally split from David and hoped it would encourage her to come back to her. But she couldn't tell David just before Christmas, which was coming up. She loved him dearly so she didn't know how she was going to tell him, let alone when. She hoped that it wouldn't come as a total surprise to him considering their history of ups and downs.

She sat up from the sofa to go to the study to collect some paperwork. She took time on her way to look at family photos taken through the years, which were lovingly framed on the walls. She was trying to be strong within herself about her final decision, but she could feel herself breaking up inside with sadness. She loved David but no longer in the way a wife should love her husband. Staying married wasn't fair on her and it wasn't fair on him. She sat down in the study and felt a sharp pain in her chest. She put her right hand to her chest to try to soothe the pain and breathed in and out deeply and slowly as Amber watched on.

'Been a long day and dinner was more dull than you could ever imagine.' David flung off his tie.

'Really,' Cara replied weakly. She had been crying so found it too difficult to look up at him. She continued to reside over her papers on the bed.

'Why are you looking so miserable?' he barked at her, standing by the bed. 'I'm so sick of this.'

With a deep breath she gathered up her paperwork, got off the bed and brushed past him. He ran his hand roughly through his hair. He was so frustrated with her; she just wasn't telling him what was bothering her. David walked after her to apologise, wherever she had run off to. He found her sitting in the reception room.

'I thought I would find you in here. We need to talk Cara . . . '

'David I'm moving out,' Cara declared boldly. She couldn't keep it in.

'Excuse me?!'

'I'm moving out and I want a divorce.'

He stood stunned in the cold silence.

'I can't carry on like this, I just can't. I've tried David. You know I care about you but . . . '

'Don't say any more. Come and speak to me when you've calmed down all right?'

'I can't do this,' she sighed as he shut the door firmly. Regardless of whether Sirena moved abroad with James or not, she still needed to get her own life back. She wasn't happy living with David and going around in the same circles year after year.

She emerged from the reception room an hour later, having composed herself again. David was sitting quietly in the drawing room watching the news and she sat down beside him.

'David, I really do want a divorce,' she said softly. 'We both know it would be for the best . . . for both of us?'

David continued to stare at the TV. 'Cara, I don't know why you're saying this. I thought we were working things out?'

'I need my own life back. I'm just not happy living like this David.'

He turned to meet her solemn eyes. 'You don't want Giles and I any more you mean?'

'No! Of course I want you two in my life, what a ridiculous thing to say!'

'Well you either want to be on your own or you don't?'

'David, please don't be like this. I'm moving to Chelsea Harbour – I've found an apartment.'

'Oh have you now? And where is Giles going to live?'

'I . . . I don't know. Here, I assume, but he can stay with me whenever he wants. I don't know David, I haven't really thought about that too much . . . '

'You've found a new place yet haven't thought about it *too much*?' He turned off the TV. 'Cara I love you, you can't leave.'

Cara felt her eyes swelling up again. 'I love you too but it's not working for me any more – it's not working for *us*. You know I've tried to make it work with you David. But we keep going around in a circle where we argue and . . . '

'Make up again.'

'Yes but it's not a healthy relationship, is it?'

David looked away, knowing that it wasn't. He chose not to respond as Cara sat beside him, her hands covering her eyes to hide her tears.

A week later, Sirena had returned from a break in Monaco. Walking along Ixworth Place to a spa, she received a call from Cara. She answered hesitantly.

'Sirena, I've told David that I want a divorce and I'm moving to Chelsea Harbour. Please – you can't move to Monaco. I need you here.'

'But you said we couldn't work? What's different now that you suddenly feel we can work for goodness' sake?'

'It can Sirena. I was scared before. I'm *so sorry* – I can't say it enough times!'

'But what if you get confused again?'

'You must understand Sirena, I got married and had a child far too young . . . I didn't know myself and through the years I've denied who I really am . . . but I'm ready now to move forward with my life, to be truly happy . . . with you . . . '

'But I'm with James now.'

'You *don't love him* otherwise you wouldn't have kissed me.'

Sirena fell silent. Cara's apparent sudden actions of divorcing David, moving to her own apartment and declaring her love for her had thrown her completely. Her old feelings for Cara were coming back in full force but she really did care for James and her time in Monaco with him was amazing. She had to stop thinking about Cara. 'Cara, I just can't take this any more. I think we both need time apart from each other, maybe a few months or something to get things into perspective.'

'You mean you're just moving to Monaco with James?'

Sirena faltered. 'Yes I am. Look, just leave me alone. I've really had enough.'

Elle walked through the front door of Lyra's apartment at Onslow Gardens. The immediate tension in the air worried her as she followed Lyra to the open plan reception room. She fleetingly admired the modern artwork adorning the white walls to escape the atmosphere.

'So I hear from my mother that you two are getting on tremendously?'

'Yes darling,' Elle said sarcastically, resting her shoulder bag on an armchair. 'We really do have a *super* time.'

'Well I'm super happy for you.'

'You know I'd rather you didn't take that tone with me. It's not like *I* invite her out, although I'm going to have to if I'm not to appear anti-social.' Elle took a seat on a black leather sofa. 'It's not a situation I enjoy being in Lyra and you should know that.'

'When she asks you to meet you should just tell her you're busy – she's got plenty of friends to have around for dinner and go shopping with.'

'You know that's easier said than done. Anyway, despite the

awkwardness and your elaborate reservations I have grown rather fond of your mother. She's a lovely woman.' Elle paused as Lyra finally sat down on an adjacent sofa. 'So I assume you've told her that I'd decided to take on my own design project by myself?'

'Yes of course.'

'Good – you know I love your work but I don't think Makram would've been overly pleased about us working together.'

'So has she asked both you and Makram to come over yet?'

'Yes and I told her that he's always so busy.'

'Just please be careful Elle. You and I cannot get out to her and that seriously means keeping Makram away from her.'

'Yes darling, I know – my concerns are much greater than yours, OK. Now let's get something to eat.' Elle sighed heavily, although she was beginning to enjoy this new form of control over Lyra. 'I want to just relax and forget about my worries for now all right?'

Chapter Forty-Two

Cara walked around her open plan living room, admiring her surroundings and the view. Giles had just left after taking Amber for a walk around the marina. She *loved* her new apartment in the Thames Quay block, and Helen was only across the marina from her.

She stood by the window, staring out at the Thames and reflecting. The past few months had gone by like a whirlwind but although she was mentally exhausted, she was relieved and happier. The divorce proceedings with David were underway and she was feeling revitalised; she was going to be free for the first time in twenty years. She walked over to the phone. She had called and messaged Sirena every day to remind her that she was always thinking about her, and her commitment to her wouldn't just be a phase.

Sirena thought deeply about her future while she used the cross trainer at Eaton Terrace. James was in Monaco and she was due to join him in just two months. Her conflicting thoughts were interrupted by a text from Cara, asking to meet her at her new apartment.

Are you coming over to see me? My apartment is empty without you x

I don't think it's a good idea to meet.

Don't think about it. Just say you'll meet me . . . I'll pick u up?

Cara parked along Eaton Terrace. Sirena emerged and hesitantly stepped into Cara's Bentley.

'Hi,' Sirena said in an annoyed tone.

'Thank you for meeting with me,' Cara sighed. She pulled away towards Chelsea Harbour, disappointed with the negative air.

Sirena felt annoyed but also flustered sitting next to Cara. She followed Cara from the private car park to a lift up to her apartment in the five-storey building. Her apartment was immaculately presented as Sirena knew it would be, with minimalist decor, wood flooring and clear white walls decorated with lit artwork.

'Do you like it?' Cara asked. She stepped back so Sirena could get a full view of her proud apartment.

'It's *really* nice . . . your view is so amazing.'

'I know.' She smiled lovingly at Sirena. 'I love it here. You know I'm glad we're going to have a chance to talk about things before you leave London.'

'So how's the divorce going?'

'As well as a divorce can go really.'

'How's Giles taken it?'

'Well. He's nineteen next week . . . he's old enough now to understand, which is good.' Cara sighed. 'Of course it hasn't been easy for anyone but it had to happen.'

Sirena noted the sad look in Cara's eyes, which stood out when she first met her two years ago. She wanted to hug her. 'I hope you're all right,' she said sympathetically.

Cara's eyes became tearful and she turned to walk away from Sirena so she wouldn't see. 'Do you want a drink or something to eat?'

'No I'm OK . . . well, I'll have something if you are?'

'Yes, I haven't eaten much all day . . . I was going to cook pasta.' She discreetly wiped her eyes with her sleeves. Being with Sirena in her new place was making her feel emotional. 'Sit down Sirena.'

Sirena gazed around at the furnishings in the open plan reception room. Cara sat down on a sofa and patted the other side for Sirena to sit beside her. 'So are you looking forward to moving with James?'

'I really am although it's quite daunting at the same time,' Sirena said, sitting down. She tried to ignore the tense sexual energy between herself and Cara, which felt as strong as when they were in a relationship.

'I do like Monaco but I must say that I wouldn't want to live there myself.' Cara tried to look happy for Sirena, but she couldn't quite manage it. 'Sirena, you can move in here with me . . . and Amber. It'll be the three of us!'

Sirena looked away. She knew it was a bad idea to see Cara. 'Cara, I can't.'

'Why not? You love *me* – not James!'

'I can't throw away what I have with James – my life is on track and he means a lot to me.'

'You want us to work otherwise you wouldn't have agreed to meet with me.'

Sirena looked at her. 'I like you Cara, I always have but I can't take risks. How am I supposed to trust you after everything?'

'Darling, I'll take care of you and give you everything you'll ever need – you can trust me now, I truly mean it. I've learned a lot about myself through everything that's happened.'

Sirena glanced away. She loved Cara and she was attracted to her, more so than to James who just didn't ignite the same passion that she felt for Cara. She was in disarray. Cara lightly brushed her arm over Sirena's thigh as she reached for an empty glass on the coffee table.

'I'll get you a drink.'

'Cara, I agreed to see you to just see how you're doing. I'm not going to leave James.'

'Sirena I've bought this new apartment, got a divorce and I'm ready to be with you properly. And James isn't the one for you – he's not the one for any woman because he's never with just one woman!'

'Piss off Cara.'

'James has been teaching you bad language?'

'You're being your usual selfish self and trying to put me off James for your own needs.'

'I'm telling you the truth. Just ask anyone who knows him, *especially* his ex-girlfriends. Maybe I can introduce one to you over a coffee?'

Sirena avoided looking at Cara. She had heard about James's playboy reputation more than enough times from various people but chose to ignore it. 'Look, I didn't come here to listen to you criticising James.'

'Yes, you came to see how I'm doing – thank you.' Cara stood up to get Sirena a drink.

*

Elle wandered leisurely around Peter Jones in the babywear department, shopping for her nephew's birthday. She received a call from Lyra and answered quickly. 'Hey baby girl.'

'My mother tells me you're going to a party with her tonight?' Lyra asked sternly, which Elle found quite comical. When Lyra was angry she found her rather sweet.

'Yes that would be correct – well done darling,' she replied, flicking through a row of T-shirts.

'Look, I cannot take this any more, I really can't . . . '

'Oh Lyra it's nothing to get upset about, we're just . . . '

'No this has to stop Elle,' Lyra demanded. 'It's giving me a headache. I don't like you being friends with my mother, all right?'

'Well I'll cancel on her then and tell her I don't want to hear from her again – that'll be pretty normal won't it?'

Lyra groaned excessively. 'I think I'm more worried about your husband finding out than you are.'

'OK I'll call and cancel on her *yet again*. Happy?'

'No I'm not – I've had enough,' Lyra sighed. 'You *know* it wouldn't be hard for me to find a girlfriend. Did I tell you the time when I was hit on by a girl in Boujis? She was with the Royals.'

'I think we both know how prone you are to being a little *over dramatic* Lyra. I'm so completely tired of your complaining when it's me who has to . . . '

Lyra disconnected the call in frustration. Elle shrugged off the brief conversation and carried on shopping. Lyra could never possibly lay down the rules in their relationship so her threat was not worth getting worried about.

Chapter Forty-Three

Sirena tried to call James but again there was no answer. She assumed he was in one of his series of meetings that afternoon, which he had briefly told her about the previous night. During the late evening, she called again.

'Hi princess, I tried calling you in the morning – where were you?'

'Did you? I tried calling you but you didn't answer. Anyway, how are things going in Monaco?'

'Yes, very well. Things have been so hectic but the villa is being refurbished so it's all ready for you when you . . . '

'James come back . . . ' came a whiney woman's voice. James cleared this throat and the woman spoke again. 'You're boring me!'

'Who was that?' Sirena asked.

'Who? Oh you heard my friend, Isla. I've got some friends over this evening. Excuse me darling, I'm entertaining this evening so got the old guitar out.'

'Poor them! What friends are they?'

'Associates and friends who I invited over. I need to make this place seem more like home . . . I've hardly been in with work and so on. It's just been so mad here.'

Sirena pressed the phone closer to her ear as James seemed to be walking around. 'James I can't hear you properly, your signal is going funny.'

'Sorry, just walking away from everyone so I'm not distracted. I'm in a quiet spot now.'

'OK well, I'll see you when you're next back in London?'

'Yes, I should be back in two weeks to help sort everything out but why don't you come out here for a few days? I'll book your flights then you can meet my friends out here? Although things really are hectic here so I can't guarantee you'll see much of me – probably see more of them than me!"

'Well you'll have to *make* time for me! I'll let you get back to your friends before they get too bored!'

'Good idea. I'll call you again tomorrow my princess, take care.'

Sirena got off the phone feeling dazed. James was drunk and she didn't like the sound of that woman's voice in the background at all. Was James cheating on her with another woman in Monaco? Cara had warned her but she didn't want to believe her, seeing as she wasn't exactly truthful to her when they were together.

She sent James an accusing text asking who the woman in the background was. He replied quickly.

She's just a friend – I told you I have friends over! What's got into you???

Maybe she *was* over-reacting. He was so supportive and caring, and offering her an amazing life. He had bought a villa especially for them to live in together – that was evidence enough that he loved her and wanted to be with her. But her heart was always with Cara despite the dishonesty, served cold in front of her at James's party.

She quickly replied to James, apologising – but then read through messages from friends, telling her to stay with James and to forget about Cara. If she allowed herself to be ruled by her head, she would stay with James for he had never expressed doubt in them as a couple, nor had he been dishonest, as far as she knew. She needed that stability. But like tossing a coin for a decision and not being happy with the side facing up, the advice from friends was not what she wanted to follow. She knew in her heart who she truly wanted so asking friends for their opinions was just pointless. She yearned to be in Cara's sensuous arms again; to wake up with her every morning and to enjoy the intense physical and emotional connection they had together. She missed her alluringly mature yet mischievous company and her exciting flamboyant friends. Thoughts of making love with Cara again were overwhelming her. Cara was her first intimate experience with another woman and she had never wanted it to end. She couldn't leave with James when the life she really wanted deep down was in London. She received a usual message from Cara, encouraging her to be with her. Cara was certainly fighting for her to be in her life again. She could grow to trust her again, eventually, but this had to be at the risk of everything. And she was giving up *a lot*. She loved James but not enough; if she moved away with him she would only be thinking about Cara. Cara had made her realise how it really felt to be in love but *also* the deep pain that can go with it. She collapsed on to her bed, going through her thoughts before making the biggest decision of her life.

Elle sent her eleventh unanswered text to Lyra. A week had gone by since she'd cancelled the party Lizette had invited her to and, during that time, she also hadn't heard from Lyra.

> Lyra how long are you going to be in a mood for? Are you free to meet me Thurs night? x

After a long hour, there was still no reply. She pulled a face at Cara.

'What's wrong with her?' Cara asked, walking beside Elle into the main gallery at Sotheby's.

'She's in one of her world class sulks darling. One never gets used to them.' They took their seats before the auction was scheduled to begin.

Cara scanned through the brochure of the lots to be offered. She had her eye on a couple of paintings. 'What's happened between you two now then?'

259

'I don't know . . . ' Elle hesitated. 'Well, she doesn't like me being friends with her mother but it's difficult for me to just ignore her you know?'

Cara nodded in agreement, although she had a feeling that Elle was exercising her playful nature on poor Lyra. They quietened down when a couple of people sat near them in the quiet gallery. Elle shuffled in her chair causing her brochure to fall off her lap. Deep down she felt bewildered and immensely worried that Lyra still hadn't been in touch with her.

Cara sent Sirena a message before the auction started.

Do you want to meet for a final time before you leave? x

Are you really happy for us to be together as a proper couple?

Yes of course, Sirena. I love you and want to be with you x

I'm going to end things with James. I'm not moving to Monaco x

Cara smiled brightly to herself while Elle remained fixated on the brochure. Just when she thought she had lost the one she loved, Sirena was coming back to her.

Darling I'm overwhelmed with happiness and relief. Let's meet tonight for a private night in? We have lots to talk about. Lots of love xxx

I would love to see you but need to be alone and stay at home tonight to speak to James. I haven't told him yet x

Chapter Forty-Four

'I feel so tired tonight,' Cara commented in the traditionally designed double reception room. She was at a private party in Belgravia.

'Whatever dah-ling – how's your new apartment?' Valentina asked, gazing around at her surroundings. She turned to face Cara for her answer but clearly she didn't have her full attention as Cara fiddled with her phone. 'Are you all right?'

'Sorry yes I'm fine. My place is great – love it.' She took a moment to look around the room, filled with attractive men and women. She wondered if any of them were going through testing times, as they laughed and spoke with one another.

'Cara you need to put a smile on your face or no one will speak to you tonight.'

'Valentina, what if Sirena actually does move to Monaco?'

'What? She told you earlier today she wasn't, but if she does do the right thing then you'll move on and forget her. You need a strapping man to take care of you – not a little girl.'

Cara forced a smile. Michael appeared to her right with a cocktail for her.

'Michael, are you going to Antibes next week?' Cara asked.

'Probably going in the next couple of weeks so care to join me? The more the merrier, apparently!'

'I may do actually,' she smiled warmly.

Helen approached the group and noticed the flirtatious atmosphere. She knew Michael would be after Cara again with her divorced status, although he still remained unaware of Sirena.

'Good, we used to have such fun times together and now is

certainly the time to revive them after everything you've been through.'

Helen cringed at Michael's feeble attempt. 'Why don't we all go on the Inca Trail? It'll be something different!'

An hour into the party, Helen had found herself stuck talking to a couple who were old acquaintances through her ex husband. They kept talking to her as if she were still with him but she refused to remind them again that she now lived alone with her daughter. She scanned over the crowd but couldn't see any of her close friends.

Michael was standing by the grand piano with Valentina. He picked the cherry off his cocktail and threw it into the air to catch in his mouth, but missed and it fell to the floor.

'Didn't expect you to be careless with cherries Michael,' Valentina laughed. She kicked the cherry lightly with her Versace heel so it rolled away from them. 'The one that got away!' She laughed louder.

Michael blushed a lighter shade of cherry. He looked over at Cara who stood close by to check that she hadn't witnessed the amateur incident. Valentina noticed.

'Unless, of course, you do something about it,' Valentina said quietly. She took the cherry off her cocktail and placed it flirtatiously into his mouth. She would so much prefer Cara to be with Michael. He was such a gentleman and would certainly give her what she needed in a relationship.

Cara finished her fourth cocktail by 1.00am, and cheerfully used Michael's strong shoulder to balance. Helen took Cara's empty glass from her and sat down on a nearby sofa to rest her feet in her five-inch heels. She felt a bit tipsy, and watched Cara laughing hysterically with Michael through the crowd. Their arms were wrapped around each other. They would certainly make a lovely couple. They had known each other for years, been on holidays together and made each other laugh whenever they were in each other's company. Cara turned around and caught Helen watching. Helen smirked in her direction and Cara instantly knew why; she looked at her arm across Michael and his arm across her waist. She turned back to smile at Helen.

'She asked me if I was sailing towards relaxation or adventure,' Michael shrugged with a high-pitched giggle. 'I didn't know what . . . '

Cara interrupted him with an equally high-pitched cry. Her diamond bracelet had become loose and fell from her wrist. She managed to catch it before it left her fingers.

Michael giggled at her. 'You don't want to drop that, let me put it back on for you.'

'Thanks.' Cara stared into the sparkling diamonds as Michael's strong hands clipped it back on for her.

'There, now be more careful next time.'

'Thank you,' Cara grinned drunkenly. Michael had put it back on perfectly.

Chapter Forty-Five

Cara lay awake in Michael's bed. She had a thumping headache from too much alcohol at the party, although she remembered how the night had gone. She reached out for her watch and squinted; it was 9.00am. She put her arm back under the covers and snuggled into the blankets.

Michael had taken good care of her throughout the night, which she was more than grateful for. She hadn't been that drunk for so long, but she sure needed it after everything she had been through. She tiredly rubbed her eyes. The large bed was so comfortable. She pulled the sheets up towards her to sleep for a while longer.

*

Elle raised her eyebrows in disbelief at Helen's text.

Cara went back to Michael's last night. Here we go again . . . x

She placed her phone back on the bedside table; she really didn't see that one coming. She cuddled back up to Makram who lay asleep and trailed her fingers around his chest thoughtfully. She knew of many men who had mistresses but, for her, having a mistress brought her variety – the enjoyment of love and sex with a man *and* woman. She wrapped her arms and legs tighter around Makram as she thought about her date with Lyra later that day.

Michael threw on a jumper and long shorts after his quick shower. He felt elated that Cara had gone back with him. He had waited years to get her in his bed – if only she weren't so drunk. He hoped she remembered every moment of the night they spent together – the way he looked after her and held her in his arms. He walked to the kitchen to make some coffee, leaving her to rest.

'Good morning you. What a night.' Cara emerged into the kitchen in one of Michael's shirts. She wrapped her arms around Michael's waist as he stood by the sink washing cutlery after his breakfast.

'What a *great* night.' Michael turned to grin at her. 'Did you sleep well?'

'Did you try to kiss me last night Michael?' Cara replied with a smirk, bypassing his polite question. She drew away from him.

'No . . . I have no idea what you're talking about.' He bit his lip. He had carried Cara into his spare bedroom in her drunken state and then slept in his own room. He was terribly embarrassed having failed in an attempt to seduce her at the party.

Cara giggled. 'Michael I don't know where my phone is, have you seen it? It's not in my bag . . . '

'You dropped it in the entrance hall last night so I left it on the table for you. I didn't want to disturb you as you were a little worse for wear!'

'I'm never drinking again,' she groaned. 'I haven't been that drunk for so long.'

She left the kitchen to fetch her phone and immediately saw the missed calls and texts from Sirena. Oh gosh, she thought in the entrance hall, reading each text. Sirena had really gone through with it and told James. She contained herself from running to Michael in happiness – she really was going to be in a proper relationship with Sirena now.

Chapter Forty-Six

Michael drove Cara back to Chelsea Harbour, singing along to the radio. He glanced over at her. She was sitting beside him in a quiet, contemplative mood. 'Are you OK?' he asked, turning down the music.

'Yes I'm fine, just thinking about something.'

'About David I guess?'

'No, about your attempt to kiss me actually.'

'Oh great.'

Cara giggled and nudged him. She couldn't discuss with him the real reason why she was being quiet – not yet anyway. She just needed to get back to hers quickly to gather her excited thoughts.

Cara walked back into her apartment, quickly took off her heels and threw her bag on the floor. She flopped down on the sofa in silence, thinking deeply about Sirena. Sirena had done what she had asked her to do, what she desperately wanted her to do.

The whole situation was making her think about her relationship with Alessandra. She'd thought she could make a real go of things with Alessandra, but when she found out that she had told her husband she would be leaving him for her, she got cold feet. Alessandra had told her while they were on a break in Tuscany. She had just given Alessandra an orgasm and, in the heat of the moment, Alessandra said that her husband knew and she was going to divorce him. Giles was only thirteen years old at the time and she just couldn't start a new life with Alessandra, another woman, despite her on-going rocky relationship with David. She hadn't exactly asked Alessandra to declare her affair, but she acknowledged that she had encouraged it.

After they returned from Italy, their relationship took a turn for the worse as Alessandra realised she had made a mistake in wanting to end her marriage for someone who couldn't commit to her. She had only been in touch with Alessandra a few times since and last heard that she had moved to Lake Como with her husband, who had eventually forgiven her.

'It's been such a busy day so far,' Elle remarked, walking into the entrance hall of Lyra's apartment. She took off her scarf.

'I've been very busy myself,' Lyra said distractedly.

'Seems like you have – you've been very quiet.'

Lyra gazed over at the wall clock; it was 4.15pm and she was expecting a call from her sister at about 6.00pm so she couldn't hold back on telling Elle her news that afternoon. 'I know, I've just been sorting various things out.' Lyra walked through to the reception room with Elle following behind.

'You seem rather down?'

'No no I'm fine.'

'OK then,' Elle sighed, confused as to why Lyra was being closed. She dropped her shoulder bag and scarf by the sofa and sat down, pulling down the sleeves of her tight-fitted jumper. 'I was going to bring Sebastian over but a friend refuses to give him back! I don't know why she just doesn't get her own . . .'

'Elle, I do have something to tell you – I just don't know how I'm going to say it,' Lyra groaned.

'Oh that sounds very suspect!' Elle laughed a little. 'What is it?'

Lyra sat down next to Elle but found it difficult to look at her. 'I've just been doing a lot of thinking recently.'

'Has something happened?'

Lyra rubbed her forehead tiredly. 'I just don't know how I'm going to . . .'

'Lyra you're beginning to worry me – what's wrong?' Elle pushed in, but she didn't want Lyra to go on, feeling scared as to what she was going to tell her. 'You know, I *am* sorry for causing you stress with your mother but it was very awkward for me – she was so enthusiastic about getting to know me.'

'I know it's just something that happened.'

Elle examined Lyra's solemn face, trying to read what was on her mind before she spoke again. 'Well shall we go out then and do something exciting? I think you need to be cheered up!'

'Listen Elle . . .'

'Lyra, just tell me what's going on – what's the matter with you?'

'I'm moving to New York. I'm staying with my sister for a while.'

Elle took a few seconds to speak. 'You're *what?*'

'She's helping me with clients there and she's making arrangements . . . I'm leaving in a couple of months. Everything's been confirmed.'

'Everything's been confirmed? This is the first I've heard of all this! What *on earth* are you talking about?'

'Elle I have to . . .'

'Darling I see you to feel good, not to feel bad!' Elle exclaimed.

267

'Why are you doing this?' She looked deep into Lyra's steady and serious eyes. 'You *really are* leaving me?'

Lyra moved her hand over her face, looking away from Elle. 'I just need this move. You know I love you but I need to just . . . I just haven't been happy lately at all and everyone's noticed . . . ' She turned back to Elle. 'You can visit me whenever you want and I'll be back at my place every now and again so it's not like we'll never see each other . . . '

'Lyra stop this, please don't leave – please darling *I need you here.*'

'Elle don't, please don't make this harder for me . . . '

'But you're part of my life?'

'Just don't do this – you know I care so much about you.'

Elle moved towards Lyra, wrapping one arm around her shoulder with her other hand holding Lyra's thigh. 'Darling just *think* about this properly, OK. You love your life here . . . '

'You need to focus on your family Elle. You can't keep risking what's important to you. You and I . . . we just can't carry on.'

'Goodness knows why you're talking like this. You know how much I need you . . . I love you Lyra.' Elle rubbed her own arms protectively, feeling weaker by the second. 'This is so unexpected – I just don't know what's going on.'

'We'll keep in touch . . . I'll message you every day . . . '

'This is too much to take in Lyra.' Elle rubbed her forehead wearily, feeling dazed with her scattered thoughts. 'How long have you been planning this without telling me?'

'Only very recently.'

Elle turned her face away from Lyra, trying to stay strong. She was also feeling an unexpected release of emotional weight, as she recalled her early years of marriage to Makram before she had met Lyra. A time when she felt proud of herself as a devoted wife, as her own mother used to pride herself in. 'Sorry

Lyra, give me a few seconds – you just can't throw something like this on me and I don't think you really *have* thought this through . . . '

Lyra stroked Elle's arms, afraid that she would start crying as she could see Elle becoming tearful. 'Please don't make this harder for me.'

Elle drew Lyra in and wrapped her arms around her tightly to prevent Lyra from seeing how upset she was. She knew she was losing Lyra.

Chapter Forty-Seven

'I thought you and Michael had acted on your desires,' Helen laughed. 'I've told *everyone*.'

'Oh great – thanks,' Cara rolled her eyes. 'You're a *friend*.'

'True,' Helen giggled. 'But you must be excited about seeing Sirena later?'

'Helen, I am *so* excited,' Cara exclaimed, twirling her hand in the air. 'I need to buy the best ingredients for our dinner later so run around with me!'

Helen followed Cara into the Food Halls in Harrods, amused by Cara's enthusiasm. 'Seeing as she's giving up a lot for you – you need to treat her *very well*.'

'Don't I know it,' Cara smiled, nudging into Helen as they pushed through the crowds. 'Come with me to Womenswear after. I want to surprise her with something.'

After buying a dress, Cara left Harrods while Helen went to meet a friend at the Harvey Nichols Fifth Floor Bar. Sirena was coming over to hers in just under two hours and she needed to start preparing.

Cara ignored her vibrating phone on the passenger seat as she drove out of Knightsbridge towards Chelsea. She needed to start cooking and style her hair – she wanted more volume. Amber also needed to be taken for a walk. She stopped at a traffic light and watched the people walking past her car. She felt lucky. None of these people can possibly feel as happy as I do right now, she thought humorously. She was engulfed with passion. She glanced back at her shopping bags; every item bought with care and love. Before the light changed, she quickly reached for her phone to satisfy her curiosity.

Alessandra came by asking for you earlier. We need to talk.

The traffic light turned to amber. Cara reached for her hand break and stalled, her mind numbed with shock. The hooting of horns behind forced her mind to jump back into action and she restarted her engine, quickly finding a side street to park on. Alessandra? *It couldn't be.* She frantically called David but there was no answer. 'David!' she groaned. She threw her phone back down in frustration. Pulling herself together, she drove away to Wellington Square. She had no time to see David but she was beyond baffled – why would Alessandra want to see her after everything that had happened? It had been years since they last spoke.

She parked at Wellington Square, sighting David's Porsche. He'd sold his Maserati during the divorce – he knew she loved that car. She gazed up at her family home, wondering whether to go in. Giles was away at university so only David would be in, she presumed. She fumbled about in her bag for the key; she didn't like the idea of having to knock on the door. But she couldn't stay at Wellington Square for long. Too many memories were resurfacing, and she couldn't get emotional before celebrating with Sirena. A message arrived.

I'm in PJ.

Zipping her bag back up, she stepped out of her car, feeling almost faint as she breathed in the nostalgic air. But she was much happier now, and that was better for everyone. She walked briskly to the King's Road towards Peter Jones. Her earlier excitement was clouded with confusion. She *really* didn't need this after everything she'd been through emotionally. If she was to ever stand alone, laughing manically in the middle of the King's Road, today was it. But she had to get to David; she couldn't bear it if he found out about her sexuality from anyone but her. She had to find him quickly if only the overly relaxed shoppers would just move out of her way.

'Cara . . . '

Cara glanced over at Duke of York Square to her right. Her eyes darted around for a familiar face. Her heart and throat numbed. 'Alessandra?'

'Hi.'

'Alessandra . . . ' Cara continued, unable to speak. 'Oh my . . . '

'Come here – you're in the way!'

'Gosh!' Cara smiled awkwardly. Her mind was racing but she struggled to walk in and around the shoppers. 'Alessandra!'

'Yes it's me,' Alessandra exclaimed. 'Come here.' She held out her arms and embraced Cara. 'Darling you haven't changed at all – you look so well.'

'Thank you – so do you,' Cara replied with dipped eyebrows. 'I'm in shock!'

'I dropped by your home earlier, but you weren't in . . . '

'David told me.' Cara intercepted. She couldn't believe Alessandra's arms were wrapped around her, as she tried to make sense of the situation she was in. She let go of Alessandra. 'This is so crazy – I never thought I'd see you again. What are you doing here? Are you visiting family? I heard that you were living in Italy?!'

'I *still* live in Italy,' Alessandra beamed, creating space between herself and Cara. 'I had a very long break from here but now that I've bought a place in . . . '

'Where?' Cara asked with enthusiasm. She couldn't help but stare at Alessandra, familiarising herself again with her adorable face, which had been fading in her memory. She looked more mature but her eyes retained that fiery glow she once loved. She glanced away momentarily to collect herself.

'Knightsbridge.'

'With your husband? Gosh have you started a family together? It's been years . . . '

Alessandra gazed away, grinning at Cara's liveliness. But she knew it was to counteract any awkwardness. Cara was always good at appearing composed when, inside, she was anything but. 'I live alone – here *and* in Milan. My marriage didn't work out, Cara. I've been through some really tough times, but in the past couple of years I've worked hard to make a success of myself and life has been *very* good to me.'

Cara used her eyes to express her sorrow, which was too difficult to voice in public. She instantly felt guilt, but she couldn't have agreed more; life seemed to have been Alessandra's best friend. She looked *stunning*. Her tight jeans showed off her long shapely legs and her fitted jacket with a slightly upturned collar, mostly covered by her wavy hair, exuded confidence. Alessandra was back in town and had brought Mediterranean paradise with her.

'You've made a *success* of yourself.'

'Cara don't sound so surprised – I was never an idiot,' Alessandra frowned.

'I never said you were – I'm just so shocked to see you and to hear what's been going on with you! I just never expected to see you again. You look so well . . . '

'After my divorce, I just gave my life a complete overhaul – for my sanity. You might know this already, but I've been presenting – in Italy. Plus with some inheritance, I've been enjoying life as much as I can. After everything.'

Cara puffed out her cheeks, overwhelmed. 'I'm no longer

with David now. Not sure if he told you when you spoke to him? And you didn't mention anything about me – or us – did you? I was so worried when he messaged me . . . '

'No I just said we were old friends. I gathered you'd gone separate ways when he said you'd moved out . . . '

'Yes, of course. I don't want to talk about *any* of that now, though – but you seem to be doing very well! I'm so happy for you.'

'When life is good to you, you can wonder what you did to deserve it – I often thought that about you. But I always had a good heart. I just wanted to fill it with love but clearly I messed that all up for myself.'

'I have a good heart, too,' Cara exclaimed. 'I never told you to tell your husband – you just did it and *then* told me. I couldn't believe it.'

'You *knew* I thought a lot of you. We were making plans together . . . '

'Plans I was willing to go through with in the *future*. I wasn't ready to be with you and leave David – plus Giles was so young! Maybe I could have been a bit clearer with you but . . . '

'*A lot* clearer,' Alessandra interrupted.

'But you shouldn't have told your husband before speaking to me first . . . '

'Cara, I was excited about us – about our future – and you acted like you were, too. But after all these years, the annoying thing is that I've never met anyone since who's made me feel the way you did – *tradita*.'

'Oh I never used you darling . . . '

'But also so needed and *alive*,' Alessandra continued. 'I've moved on with my life but I *have* missed you – *and* not thought well of you. I feel like I've been trying to run from you, all this time.'

'So you moved back?' Cara laughed a little.

'I missed London and family – I haven't come back for you,'

273

Alessandra replied sternly but with fondness in her eyes. 'I also have good prospects here . . . '

'Darling, we need to talk properly – about everything,' Cara interrupted, suddenly conscious of the time. 'I have to go – I've got plans. Why don't you . . . '

'Why don't *you* fly to Milan with me for the weekend?' Alessandra jumped in. 'I've got plenty of room for you – I remember you don't exactly travel lightly.'

Cara paused.

'Cara, take time to think about it. We can get a coffee here tomorrow or something. We haven't seen each other for years, but I'm enjoying life now as much as I can – no pressure, OK?'

'I would love to go but this is all so sudden. You know I love going to Italy whenever I can . . . '

'I could never forget. After all, that's where we met and share our heritage.'

Cara smiled warmly at her, pondering her answer. 'Let me see what I've got on and I'll let you know – send me a text so I have your number, OK?'

Cara sat back in her car, dazed and flustered. Alessandra was everything she'd ever wanted in a partner but when they were together it was just bad timing. Sirena had captured her heart in a way no one else ever had. She gave her the courage to change everything to be with her, which Alessandra didn't. But times had changed; her circumstances were different and Alessandra was shining brighter than ever before.

'Darling, I've been bursting to see you all day. What time do you call this?'

'Can you believe it?' Sirena walked through the door into her new life. 'I feel so all over the place – I've just changed my *whole life* in the last twenty-four hours. I'm going to pass out with everything that's happening.'

'Oh no you're not – come here, babe.' Cara hugged Sirena

tightly by the door with Amber rushing around their feet. She breathed in Sirena's fresh scented hair around her face, instantly making her feel relieved. 'I'm never going to let you go again.'

'Let's just stand here like this all night then.' Sirena pressed herself tighter into Cara for comfort.

'Although I will need to breathe at some point,' Cara quipped. 'So what have you been up to all day? Explain yourself – pronto!'

'I've been packing up all my things in case James comes back tonight . . . everything's just happening so quickly – I feel *so* guilty about him and . . . '

'Where are your things now?' Cara interrupted.

'Still at James's – a friend's going to drive my things to Reigate tomorrow.'

'What made you change your mind about us? I was so surprised to get your text – I was . . . well, I was just so taken aback after everything you'd said.'

'I'd been doing a lot of thinking – I just couldn't move to Monaco. I couldn't leave you for someone else, although I *did* try.'

'Oh darling, I couldn't be with anyone else either – even Amber has missed you!'

'Aw I've missed Amber, too! How's she been?' Sirena looked down at Amber fondly.

'She's been doing very well,' Cara beamed at her proudly.

Sirena smiled at Amber then at Cara, feeling overwhelmed at ending her life with James and now settling into her new one with Cara.

'Are you all right?' Cara drew her body a little from Sirena so she could face her. 'I know the past few months have been difficult for you – and me – but you are happy about all this aren't you?'

'Yes of course I am – *really* happy.' The touch of Cara made her body tingle all over.

Cara held Sirena's face and kissed her more intensely. 'This is how it'll always be.' She kissed her tightly on her cheek. 'Listen – tell your friend to bring your things over here, OK? I want you here all to myself.' She moved her hands lovingly up and down Sirena's arms, wanting her to feel as secure as possible with her.

'I'll arrange a bit later – just need to take everything in first now that I'm here!'

'Darling, you know I've given all of this a lot of thought. I've been so excited about moving you in I've bought *hers* and *hers* bathrobes! Now come and sit with me . . . we have a lot of catching up to do.' She smiled, leading Sirena by the hand to a sofa. She missed her hands, the way they felt against every part of her naked skin.

But Alessandra was on her mind. She had Googled her earlier and found numerous articles and photos of her. She was doing *very* well. Achievement was a big aphrodisiac.

'So have you told your family about me then?'

'I haven't told family yet, but David will no doubt hear about James's break-up with you and questions will be raised when everyone finds out you're now with me.' Cara took Sirena's hand. 'Being with you will bring complications . . . just don't know *how* I'm going to tell Giles that his mother is now with another woman. But I'm sure when my family see how happy I am, they'll be pleased for me. And if not then we'll work through it – the same goes for your family, OK?'

'Goodness I've no idea how I'm going to tell family . . . '

'We'll go through it together.' She smiled reassuringly.

'OK,' Sirena smiled happily. 'Why don't we spend the week-end in Reigate so I can show you around where I grew up?'

'Oh that would be so lovely, but . . . well, I may actually have to go to Milan this weekend . . . '

Cara hesitated, stroking Sirena's face lovingly. She smiled.

'Then again, nothing's certain.'